D0457713

BREACH

ALSO BY ELIOT PEPER

"True Blue" (A Short Story)
Neon Fever Dream
Cumulus

The Analog Series

Borderless
Bandwidth

The Uncommon Series

Uncommon Stock: Exit Strategy
Uncommon Stock: Power Play
Uncommon Stock: Version 1.0

BREACH

an Analog Novel by
ELIOT PEPER

47N⬥RTH

Text copyright © 2019 by Eliot Peper
All rights reserved.

Published by 47North, Seattle

www.apub.com

Amazon, the Amazon logo, and 47North are trademarks of Amazon.com, Inc., or its affiliates.

ISBN-13: 9781542044592 (hardcover)
ISBN-10: 1542044596 (hardcover)
ISBN-13: 9781542044615 (paperback)
ISBN-10: 1542044618 (paperback)

Cover design by The Frontispiece

Printed in the United States of America

First edition

To all who wrestle with hard questions instead of settling for easy answers.

CHAPTER 1

Emily Kim admired the exquisite control with which the food-stall vendor prepared *teh tarik*. Reaching one stainless-steel cup high over his head, he poured the hot milk tea in a steaming arc and caught it in a second cup by his knee. Then he extended his arms and threw the liquid sideways from cup to cup. The next stream flew right past his ear. He accelerated, contorting his body and flinging the liquid between the cups from impossible angles, his speed and skill turning the simple maneuver into a dance, crosshatching the air between them with flickering curves of fluid amber before depositing the entire frothy flow into Emily's waiting mug.

He didn't spill a single drop.

Emily took a sip, savoring the creamy sweetness.

"Better than KL," she said.

"Even Filipinos need their *roti canai*." He handed her the flaky flatbread, hot to the touch and folded around an egg.

"You ever miss Malaysia?"

"Same same but different." He shrugged. "Camiguin's got everything."

Emily looked around, trying to see the tiny island she'd called home for a dozen years through fresh eyes. Elegant timber-and-glass buildings lined the waterfront with tropical cumulus clouds massing above the turquoise sea beyond. The center of the island was a protected nature reserve, thick jungle covering the slopes of the three volcanoes.

Camiguin was beautiful and offered all the amenities tourists might desire, but the engine that drove the local economy wasn't diving lessons or honeymoon packages. Instead, the lax laws and even laxer enforcement made this a premier destination for those looking to escape the overeager eyes of more demanding governments or seek an illicit thrill. Its location in the southern Philippines was just far enough away from megacities like Taipei, Hong Kong, and Singapore to avoid undue attention yet close enough to be convenient.

Emily wasn't the first person who had come here to hide.

Summoning her feed, she paid the vendor and moved on. She hoped the afternoon snack would take the edge off her burgeoning anxiety, dull the anticipation of imminent violence that made her so twitchy. But soon she held nothing more than an empty mug and a greasy square of wax paper, and her nerves were still as raw as ever. It was like public speaking. No matter how many times you did it, the butterflies never went away.

Javier had always hated public speaking, preferring to craft algorithms in the safety of his feed, where mathematics could soar unimpeded by the mess of everyday life. She pulled up the stream from this morning to watch him deliver an impassioned commencement address to the assembled graduates of UC Berkeley. A protest demanding that Commonwealth intercede in the Russian civil war had delayed the talk, and a counterprotest demanding they remain neutral delayed it further. But the commencement had finally commenced, and in a conclusion that had taken the headlines by storm, Javier invoked his role as a Commonwealth board member to publicly pressure the conglomerate that ran the feed to tackle the enduring problem of global inequality.

Emily had to admit, it was impressive what Commonwealth had accomplished since the feed blackout a decade before. After the US government had tried and failed to nationalize Commonwealth in a misguided attempt to establish a global empire, the conglomerate that ran the feed had declared itself sovereign, making its ubiquitous information infrastructure even more integral to the global economy as it secured its independence and later its quiet dominance in the new world order.

Javier's arguments reminded her of countless late-night debates fueled by fervent idealism and ample quantities of Bordeaux. How they had both loved that heady rush. But now Emily didn't dissect Javier's ideas as she would have all those years ago in front of the fire at their sanctuary in the Pacific Northwest. Instead, she listened to the familiar inflections of his voice, noticed the streaks of gray running through his dark-brown hair, and smiled when he fiddled with his long fingers as he always did when he was nervous. She imagined that he was speaking directly to her, that this was a live video conversation instead of a recorded speech, that this was real, *real*, and she could interrupt to tell him how proud she was of him, how much he and Rosa meant to her, how much she missed him.

Emily dialed back the opacity on her feed, and Javier faded into an apparition. The setting sun transformed the clouds into piles of blood-soaked wool. Flocks of drones and bats vied for aerial dominance overhead. This island was a candy apple with a rotten core, a paradisal parasite that fed on corruption and sheltered those broken souls who found solace only in pain.

She crumpled the greasy paper and threw it away in disgust.

Souls like hers.

Her feet had carried her through neighborhood after neighborhood until she reached that liminal zone that seemed to exist in every city, the place where shadows thickened, where you could score whatever your sordid heart desired and people minded their own damn business. A pair of junkies were draped across a bench, murmuring in blissed-out oblivion. Someone had carved an ejaculating penis complete with hairy balls into the wooden wall of a low-slung warehouse. Down the street a woman screamed obscenities—whether to someone in her feed or to the universe at large, Emily couldn't tell.

Emily slapped at a mosquito and examined the gory smudge its carcass left on her palm. That was all she might amount to after tonight. Time to get her head in the game.

Dismissing Javier, Emily cycled through her playlist and jacked up the volume. Big bass wrapped her in a reverberant embrace. High-pitched loops and flourishes added spice and texture. And then the lyrics hit, raging against the broken system, glorying in rebellion, asserting identity in the face of oppression. Classic hip-hop was a forgotten genre, detritus from a previous century, its aesthetic subsumed into the intervening stages of musical evolution. But it was also raw and angry and the truest thing Emily knew.

Emily looked down at her hands. The dying light caught the puckered flesh of the scars, the thickness of the calluses, and the crooked hitch in her thrice-broken pinkie. She couldn't do this forever. She was too small, too old, too amateur. One day soon, it would all end. That was the whole damn point.

The narrow gate recognized her and popped open as she turned into the alley. She stepped under the barbed wire and over shards of broken glass. Rizal really needed to work on the ambiance. Then again, maybe this was the ambiance he was going for.

Beats thrummed through her and the song ascended to its fiery climax as she reached the battered concrete stairs leading down into darkness. This island was shit. This world was shit. And she deserved nothing less. The sweet aftertaste of the teh tarik was suddenly nauseating. The vendor hadn't spilled a drop. Not a single drop. Perfection. That was what this fucked-up universe demanded. That was what she hadn't been able to deliver.

Emily squared her shoulders and descended into the fight club.

CHAPTER 2

A hush fell over the crowd as all the lights went out.

Emily welcomed the silence and darkness. She wiggled her bare toes in the sawdust, adjusted her leotard, and felt the current of electric bloodlust running through the eager spectators. Every cell in her body screamed at her to run, to hide, to yield. What was she doing? Why would anyone subject themselves to this? From what dark recess of human nature did such horror stem? The abyss yawned before her, terrifying and enticing.

The stillness reached its apex. The bets had been placed. It was time.

"Ladies, gentlemen, and everyone in between." Rizal knew how to read a room. The darkness made his low growl feel intimate and otherworldly. The audience held its breath. "Society has forgotten the hard truths that ancient civilizations took for granted, truths written in blood and steel. We have grown soft. We have grown comfortable. We have grown weak. But not *you*." The syllable came out harsh and guttural. "Your presence here tonight proves that you are among the special few prepared to face the darkness. After we are done, as you go forth from this hall, look around you, and know those timid people too scared to attend this ritual for the sheep they are. This contest is more than entertainment—it is sacred."

A single light snapped on, its beam transfixing the boxing ring and Rizal standing at its center, head bowed. Emily suppressed a snort. Sometimes Rizal was such a showman. A retired mixed martial artist, he'd opened this joint after aging out of competitions, and taught Emily what he could after she washed up here more than a decade ago. Rizal looked up, gray dreadlocks cascading around his broad shoulders.

"And now," he said, "let me introduce this evening's heroes."

A spotlight speared through the darkness to illuminate her opponent as he approached the ring. Emily ignored Rizal's spiel and focused on the man she would fight. Niko. He wore nothing but a loincloth, displaying the extensive tattoos that turned his skin into a tapestry of Maori mythology. His stride betrayed a certain bluntness, a tendency for compensating for insecurity with aggression. He had been a rugby player before trying his hand as a fighter, a middling athlete in a sport where his short, stocky build was an asset. As Rizal sang his praises, Niko stomped through the crowd, pulled apart the vinyl-sheathed ropes, and stepped into the ring.

Rizal paused to allow for a round of fevered applause.

Then the spotlight found Emily, blinding her as it shattered off the iridescent glitter that covered every centimeter of her skin and leotard. Even after all these years, it took ages to prep in the greenroom. She would sit in front of the mirror applying every shade and hue of glitter into interlocking fractals that resolved into finer or coarser resolution depending on the distance of the observer.

Every time she went through the painstaking ritual, she entered a kind of fugue state that orbited around Dag. He could have been sitting right there with her, illustrating her as if her flesh were one of his beloved sketch pads. She had spent so many years scraping data from his feed, distilling the results into insights and hypotheses about why he did what he did and testing those hypotheses through subtle manipulation of his digital universe. Rinse and repeat. To bend him to her will, she'd had to know him better than he knew himself. That took more than dedication. That took obsession. In the process, Dag had become a part of her, his instincts and intuitions fusing with her own until she was able to exercise ever-finer control by tweaking his feed, knowing what would work through internal reflection as much as external analysis.

Such intimacy made her betrayal unforgivable. She had over-reached, and fate had whipped back to strike her down into this hell-hole. It was precisely what she deserved.

Before each match, Rizal would pound on the greenroom door with a five-minute warning. She would emerge from the trance to see a psychedelic daemon staring back out of the mirror. Hot-pink capillaries spiraled out from her eyes, neon-green tendrils grew from her navel, and everything laced together into a riot of color that was dazzling and absorbing, running the eye through a roller coaster of strange loops and generating a gravity well for attention.

Reeling herself back to the present, Emily curtsied and pushed her oversize lucky glasses up her nose.

The crowd howled.

Rizal launched into his pitch and Emily skipped toward the ring, careful to keep her movements loose and childlike, throwing in the odd pirouette to enhance the whimsical aesthetic. It was as if she had leapt from the pages of a fairytale that, like so many of its ilk, was about to turn gruesome.

CHAPTER 3

"May fortune favor the bold."

Emily closed one eye to protect her vision as Rizal fired a blank from his antique Colt .45 to start the match. Fighters sometimes charged right off the gun, hoping to use the element of surprise to catch their opponent unawares. Emily had lost a fight that way once and suffered a severe concussion that had resulted in six months of unpredictable attacks of vertigo, dizziness, and nausea. She would never again let the afterimage of the pistol's flash impede her view of her adversary.

But as Rizal slipped out of the ring, Niko kept his distance. Maybe he'd heard stories about the crazy girl that prowled Camiguin's fight club, or maybe he just wanted to suss her out.

They circled each other.

Emily had watched game after mediocre game of his rugby career, looking for clues that might indicate what made Niko tick. He didn't distinguish himself through skill or athleticism, and he never had a chance to advance to the big leagues. But there were certain times when he made unexpected plays. During the first stage of a tournament when a sleet storm had turned the field into icy muck, Niko had tackled a fly-half with surgical precision at a critical juncture. In the last few minutes of a rout, Niko had rucked like a maniac even though his teammates had already given up. Once, during a scrimmage in the off-season, he repeatedly plowed through the defensive line with vicious and almost inappropriate tenacity. Emily had stitched the segments together in her feed and let them loop again and again as she tried to work out what connected them, what particular catalyst transformed Niko from a lackluster prop into a raging bull.

Now what she saw behind his deep-set brown eyes confirmed her hypothesis. His thick muscles and heavy bones were nothing but a reactor vessel for the nuclear fuel rod that was his slow-burning ire. He excelled only when weather, imminent defeat, or certain victory set off a chain reaction that sent him into emotional meltdown, loosing his fury on an unsuspecting world. She could feel the vibrations every time his feet hit the mat, as if he were trying to pound the earth into submission. He was a mastiff straining against the leash of self-control.

Emily would sever that leash.

"They told me you were going to be so big and strong," she said in a singsong voice pitched to carry. "An all-star athlete turned gladiator, they said, a man who could strike down enemies with a single glance." She giggled brightly. "Can you, really?"

She paused as if waiting for his gaze to smite her.

"Here, I'll try too." She pushed her glasses up her nose again and squinted at him with feigned intensity.

The audience tittered.

Niko's Adam's apple bobbed up and down.

Emily sighed. "No luck. Well, I guess I shouldn't have gotten my hopes up. When I dug deeper, I discovered that *all-star* might have been overstating it just a teeny tiny bit." She held up her thumb and forefinger. "I mean, the only record you hold is for the second most consecutive losses of any player in the league. Second most." She shook her head sadly. "You can't even win at losing."

A laugh rolled around the room. Emily covered her mouth and opened her eyes wide. "Oh shoot, Rizal told me not to mention that in front of everyone. Eek, my bad. It'll just be our little secret, okay, Nikito? Cross my heart."

Muscles bunched along his jawline, distending the facial tattoos.

"Cunt," Niko spat, the word dropping like a brick from a second-story window.

"Ooo!" Emily waggled her eyebrows. "Is that what you're here for? To eat me out instead of beat me up? That's so very thoughtful of you." She lowered her voice into a stage whisper. "I don't normally go in for the whole exhibitionist thing, but if that tongue of yours is as well developed as those biceps, it's possible that maybe, just maybe, I could be convinced." She was careful not to expend too much oxygen as she talked, timing her sentences to match the natural ebb and flow of her breath. "I'm just sayin', a girl's gotta—"

Niko lunged. He came in with a three-punch combo that could have dropped a donkey.

But Emily wasn't there.

She spun away, pushing off his forearm as it careened by and stepping forward, throwing a quick jab into his kidney as she passed him. One, two, three steps. Then she planted her feet and turned back to face him as he came around like an eighteen-wheeler turning onto a residential side street.

"Tsk, tsk." She shook an index finger at him. "That's hardly the way to approach a lover. What happened to radical consent, Nikito?"

This time he tried to grab her, knowing that if he could get her on the ground, his weight and strength would be nearly insurmountable advantages. But Emily ducked the grapple, stomping on his instep and then pushing off his hip to bounce off the ropes and back into the middle of the ring.

She blew him a kiss.

He limped on the next charge and she dodged to force him onto the weak foot, air hissing between his clenched teeth as nerves twinged.

Even so, he was close this time, a finger snagging her shoulder and coming away with a brilliant smear of glitter.

Rizal had taught her the importance of combat as theater. But at some point in every fight, the audience receded. Thoughts, anxieties, expectations—everything beyond the ring faded away. There was only this cone of light, only this mat beneath her feet, only this deadly dance.

As they advanced, retreated, twisted, and thrust, Emily felt for the underlying cadence. She imagined the 1973 house party at 1520 Sedgwick Avenue. Fires gutting the surrounding housing projects, residents fleeing a world intent on forgetting their very existence to find respite in each other, in community, in music. DJ Kool Herc had improvised at the turntable, scratching the record to extend the instrumental beat so that people could dance longer and harder to the same groove. The partiers went wild, inventing new moves and riffing off each other in what would one day be called "breaking." That dingy rec room in the Bronx was the birthplace of hip-hop, and Emily was one of the dancers.

She explored the breakbeat, let her heart play counterpoint to the bass, allowed the tempo to regulate her movements, knowing that Niko would absorb it through osmosis, unconsciously mirroring her, his reactions governed by the groove. Adrenaline flowed cold as ice. The air was sour with sweat. Emily might die tonight, but for now, right *now*, she was more alive than ever.

Block. Jab. Hook. Block. Block. Kick. Block. Dodge.

Niko responded to her, matched her, fell into the silent rhythm. They were partners. They were tied together at the hip. They were iterations of each other. And then Emily broke the pattern and landed a discordant and vicious kick to the groin.

Niko grunted and bent over.

Emily sprang forward, bringing her knee up to meet his descending face, and felt cartilage crumple on impact. She brought a hand down to strike the brachial plexus, and then pushed off his shoulder and away, already five steps ahead, extrapolating trajectories and—

An iron manacle closed around her ankle.

Her body jerked to a stop.

He had her ankle.

She tried to twist free, but his grip was a vise.

He had her fucking ankle.

Fuck.

Fuck. Fuck. Fuck.

He wrenched her ankle, and she spun her body in the air to prevent the joint from breaking, then landed with her hands on the mat. She kicked back with her other heel and hit his navel, forcing a huff of air out of him. But he yanked her ankle savagely, forcing her to hop backward on her hands until he was holding her upside down like a trussed turkey.

He looked down at her and they made eye contact. His nose was destroyed and blood poured down his face, staining his bared teeth and dripping off his chin. The rage burning behind those dark-brown irises had gone supernova and for a fleeting moment Emily wondered what tragic sequence of events had landed Niko here tonight, what past abuses, deep-seated flaws, or repressed memories might have set him on a path to kill or die for spectacle. There were so many flavors of personal disaster, so many trip wires in this callous universe. It could have been nothing more than an accident of birth, or, like her, it could be entirely his own doing.

His foot lashed out. She contorted her body, trying to avoid the kick, but she didn't have enough leverage. At the last second she threw up one arm and the kick landed on her shoulder, setting her deltoid spasming. Shock numbed her, and white-hot pain followed in its wake.

Another kick knocked the air out of her, and, as she gasped for oxygen, yet another one swiped her arms from under her. She swung freely from her ankle, a sparkling fairy in the grip of a monster.

She had to move. She had to do something.

She reached out for his knee and tried to land a grapple. If only she could get close, he wouldn't be able to hit her and she might be able to create an opportunity to extricate herself. There were pressure points she could strike, flesh she could bite, anything to take back the initiative.

But he saw it coming, snatched her other ankle, and swung her whole body around like a proud father playing helicopter with a favorite child. Air whooshed past her and the world spun, spun, spun, and then—

Wham.

He slammed her down onto the mat and fireworks went off inside her head. But before she could catch her breath, she was airborne again.

Wham. Wham. Wham.

The world faded and she was fifteen years old again, stepping into the Houston drug den where Javier and Rosa's junkie mother had taken them. The reek of piss and body odor. Limp bodies scattered around the room, their owners' minds floating in dissociative bliss. Javier and his younger sister huddling behind a rotting couch. Emily had funneled her crippling doubt and fear into a facade of fierce certainty, offered their mother a month's worth of pills, and demanded she sign the paperwork. By pretending to be in control, Emily took control.

Hard, awkward silences on the long drive back to LA. Flashes of profound weirdness as Rosa and Javier moved into Emily's house and the three of them joined forces to game the system so they could remain independent, attend school, and scrounge enough money to get by. Seeing Rosa laugh when Javier tickled her one Sunday afternoon and thinking that one day they might even transcend friendship and become a family, the prospect at once terrifying and sublime. The wonder and surprise when she looked back to see that it had come true. Establishing their own code of honor in the absence of anything to guide them. Watching as a community formed around them, the house becoming a home for talented outcasts hoping against hope to build a better future.

There was nothing more important than this strange new kinship. They had survived the system. They had subverted the system. They had changed the system. How could Emily have forgotten that? How could she possibly have risked severing those sacred ties? How could she have betrayed the family they'd built together?

A tattooed face swam back into sight. Hoots and catcalls echoed in her ears.

The ring.

The fight.

Niko.

He held her gently in his arms, supporting her head with one massive hand. He grinned when he saw her blinking groggily up at him. He leaned in close.

"Cunt," he growled, apparently lacking a certain flair for creativity. "I am going to teach you a goddamn lesson."

Emily reached for her lucky glasses, but they must have flown off. No matter. She almost wanted to thank Niko, to beg him to bring the pain. This was why she was here. To chase exquisite agony as desperately as those losers holed up in Houston.

Niko dragged her to the side of the ring and pressed her up against the ropes.

Emily struggled, but her limbs shook and her strength had evaporated.

He backhanded her across the face and stars peppered her vision.

Something strange was happening. He was pressing the top rope back with one hand while pulling it forward with the other, sliding it across her scalp. Emily didn't understand until the makeshift noose was already around her neck, the elastic tension cutting off her windpipe.

Her back arched. Her arms dangled back behind her. She was facing up, the single light glaring down at her like the eye of a disdainful god. Niko hit her. Hit her again. He was close to her, excited, pushing her back against the ropes. She could smell meat on his breath.

She urged him on. This was the fate she deserved. Emily wasn't here for glory or riches or even love of the fight. She was here to construct a personal hell on earth, an inferno worthy of Dante, a crucible that could burn away her shame. Only in oblivion could she find release. Niko was not her opponent—he was her psychopomp, ferrying her to whatever came next, whatever lay on the other side of this mortal veil.

Emily pressed herself into the rope, arched her back farther, reached her fingers behind and down, yearning for a glimpse, a touch of the unknown underworld awaiting her.

Contact.

Something smooth and cool against her fingertips. She focused, trying to push back the sparkling pyrotechnics occluding her vision.

It wasn't the door to Hades.

It was a champagne flute.

Emily was hanging off the edge of the ring a meter above one of the VIP tables that Rizal had crammed in as close as possible. She watched with detached curiosity as her fingers closed around the glass and jerked it up to grab the base.

And then her arm came up and around, flying droplets of golden liquid indistinguishable from the galaxies whirling around her. She smashed the slender, elongated bowl across Niko's temple, and when he jerked his head up to keep the glass and liquor out of his eyes, Emily stabbed the stem into the soft flesh under his jaw and all the way up into his brain, her hand stopping only when the base of the shattered flute met skin, like a carpenter driving home a nail.

Niko stumbled back.

Emily's hands went to the rope at her neck, pawing at it as black spots swam and multiplied in her vision. One finger between rope and skin. Two. Three. She ripped it over her head and gasped for air as she came free, trying to regain her balance, clawing back from oblivion.

She vomited. Sickly-sweet teh tarik and chunks of roti canai spewed across the blood-and-glitter-stained mat. Bile seared her throat. It hurt to breathe. She coughed. Coughed again. Sucked for air.

Niko swayed. His body was polka-dotted with glitter where her strikes had landed. His face was a gory mess. Thick muscles twitched involuntarily, as if his tattoos were trying to escape their doomed host. It was Emily who would offer Niko the reaper's sweet relief, not the other way around.

She reached up and flicked him between the now-dead eyes.

He toppled backward and crashed onto the mat.

Silence.

Applause grew from a trickle to a cataclysmic flood.

But when Emily looked around, she saw only roaring darkness beyond the ring.

CHAPTER 4

Emily stared into the mirror. The glass was cracked and smudged, and the greenroom itself was little more than an oversize closet. They weren't pop stars playing stadium shows. They were fighters spilling blood for credit.

That blood was caked onto her skin and leotard, the uneven splotches dark against glittering fractals. The woman in the mirror was a stranger, an evil djinn smuggled in from a nightmare parallel universe. Emily had spent years covertly seeding Dag's feed with her own visage so that her face became an object of obsession for him, a Platonic ideal against which he measured beauty. Not even he would recognize her now.

An old memory surfaced. Rosa standing in the living room of the old house in LA, practicing her mythology presentation for world-history class. Emily gently coaching her to stand up straight, make eye contact, slow down. Being unable to hold back a smile at Rosa's fierce frown when she couldn't remember how Perseus slayed Medusa. Emily prompting her, and Rosa snapping her fingers and interrupting, explaining that in order to avoid being turned to stone by Medusa's direct gaze, Perseus had polished his shield and looked only upon her reflection. The shield was a mirror and the mirror was a shield. Emily had always imagined herself to be Perseus, fighting the monsters of a broken system, but the bloody, bedazzled woman staring back at her seemed liable to sprout snakes out of her head.

Now Rosa ran a gallery in Addis Ababa and had earned herself a sterling reputation as a curator. She'd discovered Damaris Mwangi, catapulting the talented young artist onto the world stage. Emily was so proud of her. So, so proud.

Emily tried to summon her feed before forgetting it wasn't there. All she wanted to do was watch Javier's speech one more time, see what Dag was up to, read Rosa's latest post, and call up a live satellite stream of the island in the Strait of Juan de Fuca that she had once called home. She might not be able to be with them physically, but she would experience their lives vicariously, etching every detail into her memory. Her only comfort in this godforsaken place was that they still lived and breathed and loved.

They were her people. Her family. Her victims.

But here, even their apparitions were beyond her reach. This joint was feedless. Analog had been the first, of course. The infamous San Francisco social club had banned digital technology within its walls before the feed was a thing. Now the ubiquity of the feed and the global power of Commonwealth had inspired copycats like Rizal to set up feedless fight clubs in dark corners around the world. Not just venues for violent entertainment, they were places to whisper secrets beyond the reach of the feed itself.

Which left Emily bereft of the digital prosthetic that was a sixth sense. She couldn't listen to her hip-hop playlist. She couldn't call up footage of Javier's talk or access her bank account. She couldn't immerse herself in a virtual walk-through of Rosa's gallery. She couldn't view Dag's latest sketches, check the forecast, or read the news. The feed was the global brain in which every human was a single neuron. It was the forum for trillions of ongoing conversations, the library of all human knowledge, the cognition that drove every car and train and plane and drone, the source of all media and entertainment, the information infrastructure that made civilization possible, the vast and intricate clockwork on which the world ran.

And in its absence, silence.

A profound and disturbing silence that felt intensely antisocial, that put everyone on edge, but that gave fight-club regulars the initial thrill of transgression that bloodshed compounded. It forced you into the present moment, forced you to be, to exist, and nothing more.

Emily coughed and touched her swollen neck. The skin was already mottling into patches of yellow and purple. Everything hurt. The present was the last place she wanted to be. It held nothing but pain and self-recrimination. She wanted to climb those stairs into the warm tropical night and submerge herself in the digital impressions left by those she loved. She would summon the feed, endure the stares of passersby, weave through those normal people leading normal lives, hole up in her apartment, all in the company of her long-lost friends.

A migraine went off like a grenade, forcing tears.

No.

She had no right to such indulgence. She had lost control of herself. She had broken the code. She had betrayed one of her own. She would sit here and savor the agony until she toppled off the stool. This, all this, was her penance.

A tentative knock on the greenroom door.

"Pixie?" Her stage name—the only one he knew her by.

"I'm fine, Rizal," she called out. "Just leave me be."

"I'm coming in."

"For fuck's sake."

He entered, closing the door behind him.

She looked at his reflection in the mirror. Rizal wasn't quite a boss or an agent or a coach but a little of each and more. He'd gained a few pounds since he'd trained her, a layer of flab accruing as he spent less and less time in the ring and more and more time managing the fight club. Emily knew that Rizal, a devoted single dad, really just wanted to focus on raising his sons, but after the expenses and requisite bribes, the fight club earned less profit than outsiders might expect, so he was always scrounging to keep the place afloat.

He held up her lucky glasses.

"Thought you might want these."

That's right—they'd been knocked free in the ring.

"Thanks."

She inspected them and, finding them undamaged, put them on.

"Dude claimed they were his 'cause they landed on his table," he said. "I had him thrown out."

"I appreciate it."

"Look, Pixie . . ." He leaned down, wincing at her wounds.

The concern in his wide-set eyes made her uncomfortable. They had spent a lot of time together over the years. Endless hours in the gym. Occasional late nights of heavy drinking. Brainstorming new ways to make the fight club's spectacle more compelling. But through all that, Emily had snipped off any buds of burgeoning affection. She had hurt the people she cared for most, proving herself unworthy of friendship. She wasn't about to let a new person into her life and thereby do them harm. Rizal deserved better.

"I said I'm fine."

He raised his palms, placating.

"All right, all right."

A beat.

"You're still here," she said. She didn't want to walk this particular emotional tightrope right now. She needed to be alone with her pain.

"You'll get paid through the usual channels," he said. "Tonight's take was good, so I threw in a little extra."

"Great," she said. "Thanks again."

Another beat.

"Yes?" she asked. He was fiddling with the end of a dreadlock. Why was he stalling? "What is it?" Oh no, he wasn't going to try to make a move, was he? Not Rizal. Not here. Not now. No, of course he wasn't. But hinting at it might disarm him, ease him into sharing whatever it was that was on his mind. "You're not about to hit on me, are you?"

"What?" She had to repress a smile at the genuine confusion on his face. "No. God, no. Come on." He backtracked. "I mean, not that you're not—I mean—no—I—"

She barked a laugh, but it burned her throat. "Don't worry," she said. "I feel the same way. But if you're not trying to seduce me, why are you here and not shutting down the club?"

He shook his head, conflicted.

"Look," he said. "I don't want ask you to do this—it's not your job, and that was a close one, like, really close. You need to rest, recover. It's just . . . well, it could really make the difference for us. I mean, look at you." He met her eyes in the mirror. "You can't do this forever. Not like this. I mean, no offense, but you're no Vasilios the Greek. And I can't, either, but right now we're just not pulling in enough. I pay you out. I pay the other fighters out. But it all just comes around again, and we can't break the cycle."

"Enough pussyfooting, Rizal," she said. "What's this about?"

He let out a long sigh, and his nervous energy ebbed.

"There's this guy who's buying up fight clubs," he said. "It's all hush-hush, but I've heard from some of the big-time owners. Dar es Salaam, Oaxaca, Vancouver, Pokhara, Milan, Ulaanbaatar, all of them changed hands in the past year. They stay open. The show goes on. Customers never know the difference. Sometimes the old owner even stays on as general manager. But from what they've said, it's enough money to retire on, to quit the business, to start a new life."

"And?"

"And he's here, tonight, with a bunch of business associates." Rizal pointed down at the floor. "I think he's scouting the place. He watched your fight, pulled me aside to say he was very impressed. They're in the VIP lounge now, and he asked to meet you, have you pour a few drinks for them." Rizal winced. "Look, that's why I didn't want to bring it up. You're a fighter, not a waitress. You almost died out there tonight. It's not fair or honorable for me to demand more of you. But . . ." She could feel the ache in him, the weight of dreams left unfulfilled. "I just—look, if he were to make an offer, the kind of offer that would let me just peace out and spend more time with Aurelio and Isko, then you—Pixie, you know this joint better than anyone. Fighters come and go, but you've stuck around for a long time, too long. I've had a good run, a dozen years doing this. If you wanted, if the money was good enough, you could take over this place, you know, manage it. It's a way out of the ring, maybe a way to lay your hands on some real cash."

Emily could tell Rizal that she wasn't doing this for the money. She could tell him that she had more money than she knew what to do with, just a tiny portion of the fortune she and Javier had skimmed off financial markets like a careful bartender scraping excess head off a frothy pint. With root access to the feed, it had been child's play to identify hedge-fund managers leaching value from the economy and subconsciously urge them to see the wrong patterns, form the wrong theses, make the wrong bets. She and Javier would take the other end of their trades, and capital ceased to be an obstacle. But Rizal didn't know that, couldn't know that. That was a different time, a different life. To Rizal, she was Pixie, a refugee from whatever unspeakable life had driven her to spend her nights in this cursed Camiguin basement. The only way that Emily wanted to leave the ring was in a coffin, but Pixie might jump at an opportunity like this.

Turning away from the mirror, Emily looked straight at Rizal. He had taken her in, trained her, and given her the scourge with which to beat her guilt into submission. She had been careful never to find herself in his debt or cultivate camaraderie, but she could not deny him this.

"Okay," she said. "I'll see what I can do."

CHAPTER 5

As she followed Rizal up the corridor, Emily considered her options. She didn't relish the task of schmoozing with an up-and-coming racketeer and couldn't help but wonder what clan he hailed from. Triads, maybe, or next-generation Le Milieu. It was hardly surprising that somebody was trying to corner the fight-club market. Just like in any other industry, illicit startups often rode hot new trends straight into the maw of consolidation by powerful incumbents. Refusing acquisition usually meant starting a war, so only the most ruthless rose to the top.

Running an illegal enterprise meant you had no legal recourse, so crime was the ultimate laissez-faire marketplace. Emily had seen that dynamic at work in LA before the fires consumed Southern California. Navigating the world alone at fourteen years old required breaking the rules to follow the rules. She'd forged documents, smuggled stolen intellectual property, liaised with gangs, played peacemaker in battles over turf, and pulled off intricate cons whose audacity required both the arrogance and innocence of youth. She'd even had to hire a local fixer to pose as an aunt in order to register for high school. The world wasn't built for minors to make their own decisions, so to control her own destiny, she'd had to operate under the radar.

If this group was bothering with a due-diligence site visit, the decision was already made. Rizal would be receiving an offer he wouldn't be able to refuse, and Camiguin would fall under the wing of the black-market prince holding court in the VIP lounge at this very moment.

Emily would make an appearance, pour some drinks, and get the hell out of there. She doubted Rizal would receive enough money to actually retire, which was fine with her because she certainly didn't want the headache of managing the club. She couldn't care less whether it was profitably or efficiently run. She didn't want to have to bribe officials, keep customers happy, or schedule staff. The only thing that mattered to Emily was getting into that ring again and again, trying to wipe her slate clean with blood.

Ahead of her, Rizal took a deep breath and opened the door. The sound of raucous conversation spilled out into the hall. English, but that didn't mean much. Any group buying up fight clubs on every continent would have diverse members and partners, and default to the lingua franca.

"Ahh, Rizal," a voice called out, the others wilting in its wake. "Have you managed to fetch our mighty champion? We're all waiting on pins and needles to sing her praises. Well, Midori isn't. But that's just sour grapes."

Emily could have sworn she'd heard that voice before somewhere, but she couldn't place it. It was a rich tenor, thick with self-assurance. American, probably.

"The woman of the hour," Rizal said, regaining his flair for show-manship. "I give you Pixie."

Steeling herself, Emily twirled into the room, scanning the interior as she spun. Five men, four women, all in tailored suits. Tiny porcelain cups in front of each of them, bottles of top-shelf *baijiu* on the sidebar, the smell of liquor thick in the air, scratchy blues emanating from a retro vinyl turntable in the corner, walls covered in ghostly abstract prints at once violent and erotic. All they needed were some gratuitous courtesans and bodyguards to complete the set of traditional gangster glad-handing accoutrements.

And there, sitting at the head of the table . . .

Lowell Harding.

Emily froze.

Lowell raised his cup between thumb and forefinger, and everyone else followed suit.

"You snatched away my champagne earlier," he said, looking her up and down. "But I must say you put it to quite spectacular use. Midori is sulking because her money was on Niko, but I always bet on the underdog, so you're in my good graces. Bravo."

They drained their cups.

Emily covered up her stare by giving him a wink.

CHAPTER 6

They had never met in person, but Emily was all too familiar with Lowell Harding. Lowell had grown up in a ghost town outside of Odessa and followed in the footsteps of many a proud Texan by leveraging a few lucky wildcat strikes into an oil-and-gas empire. Dag had spent years in his service as an Apex lobbyist, securing drilling concessions from the Arctic Council and buying up real estate in areas least exposed to the ravages of climate change. Emily had watched it all through Dag's feed as she pushed him ever so gently toward a tipping point. The oil flowed out, the money flowed in, and the carbon dioxide emissions accelerated global warming, which caused the value of the real estate holdings to skyrocket. This was the wicked flywheel that had earned Lowell his billions.

Ultimately, Dag had sabotaged Lowell by trading Emily and Javier's precious exploit to Commonwealth in return for the promise of a carbon tax. That tax had rendered Lowell's operation unprofitable, but Emily had no idea what he'd done after the breakup of his conglomerate. At the time, she had been taking the first steps on the path that led to Camiguin. Following the downfall of a plutocrat hadn't been high on her list of priorities.

But somehow, that onetime plutocrat was right here, right now.

Lowell had put on weight in the intervening thirteen years, and his hair had turned solid gray. Lines creased his face, and his reddish nose spoke to an enduring fondness for alcohol. But there was still a mischievous spark behind his bright-green eyes and an edge to his chortle that made it difficult to judge his level of irony. He was laughing right now, as one of his colleagues imitated the expression on Niko's face as Emily's coup de grâce slid home.

Emily wanted to strangle the idiot, but when everyone looked for her reaction, she took an ostentatious bow. Now was not the time to act out of anger. Whatever was going on here, she needed more data before she could decide on her next move. Ideally, she wouldn't have to do anything at all besides wait the table. She was in hiding. She didn't want Lowell popping up out of nowhere and shattering the perfect isolation she had found on Camiguin. She didn't want the memories, didn't need the fresh infusion of guilt.

What was Lowell doing here anyway? Could he have detoured into organized crime after his business collapsed? Emily wouldn't put it past him, but given his history, it seemed unambitious. Then again, Rizal had said this was the guy buying up fight clubs in every time zone. So what was his angle?

Fighting the questions like a gardener hacking back weeds, Emily forced herself to return to the present. She would play her part, get out of here, and forget this ever happened. A few weeks of recovery, a few months of intense training, and she'd be ready for her next fight. Who knew? Maybe it would be her last.

"Who's thirsty?"

Emily hoisted a bottle of baijiu from the sidebar and poured shots to rowdy acclamation. This seemed to signal the closing of a loop, because the group picked up the conversation they'd been having before she had made her entrance.

"They won't do it," said an aristocratic woman with a Turkish accent. "It's all smoke and mirrors, just making noise to make a point.

Plus, they get to rally popular support at the same time, burnish their brand. Give it a few months and everyone will have forgotten."

"Is that really something we can leave to chance?" The speaker's nasal voice was at odds with his gigantic build, and he slouched like his size made him uneasy. "Marie Antoinette didn't take the revolution seriously until the guillotine. The best way to fend off threats is by fighting them directly from day one."

"Really, Jason? The French Revolution? Don't you think that's a little melodramatic?" said a young Japanese woman with mismatched irises. "We all know what's *really* going on here." She looked around at the others and then leaned forward. "Lowell is our little Count of Monte Cristo. He's been harboring a grudge against Rachel for years and wants to exact his revenge. This situation presents a perfect opportunity to rock the boat. Simple, really."

Just like that, Emily was invisible. These were people used to hovering underlings. Staff just faded into the background. To them, Emily was a novelty, a dancing monkey who filled their cups and massaged their bloated egos. She leaned into anonymity, pretended she wasn't there. The respite was necessary. The world was spinning ever so slowly, and her neck was growing stiffer and more swollen by the minute.

"Amen," said the Turkish woman disdainfully. "I'm not looking to get drawn into someone else's feud. I've got enough of my own to deal with, thank you."

"All right, all right, enough." Lowell slapped the table, jogging the cups. "Midori isn't wrong. You all know Commonwealth fucked me long and hard. I mean, shit, I was like the runt at football camp. They destroyed my oil interests in one fell swoop. That terms of service update cost me billions. So it's no surprise I want to fuck them back, finish them like Pixie aced that asshole earlier tonight." He gestured to Emily appreciatively. "I'd like to topple Rachel off her goddamn high horse and watch it gallop off into the night, or maybe tame it, take it back to the Ranch, and savor every smack of the riding crop. But"—he held up a finger—"this isn't some petty eye-for-an-eye bullshit. You know I wouldn't waste your valuable time for that. The people in this room, and those you represent, control nearly a fifth of total global assets. Forgive me, Pixie"—he gave Emily a faux-apologetic look—"but you folks didn't come here for the entertainment. You came because you're worried. No, not worried. You're *scared shitless*." He smacked the table again, and the little cups danced. "Freja?"

The name jogged Emily's memory. The severe-looking Dane was Lowell's right-hand woman, the consigliere and operational genius who implemented his successive schemes. *A fifth of total global assets.* Emily did double takes on the rest of the faces around the table. If only she could access the feed, she could find out who they were. But even without a digital assist, she realized that Lowell wasn't the only person she recognized. Midori Kawakami was the heiress to a biotech fortune. Jason Lewis was a legendary private equity investor. Barend Laurentien was a member of the Dutch Royal House and third in the line of succession to the throne. Lex Tan oversaw both Singaporean sovereign wealth funds. If the rest sported similar résumés, this group might as well own the planet.

Freja sniffed as if she wasn't any more impressed by the company than by what she was about to share. "We hear from our internal sources that they're calling it 'progressive membership.' You're all familiar with how Commonwealth has layered on incremental benefits for feed users since they declared sovereign independence ten years ago. Global open immigration for members, feed credits replacing national currencies, subsidized information infrastructure for critical services, blah, blah, blah."

"They're hollowing out the nation state," fumed Barend. "Governments are basically just figureheads now. They can't do their job with Commonwealth undercutting them right and left."

"Good riddance," snapped Jason.

"Please," said Freja, "*none* of us want to hear you two rehash that particular debate. The point is that whatever your political philosophy, the feed blackout demonstrated that no country could function without the feed, and since then Commonwealth has held the ultimate trump card. We're in the same boat. Our companies, our assets—everything goes poof if Commonwealth pulls the plug."

Jason downed his baijiu sulkily, and Emily refilled his cup. The argument reminded her of late-night conversations with Javier and the rest of their crew, everyone snuggled around the fire at the farmhouse on the Island, passing around bottles of grenache, and waxing lyrical about the state of the world, safe in the knowledge that they could trust each other implicitly, a luxury none of them had ever enjoyed with anyone else. It never ended there, of course. They would get up the next morning and actually do something about it. She felt an echo of the fierce pride she'd experienced when, after years spent curating the feeds of carefully selected legislators, Frances and Ferdinand had gotten their groundbreaking anti–human trafficking proposal signed into law. That single piece of legislation had saved thousands of lives and dealt a severe blow to traffickers worldwide. They were a team, a family. A family that was changing the world. Until Emily ruined everything. Pain lanced through her back, nerves sizzling like bacon, and she gritted her teeth and basked in it.

"And this 'progressive membership' thing?" asked Midori.

"A faction within Commonwealth believes that the next 'problem' they should tackle is global inequality, arguing that it is the single most important way they can improve the lives of members across the entire feed," said Freja. "So they're planning to change how feed membership works. Instead of every member paying the same amount every year for access, they're going to peg each user's membership fee to that user's net worth. The richer you are, the more you pay, and the bounty will fund an expansion of benefits for the poorest members."

"It's fucking Piketty on algorithmic steroids!" Lowell threw his cup, and the ceramic shattered against the wall. Emily twitched, training kicking in at the violent motion, but she managed to cover it. "I'm sure you've already heard whispers. Commonwealth is going to use their panopticon to tax wealth. Not income, not profits, not inheritance, not real estate, not even capital gains. Wealth! Your snazzy offshore accounts and shell companies are all on the feed. Every financial market is hosted on the feed. Every transaction closes through the feed. Your companies are run via the feed. The global economy operates on the feed. Your schmancy art auctions and wine collections are tabulated on the feed. How will you hide any of it from Commonwealth?"

"Wealth taxes were always a pipe dream because nobody had the tools to track something so amorphous," said Freja, impervious to Lowell's outburst. "So governments managed what they could measure, and people like us leveraged the loopholes."

"The feed changes all that." Lowell dropped his voice an octave. "Commonwealth will use it to calculate the live net worth of every member and algorithmically redistribute *your private property* to the fucking masses." His gaze swept across the faces around him. "It's worse than the French Revolution. It's software socialism. It's right there in the bloody name: *Commonwealth*. I know you know this already. You have your own informants. So wake the fuck up and stop complaining that I've got a goddamn chip on my shoulder."

Silence.

Emily had to give it to Lowell—his sense for theatrics was nearly up to Rizal's standards. Everyone traded uncomfortable glances. Minds were racing with desperate intensity, iterating game theory, and decoding subtext. The atmosphere in the room thickened with everything left unsaid. Emily could imagine each of them descending in a downward spiral of burgeoning paranoia, cataloging their portfolios, estimating their exposure, figuring out who to call, what resources they might be able to bring to bear, how they could head off such a nightmare scenario. Obscurity was wealth's most potent shield. Without it, the playing field became uncomfortably level.

Emily reeled in this line of thinking. She was no longer a player in the great game of geopolitics, a puppeteer guiding events from behind the digital veil. She had proven herself unworthy to bear such a mantle. She had been too easily seduced by power. No. She was a fighter. Her aching, injured body was a testament to this new truth. The ring was her realm, and this conversation, these people, bore no relevance to it whatsoever. She set down a replacement cup in front of Lowell.

"Okay, Lowell, you have our attention," said a statuesque man with a refined Kenyan accent. "And if your respect for our time is as extensive as you claim, you didn't invite us here simply to present a problem. What exactly is it that you propose we do?"

Lowell grinned.

Emily retrieved the bottle from the sidebar, leaned over, and began to pour.

"It all comes down to one very special person," he stage-whispered. "Javier Flores."

Baijiu spilled over the rim of the little cup and onto the table.

CHAPTER 7

"So sorry, sir," said Emily as she fumbled for a towel. Javier. Her heart was pounding in her ears, her body opening the adrenaline tap but finding her reserves depleted in the wake of the fight. The migraine threatened to return, like storm clouds massing on the horizon.

Lowell waved her away and addressed the table. "Pixie's right, folks. Commonwealth's glass isn't half-empty or half-full, it's over-fucking-flowing." He threw back the shot. "The Mongols conquered the world with innovative cavalry tactics. The Europeans conquered it with guns, germs, and steel. Rachel conquered it with infrastructure. It's brilliant in a sneaky-little-shit kinda way. Win everyone over with how convenient and useful the feed is. Let it spread its tendrils everywhere. And then, once everyone has become totally dependent on your freakishly pervasive system, pull the rug out from under them. *Dance, motherfucker, dance.*" Lowell drew finger pistols from imaginary holsters and held up his guests. "But while Rachel can build great tech, she doesn't see herself as a ruler, and therein lies her greatest weakness."

Instead of fading into the background, Emily was now trying to forge ahead through the murky haze of what was probably a concussion. Niko had done a number on her. But if Javier was somehow implicated in whatever this was, she needed to be able to think. She needed clarity.

"Commonwealth used to be a tech startup," said Freja. "And even now that it's sovereign, its internal organization still resembles a typical private firm. As chairwoman, Rachel is essentially a dictator. In theory, she's overseen by the board of directors, but as in many publicly traded companies, I'd characterize their role as more of an advisory council. Rome under Augustus, Singapore under Lee Kuan Yew"—she nodded to Lex—"or France under the Sun King are imperfect but illustrative parallels. And this progressive-membership proposal is being spearheaded by a single board member: Javier Flores."

Rizal had sent Emily here to win over a man who was gobbling up fight clubs in the hopes that he might add Camiguin to his collection. Emily tried to remember how Dag had described Lowell, what she and Javier had learned from observing the oligarch via feed. He might have been rich, but he wasn't driven by greed. He might have been powerful, but he wasn't fundamentally ambitious. Instead, he loved living on the edge, making dangerous bets, turning everything into a game and everyone into a pawn.

Let it spread its tendrils everywhere. So maybe that was Lowell's ulterior motive for acquiring fight clubs. He wasn't adding an illegal gladiator operation to an organized-crime ring. He was aggregating all the tiny pockets beyond the reach of the feed in order to plot the overthrow of Commonwealth. A wave of dizziness washed over Emily. She knelt to clean up the shards of the cup Lowell had thrown, thankful for an excuse to steady herself with a hand on the floor.

"The guy's a die-hard hippie," said Lowell. "Even before Commonwealth took itself off the stock market and declared independence, he was an activist shareholder. Solidifying their carbon policy, demanding feed accountability, calling for a bill of user rights, all kinds of zany shit. Drives the rest of the board up the wall. Kids lap it up, though. You know how it is with these utopian revolutionary types. Honestly, I'd find it kinda cute if it weren't the political equivalent of passing a kidney stone. I mean, let him be a feed star, give him a talk show, offer him a book deal. Just don't actually let him drive the fucking boat."

"This proposal is Javier's brainchild," said Freja. "Sofia Trevisani, Diana and Dag Calhoun, Liane Otgonbayar, Zhou Baihan, and the rest of the board and senior-management team are going along with it, but only because Javier is putting all his political capital behind the proposal."

"They've got their own priorities," said Lowell. "Rachel's on her deathbed, and the word of the day is *succession*. Javier's decided this is going to be his final salvo before the queen passes. That's why we have a chance to actually head this off. Implementing progressive membership will be a massive undertaking. If we can sow enough discord, create enough confusion, and screw up Javier's plans, they'll fizzle. Rachel has announced Sofia as her official successor, but whoever replaces good ol' Leibovitz is going to have their hands full consolidating their position. They certainly won't be able to force progressive membership. If we can delay things until the crone croaks, we're golden."

"What do you have in mind?" asked Barend.

"Our people are working to slow the effort internally," said Freja. "Raising objections, offering alternative proposals, manufacturing obstacles, things like that. We're preemptively funding a bundle of academic studies demonstrating the importance of keeping private property inviolable as well as a few think tanks that are seeding press stories explaining how inequality is the natural state of a strong economic system. We're coordinating with a group of like-minded allies, namely representatives of national governments that see this for what it is: a power play by Commonwealth that will relegate independent nation states to the sidelines as it cannibalizes their tax base and social contracts."

"Academic studies?" Midori didn't try to disguise her disdain. "Your plan is to place a few think-pieces? I'm sure everyone will be won over once they read the pithy and statistically significant conclusions."

Freja assessed her coolly.

"This is all contextual, of course," said Freja. "Just framing the narrative. The real work is much more targeted. We have a team of investigators digging into Javier's background. He's got a private island off the coast of Washington State. We'll publish footage of it, excavate a few skeletons from his closet, and paint him a hypocrite so his manifestos ring hollow."

The Island. Another migraine seared through Emily's left temple. She thought of the students there, all plucked from orphanages and foster homes to be given a real education, a real chance. Javier would not want a team of billionaire-backed muckrakers sniffing through his CV. Emily didn't either. They might raise some awkward questions about what exactly he was doing after he left Commonwealth's employ and before he returned as a board member. They had been careful to cover their tracks, very careful. But that didn't mean there couldn't be a stray thread somewhere. Emily caught herself staring at one of the prints hanging on the wall, the sensual curves and savage angles seeming to swirl ever so slightly, the ink breaking free of the long tether of reality.

"This still sounds like chickenshit," said Jason. "I mean, don't get me wrong, hopefully it'll be enough. But if even a fraction of the proposal you've laid out is true, we need a *real* insurance policy, not a PR campaign. I'm not betting the security of my portfolio on a clever disinformation ploy."

"Ahh," said Lowell, pausing to take a shot. "And Jason brings us to the heart of the matter." Emily refilled his cup and bused away the empty edamame husks. "The merely rich can afford to rely on things like the rule of law to guard their assets. But guests of your means don't have that luxury." He gave Jason an appreciative nod. "You're right, of course. We need a backstop, a guarantee. The rumor mill is already up and running, but despite our efforts, Javier has continued to champion the proposal. An obvious approach would be to arrange an unfortunate accident for him—"

"Hold on, hold on," said Barend. "Surely you're not about to implicate us all in whatever it is you're talking about."

It would be so, so easy. Emily could reach out and snap Lowell's neck. She could shatter the bottle on the edge of the table and open his throat. The world wouldn't miss him, and she'd already earned whatever retribution might be exacted upon her. Given the caliber of the company, they'd likely make her disappear even more effectively than she'd managed to do on her own account. *Curtains—please exit through the back, folks. No, there won't be an encore this time around. The suits promise that the show will be returning to town once the star achieves reincarnation.*

Then again, surely Rizal, his family, and the rest of the staff would likely suffer the same fate. People this loaded dotted their i's and crossed their t's. A supremely discreet security contractor would be dispatched to clean up the mess and would leave Camiguin looking brand-spanking-new. *Fight club? No, never. We don't approve of that sort of thing here.*

Worse, whatever designs Lowell had on Javier would be left intact. That, Emily could not allow. So instead of murdering him where he sat, she reached over and placed a small dish of edamame on the table to complement the baijiu, and let her forearm brush his, felt him register the contact.

Lowell raised his eyebrows at Barend in exaggerated surprise. He gestured around with upturned palms. "Implicate you? Here? And how exactly would I do that? That's the beauty of this joint." He reached out and smacked Emily's ass, and she had to repress her instinct to shatter his nose with her elbow. "What happens in a fight club stays in a fight club. Am I right? If it's not on the feed, it didn't happen."

Emily circled the table, refilling cups. When she reached the far end, she glanced back over her shoulder at Lowell, caught his eye, let her frank gaze hold his for a second too long, looked away without smiling, continued around the table.

"And you're hardly in a position to play Goody Two-shoes." Jason glared at Barend. "Or was the team who cleaned up the Atacama fiasco *not* under the employ of the Dutch Royal House?"

Finishing her loop around the table, Emily ran her pinkie lightly across Lowell's shoulder blades, imagining her fingernail was a poisoned razor blade. Nobody else could see the touch, but he straightened his posture marginally.

"Gentlemen, gentlemen, please," said Lowell. "We're all friends here. And friends don't let friends get jacked. Hence this little spitballing session. And while we're speculating, I'm sure y'all can imagine that security for Commonwealth board members is airtight. Diana Calhoun has seen to that. Playing hardball against Javier directly would be . . . blunt, and we'd risk significant blowback. However, Freja's due-diligence team has turned up a tasty morsel. For all his grandstanding, Javier is pretty quiet about his personal life. One person he doesn't mention in his media appearances is his little sister, Rosa." Emily's heart skipped a beat. "And yet we know that they're extremely close. Rosa's an art dealer in Addis Ababa, and her security is *not* airtight. We don't need to threaten Javier directly. We just need to threaten whatever, or in this case *whoever*, he cares most about. Our team is already in place. With Rosa safely in hand, I believe we'll find Javier to be quite receptive to our entirely reasonable appeals. Perhaps he'll be inspired to stall the project, or even change direction entirely. Family first, right? Voilà! Disaster averted."

He raised his cup.

The last time Emily had seen Rosa in person was at a ginger-beer bar in Seattle. While they sipped on the extra spicy, Rosa had enthusiastically described the new artistic talent she was scouting in Addis Ababa. But Emily's mind had been elsewhere, absorbed in constant revisions of the multiyear plan to pass new international climate-change legislation. She had been thinking about the hurricane that had ravaged the Yucatán peninsula, the water-war refugees fleeing Nigeria, what precisely she should say to win Dag to her cause, and how critically important that cause was. Emily had left early, swigging the last of the fizzy beverage and explaining that there was work she had to get back to. Rosa had assured her that she understood completely, squeezed her in a big hug, and kissed Emily on the cheek. All these years later, Emily couldn't believe how easily she had taken Rosa for granted, how thoughtlessly she had ditched their conversation to return to her own all-consuming project. Were these power brokers rubber-stamping her kidnapping?

Jason raised his cup to join Lowell's.

"Hold on," said the woman with the Turkish accent. "What exactly are *you* getting out of this? You're not asking us for anything in return. If you were going to do this anyway, why bother to call this meeting at all?"

"My dear Nisanur," said Lowell, cup still raised. "Please accept this gesture as a token of good faith. Risk nothing. Watch from the sidelines. Enjoy the fruits of my labor. Draw your own conclusions. My hope with this little project is to earn your trust." The corner of his mouth quirked up into a half smile. "And remember, *succession* is the word of the day. The end of Rachel's reign will herald the beginning of something entirely new, something I intend to have a hand in. That is when I will need your support. By then you'll know you can rely on me. None of us want to live under a technocratic despot, and the easiest way to seize control of the future is to build it ourselves."

Nisanur held Lowell's eye for a long moment, then raised her cup. One by one the others raised theirs. Midori looked delighted, like she had been admitted to an exclusive club. The Kenyan appeared bored, as if this was but one of many such meetings this week. Barend was about to say something, but then swallowed his words and followed suit.

Emily wanted to murder each and every one of them.

"To victory," said Lowell. "May we strike as true as Pixie."

CHAPTER 8

It was slow at first, a rhythm so drawn out that it wasn't yet a rhythm, a union of pleasure and pain, the ultimate realization of mutual fantasy. Emily rocked her hips faster and faster, felt Dag grow inside her, barely heard the old bed creaking beneath them. They had been orbiting each other for so long. Their relationship was a curve forever approaching its asymptote but never quite intersecting, becoming tangent only at infinity. Well, infinity had arrived, and first contact had sparked this singularity that was burgeoning inside her as she accelerated, sweat stinging her eyes, the high hat of tingling nerve endings tumbling over the accelerating bass line that could not be denied. She slapped him across the face, then locked her hand around his throat, felt the pulse at his jugular, the fragility of his precious airway. He thrust up and into her, and she met him with equal force, urging him on, every thread of the breakbeat looping into itself again and again, a recursive function collapsing into crescendo, and then he cried out and she moaned his name and she was him bucking underneath her and he was her arching her back, and they were each other and both of them and everything was sucked into the vortex, spiraling slow and fast and inevitably toward the source, and they were lost and they were found and they were one and then it was over.

Emily kept her eyes closed for a few heartbeats, clinging to the receding tide of fantasy, aching for it to be real, for all the rest to be nothing but a bad dream, a psychedelic experiment gone wrong. Could it be possible to turn back time? Could she unwind fate, undo her mistakes, respawn at the last save point and play again?

"Mother of God," he said, panting. "That was a *fuck*."

Her eyes snapped open.

Lowell Harding lay beneath her. Thick white hair covered his chest and protruding belly, which rose and fell as he sucked for air. His arms were splayed out across damp sheets stained with cum and glitter. Cicadas sang. The air was thick and funky with the smell of sex.

Emily slapped Lowell again, backhand this time, and he grunted, his wilting penis twitching inside her. Then she dismounted and retreated to the bathroom. As she peed, the migraine returned with a deep throb. Every joint complained. Every muscle burned. She hadn't wanted to hate fuck Lowell. She hadn't wanted to ever see his face again. She certainly hadn't expected to enjoy it, but maybe a benefit of spending so long painstakingly constructing other people's digital realities was that she could conjure similarly immersive fantasies for herself.

The toilet flushed with a gentle whoosh. She could still opt out. She could endure the walk of shame back to her little apartment, swallow a sleeping pill, and pretend this never happened. After a brief recovery period, she could return to the gym, coax her body back from the brink of breakdown, and eventually take on her next challenger in the ring. Rizal would try to dissuade her as he always did. Maybe Lowell would buy him out and Rizal would once again attempt to convince her to manage the fight club in his absence. She would decline, or perhaps accept but claim the joint title of manager and fighter, playing the part of both jailor and prisoner in her self-enforced captivity.

She washed her hands, splashed water on her face. Even in darkness, she could make out the whites of her eyes in the mirror, feel the water dripping off her chin, running down her neck and between her breasts, carrying sweat and blood and glitter with it. Niko wasn't the only person who had died tonight. Emily wasn't—couldn't be—just Pixie anymore. The moment Lowell had uttered Javier's and Rosa's names, something had clicked. Emily had worked so hard to hide, to banish herself so that she could not inflict more pain on those she loved, to live in this parallel dimension that was Camiguin. But if her goal was to protect her friends at all costs, even from herself, how could she ignore a blatant threat to them from a man like Lowell?

Taking a deep breath, Emily tamped down the revulsion curdling in her gut. Killing Lowell outright would create more problems than it solved, and certainly wouldn't guarantee Javier and Rosa's safety. She needed to find out what was going on, and, as was so often the case, testicles were the lowest hanging fruit. Lowell was a man who frequently thought with his dick, and Emily would do what it took to get the intel. Knowing what she did about his history and preferences, it had been all too easy to secure a booty call to his hotel room after the meeting finally adjourned. Now she had to figure out how to actually convert sex into secrets. Hopefully, stroking Lowell's ego would prove as effective as the physical equivalent.

She emerged from the bathroom.

The bed was empty. The door to the balcony was open, the delicate curtains billowing in the humid midnight breeze. She could see Lowell's naked silhouette against the moonlight, standing out there, listening to the crash of the surf. He struck a match, and Emily smelled the sharp tang of sulfur dioxide. He raised it and lit a cigar, giving it a few exploratory puffs and then a long pull.

This was a tipping point. Lowell might very well lose all interest in her now that this one-night stand had been consummated. Emily had to ensure the opposite. She needed to make herself endlessly fascinating in his eyes, a puzzle he could never quite figure out, a black hole for wandering attention. True seduction had far less to do with carnal delights than with enigmas. She would stoke his interest by withdrawing her own, treating him with a casual indifference that would corrode his brittle self-esteem and fan the flames of obsession. Eventually, he would feel compelled to draw her in, do her bidding, keep her close. From the vantage of counterfeit intimacy, she would unveil his secrets, sabotage his plans, and safeguard her friends.

"That's right," he said.

Emily startled at the non sequitur. Had she missed something?

"Yes," he said. "We have approval."

His words had nothing to do with her. Lowell was talking to someone via feed. She moved forward quickly, careful to step on the front outer edges of her feet before rolling onto the ball and heel, totally silent on the thick carpet, a phantom levitating toward the ghostly curtains. She breathed through her open mouth so that the sound of her heartbeat wouldn't interfere with her hearing.

"Uh-huh," he said. "Uh-huh, uh-huh."

He exhaled a cloud of smoke and she tasted cloves and marzipan.

"Nope," he said. "We've waited long enough. No more beating around the bush. I want you to go in and get her tomorrow. Do it at home: fewer witnesses. Once we cage the bitch, her brother is ours."

Tomorrow. Shit. There wasn't time for temptation games, or maybe she had just won this particular round. Emily summoned her feed and accessed accounts she hadn't touched in years.

"Let me know when it's done," said Lowell with finality. He took a long pull and leaned his elbows on the balcony railing, staring out into the night.

Emily retreated into the suite, a thousand variables dancing in her pounding head. She pulled on her soiled leotard and retrieved her glasses from the bedside table. Opening the closet, she selected Lowell's last remaining pressed shirt and pulled it on.

"What are you doing?" he asked, stepping back into the room.

She looked up without expression, then looked back down and continued buttoning up the shirt.

He leapt onto the bed, lying sidewise as if it were a divan. He patted the mattress beside him. "Come on, babe, we've got the whole night ahead of us. Don't worry, there's more gas in this tank."

Ignoring him, Emily put on her sandals. She heard him bounce back up, heavy footsteps padding toward her.

"Hey, I'll double your standard rate," he said. "Sex, violence—all you need is drugs and rock and roll, and you've got the whole package, Pixie."

He pinched her ass.

She spun, shooting one hand up to latch around his throat again, actually squeezing his larynx this time, and reaching the other hand between his legs to grab his balls. As he went up on tiptoe to relieve some of the pressure on his neck, she pulled down on his scrotum, trapping him between discomforts, establishing control.

"I have a car waiting," she said in a bored voice. "And I'm a fighter, not a courtesan." She cocked her head to one side like a bird of prey assessing a trembling rodent. "So if you ever want these"—she squeezed his balls—"to feel real satisfaction again, I suggest you ask yourself what you'd be willing to sacrifice to make that dream come true. Not pay, *sacrifice*. The more you have to lose, the better it feels to win."

She held his gaze for an extra moment as if to underscore her cryptic bullshit. She really should have come up with something better, but there hadn't been much time to prepare. Nevertheless, his pupils dilated sufficiently to suggest that he was taking her obscure point to heart, and hopefully entering an endless loop of conflicted interpretation.

"Good night, Mr. Harding. May you hold your ghosts at bay."

And just like that, she was gone.

CHAPTER 9

Acceleration pressed Emily into the seat as the car pulled away from the hotel. This was far from the urban malaise of Rizal's neighborhood. Luxury resorts hugged the beach, interspersed with starchitect-designed mansions. Yachts rested at anchor just offshore, a few of them still ablaze with light that flickered out across the peaks and troughs of ground swell, partiers determined to make it to sunrise.

Emily rubbed her temples. For the first time since descending into the fight club earlier that evening, she wasn't playing Pixie. Rizal wasn't here. Lowell wasn't here. Nobody was watching. The car would take her home. She would shower, scrub away the night's sins, hope against hope that her guilt might sluice down the drain.

But that would come later.

Right now, she had to warn Rosa.

Emily summoned her feed, found Rosa, steeled herself, and—could she really do this?—unblocked the communication channels that had been sealed tight for thirteen years. Her fingers dug into the seat as the scale of this hidden history became suddenly, painfully apparent. Messages, calls, years of appeals in all formats, their frequency tapering off over time as the futility of the one-sided conversation proved undeniable. Emily had blocked Rosa, Javier, Dag, and everyone else from her old life because she knew it would be impossible for her to resist being drawn back in, and she couldn't risk hurting them again. But actually seeing this chronicle of loss etched into the digital firmament hit Emily harder than Niko ever could have.

She dialed back opacity, stared out at the waves rolling up onto the beach, white water catching the moonlight as it tumbled in to shore. It felt like Camiguin was sinking even as the car ferried her silently along its empty streets. The next breaker would wash up the beach and onto the road, flooding the streets, seeping into basements and through cracks, tourists and residents fleeing upward, ever upward, to escape the rising tide until the roofs were packed with panicked crowds gawking at debris and flailing loved ones bobbing along in the flood, everyone broadcasting the emergency over the feed, the world watching the disaster play out in real time with sick fascination, knowing that no emergency responders could possibly arrive in time, that this little island in the Southern Philippines would be lost forever, drowned like a modern-day Atlantis, a geophysical anomaly ripe for scientific investigation, a tragic anecdote to commiserate over, to wonder at with shaking heads and somber tones, performative empathy for the calamities of distant strangers.

A distant stranger was exactly who Emily had become. Alienation, the process of becoming *other*. She had metamorphosed in reverse, from butterfly to ugly little grub. Looking down at herself, all she could see were the scars.

Struggling to escape these spiraling delusions, she returned to her feed, egged herself on, and initiated the call to Rosa. *Hi, love, just wanted you to know that you're the target of a kidnapping plot.* Or *So I've been on an extended sabbatical as a gladiator and guess who I ran into?* Cut to the chase with *Long time no see, do me a favor and call the police right away.* Perhaps even *I know this is unbearably weird, but we need to talk.* Or maybe just *Hey girl, I miss you.* Emily ended the call before it could connect.

"Shit," she said aloud, the spoken word making her suddenly aware of her physical body, her raw and swollen throat, the syncopated ripples of pain turning the inside of her skull into a neurochemical mosh pit.

She began to draft a written message instead.

A phrase. A sentence.

Delete.

Another sentence.

Delete.

Language wasn't built for times like this. How could mere words capture the enormity of the situation, the years of enforced isolation, the depth of the emotional fallout, the urgency of the danger? It was like trying to explain crimson to the color-blind or summarize all of mathematics in a limerick.

As the car rounded a corner, Emily had to quell rising nausea. When she blinked, she saw flashes of Niko spinning her around the ring, slamming her against the mat again and again.

Maybe she didn't need to contact Rosa directly. Emily could send an anonymous tip to the Addis Ababa police, or even Commonwealth security. She could reach out to Diana, explain the situation, ask her to protect Rosa but keep Emily's role secret. She could even message Dag and he could get the ball rolling. She could bite the bullet and ring Javier, leaving him to call in the cavalry.

She conjured these prospective recipients one after the other and dismissed them just as quickly. With the resources Lowell was bringing to bear, could Emily really trust the police not to be on the take? Would she stake Rosa's life on Commonwealth's technocracy? Was it any easier to contemplate what she might say to Javier or Dag or even Diana? Why would anyone trust her anyway? She would be a specter emerging from the mists of time to whisper paranoid delusions in their ears, a villain straight out of one of Rosa's samurai serials, a wraith whose word was worthless and whose presence was poison.

And yet inaction was impossible. She would not, could not, leave Rosa at Lowell's mercy, let this shitty world have its way. She lacked the means to sound the alarm, but she was the only one who could. A flash of Rosa, thirteen years old, expression preciously sarcastic, declining Emily's offer of frozen yogurt with teenage haughtiness, rolling her eyes when Javier tried not to smile.

The car pulled up in front of her apartment. The car door opened, briny tropical humidity invading the air-conditioned interior. Emily looked up at the unexceptional building, found the window of her studio apartment on the third floor, considered the neatly stacked dishes by the sink, the photos she'd pasted all over the walls, the well-stocked first-aid kit. She thought about the little gecko who liked to hang out up in the corner of the ceiling, the faint smell of cat piss that she'd never entirely been able to get rid of, the occasional thumps and moans of her upstairs neighbors trying to get pregnant again after the miscarriage that still cast a melancholy shadow.

Emily reached out and slammed the door shut, the sharp noise setting off another migraine. Forcing through the headache, she summoned her feed and input a new destination. Acceleration pressed her into the seat once more. There were battles far more daunting than anything she had to face in the ring, and she was running out of excuses.

CHAPTER 10

Camiguin receded as the plane gained altitude, a shrinking halo of lights against an ocean of darkness. Emily's exhale fogged up the plexiglass, and when she wiped it clean, the island that had been her home for a decade had disappeared.

Even Filipinos need their roti canai. That vendor had prepared her teh tarik so expertly, the boiling liquid arcing from cup to cup in a sort of magic ritual, a simple offering to the gods of hospitality. If trains, planes, and automobiles had made the world smaller, the feed had distilled it into a single instance. Emily could remember a time when a Malaysian street vendor would have had a hard time getting a visa to set up shop in the Philippines, and he wasn't the only one. Rizal's heritage was Filipino, but he had grown up in New Zealand, and he'd needed a visa in order to settle on Camiguin. Emily herself had gotten her paperwork approved at the embassy when she first arrived. She remembered her parents' anxious conversations at the dinner table about their American green-card status. As a child she hadn't understood the details but had picked up on their simmering fear of returning to Seoul in disgrace.

That age was over, one of the cascading paradigm shifts that had swept across the world during Emily's violent hibernation. The feed ignored national borders, and Commonwealth had negotiated global open immigration for all feed users. If you were on the feed, and essentially everyone was, you could move wherever you could afford to move. Seamless international mobility was no longer the province of the elite. The apocalyptic prognostications of nearly every government had not borne out. After an initial uptick, immigration rates had returned to relatively normal levels. The economy was already global, and people's lives and families were still local. The impact might be important over the long term, but it was undramatic in the short term. Or at least undramatic to demographers. It mattered far more to the millions of refugees whose status was rendered legal overnight, and to nativist groups whose riots laid waste to the homes they professed to protect.

Open immigration had been another of Javier's projects as a Commonwealth board member, and it was thanks to him that Emily could so easily find her favorite snack far from its homeland. But between that, the carbon tax, and the eclipse of national currencies by universal feed credits, the changes were coming hard and fast, and while they might create more winners on net, that was cold comfort to the losers. *Once we cage the bitch, her brother is ours.* Emily shivered. Was Javier taking a step too far with this new wealth-inequality initiative? Would he finally earn enemies powerful enough to crush it and him? The feed underpinned the operations of the companies that plutocrats owned, the financial games they played, and the assets they held. It was the fascia that stitched their wealth together. The megarich did not like to see their fortunes threatened and, if history was a guide, would go to great lengths to defend them.

Emily had lived to see her personal sense of manifest destiny collapse under its own weight, taking everything else with it. When ambition became an end in itself, even in the service of the greater good, it stripped you of your humanity. But this was different. Javier wasn't betraying his own to achieve his dream. He was brilliant, and if there was one thing she was totally sure of, it was that he would never break their code for any reason, never risk the family they had made for the sake of the high ideals that united them. Javier was taking yet another leap of faith because that was what progress demanded, and Lowell would do anything to bring him down in flames.

Craning her neck, Emily peered up. A dome of stars wheeled above, light finally arriving after countless centuries spent traversing the void separating earth from distant suns, photons from the past illuminating the present, a cosmic time machine that confirmed human insignificance, a guard against the hubris that had ruined her life.

Emily stood. Her legs trembled. Her nerves flared. Her muscles rebelled. Her aches compounded. She stripped off the leotard and walked stark naked up the center of the cabin to the shower, fighting back vertigo, feeling the plane shift slightly under her feet as the feed piloted it across continents whose borders were not gone but fading, and whose peoples saw so many of their assumptions, their entitlements, crumbling and knew not whether this was a promise or a threat, sensing in their heart of hearts that you could not have one without the other.

And as steam filled Emily's lungs and water cleansed her skin, the threat of a promise became the promise of a threat.

CHAPTER 11

The thing that made Emily's heart skip was the smell.

She had known it would be strange, standing in Rosa's apartment for the first time. Emily had been forced to revive burglary skills she hadn't practiced since she was a teenager, but apparently some things never change, and now here she was.

Jasmine, peat, a hint of cumin, and maybe makrut limes? She'd never tried to identify a person's smell before—not their perfume or deodorant but that faintest of scents that was tied to them specifically, their body, their biological terroir, as unique as a fingerprint. Emily closed her eyes and inhaled, the theater of her mind filling with scene after scene. Squeezing Rosa in a hug when she moved away from home for the first time. The way the corner of her mouth quirked when she smiled. The sadness and quiet pride Emily had felt when Rosa decided not to dedicate her life to the Island's various initiatives but pursue a career in art instead.

Yes. This was Rosa's apartment. No doubt about it.

Emily opened her eyes, looked around.

Paintings, photographs, etchings, charcoals, tapestries, and reliefs covered the walls. The effect should have been disjointed and overwhelming—there was so much to look at, so many perspectives at play. But instead of a visual cacophony, the diverse media and styles felt somehow of a piece, as if there was an emotional tone, an underlying aesthetic that unified them. As Emily's gaze flickered across the various pieces, poignancy kindled inside her, and she imagined an unrequited lover throwing one final bittersweet glance back over a shoulder at the object of their spurned affection.

Emily explored the apartment, unable to disentangle wonder from dread.

The kitchen was clean but not neat, dishes in the drying rack, spice jars pushed up against the backsplash. The wooden cutting board was stained and scored. She ran a finger along the granite countertop and noticed that the sink had a slow leak, a single drop of water distending off the faucet before dropping into the stainless-steel basin.

A notification pinged in her feed. A message from Lowell.

Last night was fun. Let's do it again sometime. Sacred bulls, virgin princesses, hoards of treasure, I can supply whatever sacrifice your heart desires. Bloodlust is the best kinda lust, am I right?

Asshole. Well, at least she had successfully captured his interest. In this case, no response was the best response. Emily dismissed her feed and continued to explore the apartment.

One of the bedrooms had been converted into a home office. The other was . . . Emily smiled. Rosa had always refused to make her bed on the basis that she would simply mess it up again come bedtime. Some things didn't change. A floppy stuffed animal lay amid the tousled sheets. Otto the otter. An unbearable brightness filled Emily's chest, like the sun emerging from behind a storm cloud. Otto was the only thing Rosa had seized when Emily had rescued her and Javier from their deadbeat mother. Stoic and pensive, the little girl had clutched Otto and stared out the window the entire drive back from Houston to LA. *It'll be okay,* Javier had reassured his sister while he glanced at Emily, desperate for confirmation, his expression enhancing both Emily's conviction and terror at the responsibility that now rested on her shoulders. *It'll be okay. I promise.*

Emily forced herself to exhale. She exited the bedroom, closing the door softly behind her.

The living room was spacious. Designer rattan furniture accentuated the airy atmosphere, almost implying that this room was in fact a veranda, that fireflies might be the only light source the apartment required. Wide windows looked out onto the city, and Emily understood why Rosa had been so adamant about building a life here.

Addis Ababa was green. Eucalyptus groves lined citywide bicycle and pedestrian boulevards, cars banished to the network of tunnels that burrowed under every major thoroughfare, visible only where they emerged like breaching dolphins at designated drop-off zones. The massive Commonwealth embassy complex crowned a nearby hill, one of its globally distributed coequal headquarters. Closer at hand, a large park had been converted into a semipermanent outdoor market with hundreds of vendors hawking their wares. Above it all, high-altitude cirrus clouds were smeared across the baby-blue sky like butter on toast.

This was the jewel of East Africa, the region's economic hub. Addis generated its own gravity, and residents and visitors alike fell into its orbit. It wasn't just the ubiquitous *injera*, khat clubs, or unparalleled high-fashion culture. Ethiopia even had its own time, a twelve-hour clock with one cycle running from dawn till dusk, and the other from dusk till dawn. Even with seamless feed conversion, tourists still found themselves confused. This was a city full of intrigue, a place that easily absorbed outside influences and claimed them as its own. It had offered foreign aid and accepted refugees from war-torn Italy with understated irony after the dissolution of the European Union, established a peerless education system that powered innovation and commerce despite or perhaps accelerated by the national government's waning influence, and reinvented itself again and again until a flight from Addis to anywhere else seemed to be a journey into the past, the rest of the world's cities being but a shadow of this storied megalopolis.

How could Rosa have wanted to build a gallery anywhere else?

From this vantage, Lowell's secret meeting, the kidnapping plot, Emily's entire life on Camiguin — all of it seemed a flimsy and over-wrought fantasy, perhaps the script to a blockbuster feed drama dreamed up at Disney's Singaporean headquarters. For a vertiginous moment, Emily questioned her own sanity. Was it possible that the past decade had been nothing but an extended psychotic break? Would her eyelids flutter open to reveal the inside of a Canadian hospital ward? Could she be weaving grandiose delusions to feed an insatiable narcissism?

She swallowed, her bobbing Adam's apple demarcating a line of white-hot pain up and down her swollen throat. No. She wasn't insane, or at least she wasn't imagining things. Niko had wrapped the elastic rope around her neck and beaten her to the brink of death in the ring. That wasn't a dream or a delusion or a drama. That was real. She was real. And she was really here.

The front door of the apartment clicked open, and Emily's heart skipped again even as her stomach twisted.

CHAPTER 12

Emily opened her mouth, but no words came out. She tried to move, but her body stayed frozen in place. The door clicked shut. Sounds of bustling from the kitchen. Bags placed on the counter. Fridge opening and closing. A gentle hum, no melody, a descending scale that Emily had forgotten was a distinctive tic of Rosa's.

The short speech that Emily had carefully prepared vanished from her mind. She pulled it up in her feed but couldn't focus enough to read the notes. Blood pounded in her ears. How had she thought this was a good idea? She had broken into Rosa's home and was waiting to ambush her like some kind of maniac. Why hadn't Emily gone straight to the gallery? Or even just rung the doorbell like a friend dropping by for a chat? She should have summoned the courage to call ahead. She should have sent the damn message she hadn't been able to figure out how to draft. Anything but this.

Had those alternatives ever been viable, though? What if Rosa had blocked her back? What if Rosa had been out meeting with clients when Emily dropped by the gallery? What if they kidnapped Rosa before Emily could engineer a more socially acceptable approach? Lowell had ordered them to snatch her here, today. His team already had Rosa's life mapped out, knew her routines, were infinitely more prepared than Emily could hope to be. That's why Emily had broken in hours before

Rosa would be home from work. Her only hope was to be inside before Lowell's people showed up. This wasn't a carefully formulated extraction. This was desperate, concussed improvisation.

The hum cut off abruptly.

Rosa stood frozen on the threshold between kitchen and living room, staring at Emily. Lips parting, a sharp inhale. She had her brother's slender frame, dark skin, and wide eyes, but Rosa's face was rounder than Javier's, and her hawk nose was hers alone. She had on a loose cream-colored sweater, teal scarf, artfully torn red jeans, and flat-bottomed strappy sandals that could otherwise have paired well with a toga.

Microexpressions flitted across Rosa's face like birds before a wildfire. Emily couldn't tear her eyes away, as if Rosa might vanish into thin air if Emily's attention wavered even for a moment. There were so many things to communicate, warnings and apologies and explanations, but the sheer magnitude of what needed to be said stood in the way of saying anything at all.

Seeing Rosa, a rift opened inside Emily. Thirteen years. She had spent thirteen years following Rosa remotely, scouring the feed for every image, every mention, every post, every impression that Rosa left on the digital plane like footsteps in sand. Emily had convinced herself that this one-way relationship was not only necessary to protect Rosa but somehow authentic, that playing voyeur was the next best thing to actual contact. But Rosa was not the sum of the traces her journey left on the feed. She was so much more than that, and the distance between the image Emily had built up in her head and the woman standing before her right now was as obvious as it was heartbreaking.

The rift yawned into a chasm, and Emily was falling into it. What had Rosa learned about the nature of beauty? Was she still obsessed with samurai serials? How spicy did she like her hot sauce? Why had she chosen this particular apartment, these rattan chairs? Who had helped her move in? What were her friends like? Did she and Javier still talk daily? Would she have narrated a bad date with bitterness or sardonic humor? These were impossible questions, questions that echoed and multiplied as Emily plunged ever downward until she was drowning in them, drowning in the overwhelming certainty of irreparable loss.

Then, to her immense surprise and frustration, Emily began to weep. She wept for the lost years, for the child she'd rescued, for the woman that child had grown into, for the Rosa whom Emily had abandoned and the Rosa who stood before her now, who crossed the room in three quick strides and wrapped Emily's shaking body in a hug, who was whispering Emily's own name in her ear like she wasn't sure whether it was a question or an incantation, who held her close even when the sobs racked Emily with the strength of geological tremors, who smelled like jasmine, peat, and makrut lime.

"Shhh," said Rosa in a throaty voice, stroking Emily's hair. "Shhh. Em, it's going to be okay. Shhh."

But it wasn't going to be okay. This wasn't how it was supposed to go at all. Emily wasn't even the crying type. She should be briefing Rosa on the situation, hustling her out of this apartment, taking her someplace safe. Emily was the rock, the fierce guardian who stood between her people and a hostile world, even from afar. But no matter what she did, she could not stop the tears streaming down her face, could not slow her hyperventilation, could not calm the waves of emotion that broke against her like typhoon swell against Camiguin's reefs.

Rosa gently lowered Emily onto a chair.

"Stay right here, Em," she said. "I'll get you some water."

She pressed her scarf into Emily's hands and retreated to the kitchen.

Emily buried her face in the scarf, the cashmere soft against her cheeks. She hated herself for being so ill prepared, despised the weakness that had precipitated this breakdown. She had helped raise Rosa, and a child should never have to console a parent like this, not even an adoptive one. Emily's parents had always been unshakable sources of strength and support, until their premature deaths took them from her. Could she not offer Rosa the same? What was Rosa thinking right now, seeing this shadow from her past reincarnated? Had she noticed the scars, the mottled bruises? If Emily had seen in Rosa the enormity of her own ignorance, what had Rosa seen in her?

Sounds of water tinkling into a glass.

"Hang in there," Rosa called from the kitchen.

Emily hiccupped. She had to pull herself together. Lowell's team would wait until cover of darkness. They would slip into the apartment while Rosa slept, night vision shading the apartment in flickery green, steps inaudible, nightmare creatures transported out of dreamtime complete with sedative hypodermics and professionally neutral demeanors. Nothing to see here, folks. Just a simple abduction. Get in. Get Rosa. Get out. Get paid. This would be a milk run for them. A civilian art dealer living alone. It doesn't get easier than that.

Emily let out a shaky breath. Another hiccup. She could do this. She would do this. She pinched the bridge of her nose and inhaled deeply. She would pick up the pieces. She would regain control. She would get Rosa out of here before the strike team made their move and spirit her away to safety. Emily would handle this, come what may.

Just as Emily's lungs reached their full capacity, the doorbell rang.

CHAPTER 13

Emily was about to shout a warning but stopped herself. It was probably just a neighbor, and yelling would confirm Rosa's worst suspicions about Emily's mental state and reliability, which would make it that much harder to convince her that Emily's story was actually true. Moreover, if there was in fact something sinister behind the friendly chime, shouting would just give away Emily's presence.

"Coming," called Rosa.

Just like that, Emily's eyes were dry. She crossed the distance from the living room to the kitchen in a few quick strides and then dropped to her knees behind the counter. The hard tile sent a jolt up her left leg, but she experienced the pain from an adrenalized remove. From this angle, she couldn't see Rosa at the door, but neither could anyone entering see her. If the visitor was just a friend, she would scurry back to the couch. For the thousandth time, Emily wished that there had been more time to plan, to call in backup, to arm herself.

The door opened with a click.

"Delivery, ma'am." Male voice, Amharic-accented English. "It's heavy, so we're going to have to carry it in."

"Ahh," said Rosa. "The *kintsugi*!"

"Um, can't say. They just pay us to lug boxes around."

"Of course," said Rosa, with a self-deprecating chuckle. "Please come in. *Ameseginalehu.*"

Emily checked her feed for the translation: *Thank you.* Just a courier, then. She let out a breath she didn't realize she'd been holding. Rosa was an art dealer. She'd be receiving deliveries by special courier all the time, at the gallery and at home. Emily needed to be on guard, but she couldn't afford to let paranoia blind her. As she edged back along the tile floor toward the living room, the ache in her knee sharpened and she had to fight off a sudden surge of exhaustion.

Grunts and sounds of shuffling feet, two men carrying something bulky, the door closing behind them as they bore their load into the apartment, set it down. After the couriers left, Emily would pull herself together, explain the basic situation to Rosa, summon a car to take them to the airport, and pass out once they were safely aloft. Lowell's team would break in later tonight and discover nothing more than an empty bedroom. Once she had delivered Rosa safely into Javier's care and briefed them on Lowell's scheme, Emily could withdraw into exile on Camiguin.

"If you could just confirm receipt via feed, we'll leave you to it."

"Sure," said Rosa.

A half-second pause.

"All right, Ms. Flores," said the courier. "No sudden movements, no feed alerts, no screams." Fuck. Emily reversed direction. "See this? It's a mean little fucker. It'll fire two electrodes straight through that cute little sweater of yours and pulse fifty thousand volts through your nervous system. Nasty, right?"

Looking up, Emily saw a blurry reflection in the microwave window. Three figures, one with an arm extended.

"But you're a good person," he continued. "I've got an intuition for these things, and I really don't want to use this on you. It's not just that it'd be painful, and it would be. It's that there's a small chance that it could cause you to go into cardiac arrest. Damn shame if a beautiful, talented woman like yourself succumbed to a heart attack."

Emily had been sure they would wait until Rosa was asleep. Kidnappers were always looking for the moment of maximum vulnerability. *If you could just confirm receipt . . .* They had obviously been able to piggyback on whatever delivery Rosa was expecting, and once they were in the apartment, what better moment to strike than when Rosa was helplessly immersed in her feed?

"I'm aware these kinds of situations can be stressful, and stress can make us do stupid things." Emily shut her eyes for a second and braced herself against the tile floor. She visualized the precise layout of the apartment, every object, surface, and angle. "But you're not stupid, you're smart. A great deal smarter than us two meatheads." She assessed her options, calculated lines of approach, and excised extraneous contingencies. "So I'm going to tell you exactly how this is going to go. That way you can relax, and we can get through this nice and easy." Emily eased open the drawer next to her hip, revealing nested saucepans. She gently hefted the topmost one. "You're going to stay right where you are. My associate is going to administer a mild sedative." Emily's mind shed all thought until it was blank but supple. The coolness of the tile. The faint smell of vinegar. The rush of her blood. The smoothness of the plastic saucepan handle. The sound of Rosa's terrified hyperventilation under the steel calm of the man's voice. There was no judgment, no inner monologue, no sense of time. This was the clarity of the ring. "Don't worry, we've consulted your medical records to ensure there won't be any allergic reactions or interactions with your prescript—"

Emily pushed off the ground, flinging the saucepan overhand back into the living room even as she pivoted the opposite way. She reached out with both hands and snatched the cleaver and the chef's knife from the magnetic strip along the counter's backsplash, finishing her spin by coming around the corner of the kitchen island and shoving back against it with her forearm to accelerate her charge.

One man was facing toward Rosa and away from Emily, Taser extended. The other was behind and to the side of Rosa, raising a stubby syringe like a malevolent nurse, his other hand holding Rosa's wrist. Her sweater had been pulled up to the elbow, exposing her slender forearm. Both men wore navy-blue courier uniforms, and the massive crate they'd delivered sat near the wall, covered in stern warnings that the contents were extremely fragile. Rosa was standing ramrod straight between the two men, lips pressed together into a thin line, her free hand clenched into a fist at her side, knuckles white.

When Emily was halfway across the room, the saucepan hit the front window in the living room with the sharp report of steel on glass. The men turned toward the sound. Rosa was the only one looking directly toward the kitchen, and her eyes widened as she saw Emily.

Emily reached the first guy just as he finished tracking the Taser across to cover the unexpected sound. She could see his face in profile, was surprised in a detached way at the uncommon beauty of his fine features, imagined how she might have flirted with him in other circumstances. Then she brought down the cleaver in a vicious backhand into the nape of his neck. The blade was duller than a combat weapon and cut through skin and spine and muscle only to lodge itself in his trachea. The Taser went off, its twin electrodes firing in a burst of carbon dioxide, puncturing an intricate abstract weaving on the far wall, pumping fifty thousand volts into fabric.

The cleaver stuck even when she tried to yank it free, so Emily released the handle and elbowed the convulsing body as she came around it. Shock froze the other man's face as he saw her emerge from behind his expiring partner. Emily took advantage of his moment of indecision and shoved Rosa out of the way, a shocked "Oh" escaping her as her butt hit the floor and she skidded toward the living room.

Opting for fight, not flight, the man yelled something unintelligible and came at Emily with the syringe, light glinting off the needle as it hurtled toward her face. She ducked, using her empty hand to knock his attacking forearm up and over. The needle parted her hair as it passed, missing her scalp by a few centimeters. Emily stabbed the chef's knife into his gut with the other hand, powering the thrust with her legs so that it sank handle deep. Being inside his defenses meant being inside his reach, and given his superior size and strength, she couldn't risk wresting the knife back out and getting caught in a grapple, so she left it where it was and leapt away and to the side, changing direction when she landed and bringing her leg around in a side kick that blew out his knee, cartilage and bone crunching under the sole of her foot.

And then Emily's jacked-up senses were scanning for new threats but none appeared and she half expected Rizal to burst in and announce her victory in his booming baritone and the audience to go mad but there was no audience and she was not in the ring but in Rosa's apartment and Rosa was sitting there like a crab on the floor, breath shuddering in and out of her, the whites of her eyes like blank canvases.

Adrenaline still flooding through her, Emily tried to take in the scene as Rosa might. Blood was pumping out of the first man's severed carotid artery, the Taser still gripped tightly in his hand, its wires stretching across the room to the electrodes embedded in the brightly colored weaving, making the strange impression that perhaps his spasms stemmed from his direct connection to the decorative textile, that he was communing with the artistic divine, jacked into a muse like a toddler sticking a fork into a power outlet. The second man had fallen against the delivery crate, halting, hoarse screams inspired and cut short by pain, staring down in disbelief at the handle sticking out of his belly, seemingly unaware of the unnatural angle of his broken leg. And then there was Emily herself, fragment from a previous life, a scarred avenging angel offering salvation in the form of a surfeit of horrors, tears still fresh on her cheeks and bruises livid on her neck.

"We've got a lot of catching up to do, sweetheart," said Emily, surprised at the steadiness of her own voice. "But first, we need to get the fuck out of Dodge."

CHAPTER 14

They careened through the kaleidoscopic vortex of the next few hours. Telling the injured kidnapper to self-administer the sedative to help ease the pain as Emily helped Rosa to her feet and out the door, pausing only to grab Otto. A desperate scramble down the emergency stairwell. Heading for the building's back door, seeing the delivery van waiting in the alley, reversing direction and exiting out the front. Footsteps behind them, Emily tugging Rosa along.

Faster. Faster. Faster.

They lost themselves in the maze of the open market. The smell of roasting coffee, frankincense, and sweat. A goat bleating as it was led off to slaughter. Perched on a wooden crate, a zealot in Orthodox garb yelled through a megaphone in Amharic, his finger stabbing toward the Commonwealth complex. Drones buzzed overhead, invisible satellites hurtling past kilometers higher. Emily knocked over a bale of khat as they rounded a corner, the vendor's staccato curses fading as they sprinted out of the market and picked up two public bikes.

Emily summoned her feed to map out routes. They needed flat or downhill sections to pick up speed and had to avoid Addis Ababa University where the streets were packed with students protesting the absence of mandatory human-rights provisions in the feed's terms of service. Quads burning, lungs aching, they followed the swoop and curve of intersecting bike lanes, glancing incessantly back over their shoulders. Other cyclists swerved out of their way, swearing, as Emily and Rosa hurtled past under the dappled shade.

Emily pulled up at a random corner, and they ditched the bikes and boarded a minibus. As they squeezed in, Emily actually looked at Rosa for the first time since the apartment. Her cheeks were flushed, her eyes wide, her breath coming in short gasps. Emily hadn't seen her like that since Rosa had come off the field after losing a high school soccer tournament. Emily and Javier had been there on the sidelines ready to comfort her, but Rosa had surprised them both when she shrugged it off with a quip about how playing was more fun than winning. Rosa might be younger, but she'd somehow eclipsed them in emotional maturity.

The minibus descended into the tunnel system, joining the swarming mass of feed-driven vehicles traversing the vast network of subterranean roads that burrowed beneath the city like geophysical arteries.

Rosa was trembling on the seat beside Emily, who could feel the heat that radiated off her. Emily reached out a comforting hand, but Rosa twitched away, and Emily jerked it back like a child snatching scorched fingers from a flame.

"What—" Rosa tried to catch her breath, clutching Otto tight to her chest. "What is going on? I don't . . . I don't even know where to start. I . . ."

Emily met her gaze and looked away just as quickly. Rosa's forehead wrinkled. She was assessing Emily with fresh eyes, eyes brimming with fear, confusion, and sorrow.

Emily looked straight ahead and forced her voice to remain neutral. "It's going to be okay," she said. "I'll get you out of here, and then we can forget this ever happened."

"Em." There was too much wrapped up in that single, strangled syllable. Far too much.

"Time to get off," said Emily, lunging for the door as the minibus swooped up to the surface.

Emily looked around in the sunlight and bustle of the pick-up/drop-off zone. A *sambusa* vendor hawked her wares. The sour smell of fermenting injera. A mother harangued two kids who were tuning her out, submerged in their feeds. Had they lost Rosa's prospective abductors? How could they know for sure? No way to know. Time to make their break for the airport.

Emily hailed a private car, and they plunged back into the city's underbelly. Emily sat as far from Rosa as she could, staring out at the tunnel lights flickering past, scanning through her feed for evidence of pursuit, obsessively listening to Rosa's shallow breathing.

And then, impossibly, they were at the airport and lifting off in the plane Emily had chartered back in Camiguin, the leafy streets of Addis falling away behind them. Questions whose answers led only to more questions. Questions with no answers at all. Exhaustion. Oceans and continents spinning by as the planet turned on its axis. Dreams of garden paths forking and doubling back on themselves, phoenixes rising in flame and falling into ash, an abstract tide of melancholy surging and receding. Bumpy landing in Seattle. Transfer to a seaplane. And here, now, finally, they stepped off the pontoon and onto the dock.

CHAPTER 15

Emily looked up and her chest tightened. Waves lapped against the pilings and the smell of brine was overpowering. Mist shrouded much of the Island, drifting in long, ragged fingers, punctured by swaying evergreens. A new wing had been added to the school, and outbuildings stood where there had once been lawns. But the barn was still there, and the orchard, and the vegetable garden, and behind it all the forest brooded, damp and green and full of shadow.

"They've grown," said Rosa. "There are more than fifteen hundred students, and even the nonteaching staff has tripled. Between his responsibilities as a Commonwealth board member, advocacy, and philanthropic efforts, Javi has his hands full."

Emily sensed that Rosa was observing her from a slight remove. There was uncertainty beneath her words, a mixture of concern, fear, and pity that Emily found hard to stomach. This distance hadn't been there before. She and Rosa had never been self-conscious with each other. After spending so long building a buffer between their lives, Emily couldn't help but wish that they could pick up their relationship where they had left off, like old acquaintances falling right back into friendship. That Emily was excruciatingly aware of how ridiculous such a wish was only made it that much worse.

"Come on," said Rosa. "Let's go."

She squeezed Emily's hand and pulled her off the dock and up the path. Where Emily had led Rosa in a frenzied escape through her own city, their positions were now reversed, and Rosa led Emily through the compound she had once called home.

It was difficult to hold back the memories. Endlessly tweaking the architectural plans, popping champagne bottles while initiating a new member into their cadre, getting dirt under her fingernails as she weeded the vegetable garden, staying up all night mining Dag's feed to prime him for what would be his first and only operation, hiking through the woods with lips and fingers stained purple by wild blackberries.

It was down this same path that Emily had fled after her betrayal was revealed thirteen years ago. When they opened the backdoor into the feed, giving them godlike access to everyone's most intimate digital lives, they had committed to never use their powers of suasion on each other. Having broken that sacred pact, Emily knew she could never show her face here again. When you operated outside the law, the only laws that mattered were the ones you invented. What could be a worse transgression than breaking a law of your own devising? And yet, here she was. But she shouldn't be, she needn't be. She had already rescued Rosa, hadn't she? Emily was useless, damaged, had no more to offer. The others could take it from here. She could fade right into the background, return to self-imposed purgatory.

"I—" Emily slowed her pace. "I think I'm going to . . . I should . . . You go on . . . Really . . ."

But Rosa shot her a glare that brooked no argument, a glare that the Rosa Emily had once known would have been incapable of. And so, chastened, Emily forced one foot in front of the other, tried to ignore her churning thoughts and burning cheeks, the unbearable shame that tainted every waking moment.

"Rosa!"

Javier hurried down the steps from the deck of the ranch house, did a double take as he saw Emily next to his sister, almost tripped, recovered, and came to an uncertain stop. Rosa had alerted him that she needed refuge, was en route, but Emily had refused to let her tell Javier about her own involvement, didn't want any of her blame shifted onto the wrong target, even indirectly.

Javier was dressed in his trademark tight-fitting black leather. While he had always been thin, he now flirted with gauntness, implying a shy praying mantis. His dark-brown hair had turned to salt-and-pepper gray, a wedding band encircled his ring finger, and he favored his left leg. There was also a new but quiet confidence, an air of the patrician about his bearing that hadn't been there before. The dark eyes of the man who had been Emily's best friend since adolescence were still as large and deep as inkwells, unreadable emotions flickering through them like the pages of a child's flip-book, asking, apologizing, demanding, judging, forgiving, haranguing, accusing, and searching, always searching.

"Hey, Javi," said Emily, hating the schoolgirlish timidity in her own voice and covering it with brittle humor. "Long time no see."

CHAPTER 16

"Rosa, darling," said Javier after the story was told, "could you give us a minute?"

Rosa cocked her head to one side and gave him a look with enough subtext to crash a feed connection, but all she said was, "Sure."

She stood, her hand darting in to give Emily's shoulder a quick squeeze as she passed. Emily twitched, suppressing the subconscious reaction to block what could be an attack, discomfited by how deeply the unexpected small gesture of kindness affected her. The feeling was warm, fuzzy, and unfamiliar, manna from a heaven she wasn't entitled to.

And then it was just the two of them sitting in front of the fire. The rest of the residents were respectfully avoiding the large living room that had been their center of operations during the years they had spent subverting the feed. How many times had the world been changed from this room? How many disasters avoided? How many lives saved?

Javier fiddled with his hands, his long, slender fingers lacing and unlacing like stalks of seagrass in a turbulent current. He would not meet her eyes, but then again, she might not meet his either. Again, Emily felt detached from reality, as if this were a dream and she was an observer and not a participant. Maybe all this was a dream, the entirety of the past few days nothing but a figment of feverish sleep. Dengue was on the rise in Camiguin again, wasn't it? Or maybe this was death. Perhaps Niko had won the fight after all and the great beyond consisted of nothing more than a palimpsest of memory and imagination, endlessly looping until pure thought faded into nothing.

Javier stood without a word, his body unfolding slowly from the chair. His steps were silent as he retreated to a far corner, a habit he'd picked up tiptoeing around his mother's string of abusive boyfriends. If he was a product of Emily's subconscious, what did it mean that she'd apparently rendered him mute but left so many other details intact? A migraine flared like a match struck deep in a cavern. Enough mental gymnastics. Be this dream, death, or reality, all Emily could do was the next thing.

"I figure we could both use this." Javier was back with a bottle of Château Latour and two glasses, his tone reaching for an evasive bonhomie.

She accepted the wine gratefully, swirling it and watching the purple legs bleed down the sides of the glass in the flickering firelight. Taking a sip, she tasted minerals, ripe fruit, and salty tannins, remembered sitting around this same fire imitating sommeliers with over-the-top bullshit descriptions of wine they'd never imagined being able to afford.

"I'm sorry," she said. "I didn't mean to barge back into your life. It was just that Rosa . . . Now that she's here with you, safe, I'll go. You can tell Commonwealth about Lowell's plans, or not, it's none of my business anyway. I just—I just couldn't let them hurt Rosa."

His body tightened imperceptibly, a bowstring being pulled taut, but then he forced the tension away, appraised her like an astronomer looking for distant patterns in the cosmos.

"What happened to you?" he asked, his voice somehow both gentle and edged. "Where have you been, Em? Where are you going back to?"

Her voice caught. What could she say? She imagined telling him about Camiguin, her squalid little apartment, the torrential typhoons, roti canai, the endless flow of tourists, Rizal, how she could only find peace in violence. But that was somehow impossible to articulate, too big for words, too alien in this Pacific Northwest redoubt. It all felt affected, just some adolescent noir fantasy, as if her life as a fighter was the true dream, nothing but a passing interlude in her real life here on the Island with her friends.

"Nothing," she said.

"What do you mean, nothing?"

"It's . . . better you don't know."

Emily twisted the edge of her shirt.

"Better for who?" His voice was strangely breathless.

She sipped her wine, stared into the depths of the hearth at the roiling death's-heads and vortices of flame.

"Why, Em? Why?"

She thought of how her shins had ached for the better part of a year while Rizal trained her on the heavy bag, the pain lessening only as tens of thousands of impacts dampened her nerves.

"Because I thought, I knew, it was *important*," she said, and suddenly she was back in her body, no longer an outside observer. "Every year high tide was getting a little higher, storm surges eroded a little more topsoil, the Island got a little smaller. Droughts getting more severe, floods getting more violent, summers hotter, winters colder, biodiversity collapsing, reservoirs drying up, crops failing, refugee camps overflowing, and nobody doing a goddamn thing about it. Heads of state debating like kindergarteners, only signing treaties that required no changes from the status quo, robber barons like Lowell profiting along the way. For decades and decades and decades instead of change being the only constant, the only constant was the tragedy of the fucking commons, which was no change at all. Something *had* to be done. *Someone* had to do it. And I couldn't let Dag's newfound conscience stand in the way. And—"

"What"—Javier was shaking his head—"the hell are you talking about?"

"Javi," she said, her chest tightening, "I'm sorry. I'm so sorry. It wasn't worth it. It never could have been. I shouldn't have threatened Dag. He was one of us, part of the family." An emptiness was growing inside her, a void filling her like air in a balloon. "But I broke the code. I threatened him. I lied to you, all of you. I thought that just that one time it was necessary, given the scale of the problem and how we had no contingencies left. I couldn't let so many years of work go down the drain. But I should have. I should have let it all go in order to keep my promise. We're nothing without our word. If we can't trust each other, everything falls apart. It's the same downward spiral that broke the whole system in the first place."

Javier's wineglass smashed into the back of the hearth. The flames danced and sputtered as wine went up in steam. Emily's body tensed, her back going rigid.

Why couldn't she read him anymore? It used to be that Emily could intuit other people's dreams, fears, and weaknesses with little more than a glance. That was how she'd managed to survive without adults even after her parents had died, how she'd managed to take in strays like Javier, Rosa, and the rest, protect them, help them file their paperwork, appease the bureaucratic monster, stay out of the hands of the state long enough to reach legal adulthood and set off on their own. She used to be able to finish Javier's sentences, predict his every move without a second thought. But now he sat there with his eyes closed, implacable, opaque. Had she lost her gift? Had building up her physical intuition in the ring sapped her social intelligence? Was Javier simply a different person now, a stranger? Wasn't she?

"I didn't want this," he said in a hoarse whisper she strained to hear over the pop and hiss of the fire. "I never wanted this, any of it."

Silence.

"Javi," she said, emotion thickening her words. "You're amazing. I've followed everything via feed, everything. You've accomplished more than we ever dreamed of. You've changed the world over and over, and now you're about to do it again. It's , , , I don't even know. It's . . ."

But he was shaking his head again, resting it in his hands, elbows on knees.

"Javi?"

"I didn't want this," he repeated softly. "It's not me. You were our leader. But then you were gone. Everyone was floundering. It was awful. And I'm still floundering, and it's still awful."

"But—"

"*Why?*" Suddenly his voice was harsh and his huge, dark eyes locked on hers. "I don't give a shit about your precious honor. Why did you *leave*, Em? *Why did you leave?*"

She opened her mouth. Closed it.

"Because you couldn't have picked a better time," he said with bitter sarcasm. "The biggest crisis we'd ever had to recover from, everything, everyone on the line, and poof, just like that, you vanish into thin air. Calls, messages, goddamn private investigators dissolving into the ether. Nothing. Thirteen years. *Thirteen years.*" He squeezed his eyes and mouth shut, let out a suppressed growl. "What. The. Fuck."

He leaned across the coffee table toward her, palms splayed, eyes wide. "And now suddenly you're here and you've rescued Rosa from a kidnapping and it's all part of this big conspiracy and don't get me wrong, she's my sister and I would do anything for her and I'm terrified for her and I'm so, so grateful but you nearly *decapitated* one of her assailants and it looks like someone throttled your neck and your arms are covered in scars and you've got a black eye and to be perfectly honest you look like you were run over by a bus but Rosa says they never touched you, the kidnappers, that you looked like that when she got home and you were just standing there in her living room and now that you're finally here not only will you not tell me the slightest goddamn thing but the first words that come out of your mouth is that you'll *go*."

And then Javier was standing, towering over her, firelight illuminating half his face, his entire body trembling. "You are coming with me to tell Diana what you just told me. If we're lucky, maybe that will be enough. Then you can crawl back into whatever hole you've dug for yourself. But I swear to God, you are not *go*ing anywhere until that happens. Don't you dare. Don't you fucking dare."

CHAPTER 17

An owl hooted in the distance as Emily exited the house and paused to let her eyes adjust to the darkness. The night was cold, and the skies were clear. She pulled up her hood and headed off the path, crossing the wide lawn that led up toward the forest. She moved slowly, careful not to twist an ankle in a gopher hole.

When she reached the far edge of the lawn and the buildings were comfortably distant, she skirted the woods, tasting the forest's loamy scent and reaching out to touch each tree as she passed.

The madrone must have shed its bark recently because the trunk was so smooth it could have been polished. Next were the gnarled knots of an oak tree. Then the hard resin blisters of a young Douglas fir and then, finally, the deep furrows of a mature redwood.

Emily stopped, leaning back to see the dark profile of the tree, a pillar blotting out the stars. Slowly, she removed her jacket, folded it, and laid it on the grass a few meters away. Then she summoned her feed, queued up N.W.A.'s "Appetite for Destruction," and maxed out the volume.

Rizal had run her through this routine so many times that every move was etched into Emily's muscle memory. She would get up in the morning and he'd drill her with punch and kick targets, observing and coaching every strike. In the afternoons, she would repeat the exercise on the heavy bag. The next day was more of the same. She'd make the same mistakes. He'd correct them. And again and again until days became weeks and weeks became months and months became years and slowly, ever so slowly, she learned to fight.

Now, with explosive rhymes raging over high-pitched synth, Emily unleashed every move in her repertoire on the unsuspecting redwood. *Don't you fucking dare.* Javier's twisted face swam before her. The crack of his glass shattering against the hearth had been so sharp, the wood popping and hissing where the wine splattered.

Strike, counterstrike, combo, repeat.

Victory was not a thing to savor, it was just another base camp. You reached the peak you were striving for, and the view from the summit was of the higher mountains to come. Those who bothered with self-congratulation neglected mission-critical preparation for the next ascent or, at best, stranded themselves at a local maximum.

The bark was thick and corky, springing back against her feet, shins, and knees. The bodies of her opponents were never so forgiving. In her first fight, she'd broken her hand when she landed an uppercut on her opponent's jaw. Violence always hurt the offender as well as the victim, even if the vector was subtler.

As punch after punch split the skin on her knuckles, stringy fibers of bark came away stuck to the bloody wounds. The psychological warfare she'd overseen from this very island had warped her own reality, left scars deeper than the puckered flesh that turned her skin into a patchwork. They had exploited a backdoor into the feed, and doing so had opened a backdoor into exploiting each other.

The music howled its fury at the uncaring, broken world, bass thumping in time to the beat of ten thousand shattered hearts.

Her lungs burned, her throat constricted, her joints ached, her head pounded, but she pushed through it all, pushed harder, further, deeper, demanded herself to be up to it, forced herself to persevere, to embrace the pain, to exact and receive punishment.

Something touched her shoulder, and Emily spun, lashing out instinctively, terrified by whatever unknown threat could possibly lurk on this remote idyllic island. But it wasn't an assassin dispatched by Lowell or a nightmare creature. It was Rosa, and Emily had to redirect her reactive sweep so as to not take Rosa's legs out from under her.

Rosa stumbled back, yelping as liquid spilled from one of the two mugs she carried. Emily muted the music and realized that she was soaked with sweat, that her breath was coming in ragged gasps, and that every muscle was trembling uncontrollably.

"What the living fuck?" said Rosa, holding up her dripping arm.

"Holy shit, Rosa," said Emily, heart pounding. "You scared the hell out of me."

"I was standing right there yelling at you forever," said Rosa.

Emily opened her mouth. Closed it. She tapped her ear. "Music," she said. "Couldn't hear you."

"Jesus," said Rosa, shaking her head. "You almost *kicked* me."

"Sorry," said Emily. "I'm sorry. I didn't realize it was you."

"You're freaking me out, Em," said Rosa.

"I, um, this is . . ."

Rosa stared at her for a long moment, and Emily was mortified that she had been discovered, that someone had been watching her routine, that Rosa had glimpsed Pixie. Emily shouldn't have come back here. Shouldn't have stayed. Shouldn't be invading these people's lives again.

"You're bleeding," said Rosa, squinting at Emily in the starlight.

Emily looked down at her stained hands and felt her pants sticking to her raw shins.

"Should I go get a first-aid kit?" asked Rosa. "Hang on, I'll just run back and grab one."

"No," said Emily desperately. "No, this is nothing. Don't worry about it."

"Nothing? You break into my apartment and decapitate an abductor and then beat up trees in the middle of the night?"

"I—" Emily fumbled for words. *Don't worry about it, this is just a training routine. You should have seen what I've done to people in the ring. This is what penance looks like.* But she couldn't say any of those things, couldn't say *anything*.

"So," said Rosa with that special kind of fierceness that was little more than vulnerability's veneer. "You're a fucking ninja?"

"No," said Emily. "It's . . ."

The awkward silence stretched.

"You don't want help," said Rosa. "And you don't want to talk about it." She sighed, shut her eyes tight and opened them again. "Well, I guess this is the least I can offer."

Rosa approached, and Emily was horrified to see the hesitation in her movement, the evident fear, as if Emily might lash out at any moment.

Rosa reached out—she was trembling too—and offered Emily a steaming mug. "Chai," she said. "Frances grinds the spices fresh daily. She's obsessed. I spilled most of the other one, so we'll have to share."

At a loss, Emily accepted the mug and was grateful for the warmth of the ceramic in her hands. She smelled ginger and cardamom.

"How'd you know where I was?" asked Emily.

"Ooooph." Rosa sat down on the ground and patted the grass beside her. "Every time you had a new guest visit the Island, you woke 'em up in the middle of the damn night with cocoa and dragged 'em out here to look at the stars. When I was your victim, we talked about why I was moving out to get into the art scene. I distinctly remember that there weren't enough marshmallows in the hot chocolate."

Emily sat, heart still pounding in her ears, every centimeter of her body complaining.

"Shame on me," she said.

"Quite."

Emily took a sip, savored the creamy concoction. "It's delicious, thank you."

They passed the mug back and forth. Thoughts rolled around Emily's head like marbles. Where to start? How to start? Whether to start at all? Who was Emily but a nexus of memory and anticipation, a passing shadow in the heave and flow of Rosa's life? Emily shivered against the deep chill of cold air on drying sweat. There were so many things she couldn't say. So many things she should have said but never did. Sometimes the only real answer was a deeper truth, no matter how painful it was to acknowledge.

"Rosa," said Emily, "I want you to know how proud of you I am. No, really. I gave you a hard time when you opted out of our crew because I had a difficult time understanding why anyone who could wouldn't devote everything to helping our cause. After you left, I was always so consumed with our mission that I didn't make enough time for you. But now I realize how big a mistake that was. What you've built, who you've become, it's just . . . It's beautiful. You're beautiful. I'm not good at this kind of thing because I assume you already know, but I love you."

"You're a jerk," said Rosa, her voice catching.

"I know," said Emily.

Rosa nudged Emily's shoulder with her own, and there was a moment of contemplative silence.

"When I was little," said Rosa, "our mom would go on binges, disappear for weeks at a time. You know that, obviously. Javi did his best to take care of me. An eight-year-old trying to be a grown man. I was a total brat, of course, whining about why we were having cornflakes for dinner again." Her laugh was throaty. "Then Mom would come back, and there were tears and apologies and promises we knew would be broken but we believed anyway because how could we not? I handled it okay, probably because I had my older brother to rely on. But Javi had this tension in him all the time, like an overinflated balloon about to pop. The disappearing acts were bad, but the worst part was the *uncertainty*."

Rosa sighed. "When we got home from school, would Mom be there? If not, would she be gone for an hour or a month? Were other kids' parents like this? Was her absence better than her string of violent boyfriends? When they beat her, should we call the police? Which soup kitchens were close enough that we could get to them on the bus but far enough away that none of our friends from school would see us? And on and on and—Oh! Look at that."

A shooting star flared.

"A few months after we moved in with you, that old tension began to ebb. Javi's always wanted to be a good lieutenant, not a leader," Rosa continued in a lower voice. "Now, though . . . Javi's hard on himself. He's the only one who doesn't see all the great things he's accomplished. He just sees the work left to do, the impossible magnitude of it, the maddening politics, the stupid half measures. It's a burden, not a joy. I wish it weren't like that. He's my brother. God knows I love him more than anyone, but I can't change who he is."

The accusation was all the more heart wrenching for being left unsaid. It explained all the anger and resentment pent up inside Javier. How could an unwilling captain fail to resent the predecessor who had forsaken the ship, forcing him to take the helm? She had assuaged Javier's fear of abandonment just in time to fulfill it herself.

"When did you get so goddamn wise?" Emily choked on the words.

"When did you turn into such a crybaby?"

"Screw you."

"This is a romantic spot, but I prefer men."

Rosa leaned her head on Emily's shoulder.

Emily had never been more grateful for anything in her entire life.

CHAPTER 18

Rosa returned to the house, but Emily begged off, wrapping herself in her jacket and lying back on the grass. There was so much to process, far more than her head or her heart could contain.

Undiluted by city glow, the sky was thick with stars. Emily's feed tagged distant nebulae, projected a spaghetti of satellite orbits, and indicated where to look when a shooting star was about to burn through the atmosphere. She was about to dismiss it, disintermediate the final frontier, when she saw a message from Rizal.

Hey, girl, I know you value your personal space, and I normally wouldn't do this, but I haven't heard from you since fight night (as your account testifies, it was a lucrative evening). I dropped by your apartment, but your neighbor, the depressed Aussie kid, said he hadn't seen you in a couple days. Everything okay? If you come on down to the gym, I'll help stretch you out. Please forgive my irritating protectiveness, but you're an earner. Oh, and you must have been convincing because Mr. Harding's people made an offer on the club. Kisses, Rizal

Lowell didn't need convincing. Accruing a global network of feedless fight clubs was the perfect investment for someone plotting against Commonwealth. Sure, the feed was officially inviolable, but how long would that last if things got nasty? After all, Lowell's entire plan was to ensure that things got nasty. Emily had derailed the kidnapping, but surely he must already be executing contingencies aimed at sabotaging Javier's initiative and setting the stage for a coup. She tried not to remember the way the man had twitched on the floor, cleaver still lodged in his neck.

Rizal didn't know any of that. He didn't see the larger game of which he was but a pawn, had no idea who Emily really was. She made every effort to be just another fighter, keeping him at arm's length. Imagining him knocking on the door of her empty apartment inspired both indignation at his snooping and gratitude that anyone cared enough to check on her.

She ought to respond to Rizal, at least let him know that she was fine and that she wouldn't be back for a few days. But just like it had felt impossible to bridge the gap from Camiguin to her old life, now that she was back here on the Island, she couldn't channel Pixie, couldn't find the words to assuage Rizal's worry.

Dismissing her feed, Emily stared up at the naked stars.

She hadn't meant to build a shadow empire. It was just one of those things that sort of happened, like repetitive-strain injury. She helped out a friend in a bind. Then another, and another, and another. What could be more important and innocuous than that? Before long, the favors grew from a trickle to a flood, and Emily sat at the center of a vibrant karmic web that spawned opportunity after opportunity. Ultimately, everything she had accomplished was built on doing and trading favors.

On Emily's seventh birthday, her mom had given her a telescope. They'd set it up in the backyard, and Emily had been shocked at the new intimacy of the cosmos. The next day, Emily had lugged the telescope into the garage. Tools, workbenches, and projects in various degrees of completion filled the space, everything clean, organized, and worn with loving use. Together, they had taken the telescope apart, examining every piece as her mom explained optics and how diamond cutters had once been recruited to grind glass lenses by hand. Then they put it all back together. Emily remembered the feeling of satisfaction when she reattached the azimuth clamp, the burgeoning sense that if she paid attention, the world could make sense, that its secrets could be understood and mastered.

The next night, her parents drove her out to Joshua Tree National Park. There, amid the empty desert, they'd sipped hot chocolate and peered up at the universe. Emily had worried that understanding the inner machinations of her telescope might diminish the wonder it provided, but when she gazed through the eyepiece, she realized that the brief glimpse from the backyard had been nothing but a smog-shrouded preview, that the number and scale of whirling galaxies were far greater than she could ever hope to comprehend, that knowing how the telescope functioned enhanced its magic, that humans had made this thing that brought them closer to infinity.

By the time Emily entered high school, her telescope wasn't getting quite as much use as it once had but still occupied a place of pride in her bedroom. Her parents had pushed to her test into a local charter school. Only a few months into her freshman year, Emily had already realized two things. First, the students were smarter than the teachers, and way smarter than the administrators. Second, her peers would go to extreme lengths to procure booze and pills.

Knowing it must be good if all her friends were so enamored, Emily wholeheartedly experimented with the narcotic cornucopia, doing her best to hide her misadventures from her parents. But the appeal soon wore thin. She just couldn't get that excited about chemical-enhanced experiences. They weren't *bad*, most of the time anyway. They just weren't that *interesting*. It seemed to her like a crutch for boredom.

Boredom wasn't a feeling Emily was accustomed to. The world was an endlessly fascinating place. Physicists probed the origins of the universe. Journalists chased stories to the end of the earth. Hackers pried open cracks in monolithic systems. You could follow any hobby down a rabbit hole of obsessive curiosity. Emily loved learning. Which was why she hated high school.

For Emily, high school sharply delineated the fault line between scholarship and institutional education. She would geek out with her classmates over some new, luxuriantly obscure topic, reveling at the wondrous complexity of the world. But that was *after* school. In class, they suffered through curriculum that was neither compelling nor comprehensive.

The situation perplexed Emily, so she started asking people about it. It wasn't the teachers' fault. The school qualified for funding based on standardized test performance, so the administration naturally required instructors to teach to the test. The higher the scores, the bigger the checks. All the better if students went on to attend top-tier universities. But when Emily chatted up alumni, they told her how much student debt they were racking up. That's when Emily realized she was halfway down a new rabbit hole.

School was boring her out of her mind. Her classmates were brilliant and similarly frustrated, but they viewed it all as a big game. It wasn't a game that appealed to Emily. She found her friends much more interesting. Life was a screenplay to Florence, who had been shooting and editing footage since she was eight. Even though his home life was fucked up, Javier played math like a violin, and Emily imagined his head was filled with endless glyphs. Carolyn had read more or less the entire library of classics in the original Greek and Latin.

Unlike academic topics, people were just weird. They couldn't be categorized, not really. They were a strange agglomeration of habits, hopes, dreams, foibles, memories, and DNA. There were no clean cuts. Everyone really was a special snowflake after all. Listening was the best way to get to know people, and questions greased the wheels.

Which was why Emily hadn't been paying attention when the assistant interrupted Ms. Randolph's physics class, whispered in the teacher's ear, and beckoned Emily. As she was escorted to the principal's office, Emily's questions multiplied: What had she done? Did they know she'd bought those pills from Dane? What would she do if they pressured her to rat him out?

The principal's face was tight. *I'm sorry, Emily, I don't know how to say this. There was an accident. Your father was killed, and your mother is in the ICU. Is there someone you can call?* Frank disbelief. What a ridiculous thing to say. She had downed a bowl of cornflakes that morning while her dad told her to hurry up because they were going to be late and her mom prepped to give her big presentation. But even as Emily marshaled her arguments against the obvious inaccuracy of the principal's statement—surely there must have been some mistake—she noticed how genuinely ill at ease he was. His discomfort was so profound that it gave her pause, and the second she stopped to consider whether there was any chance what he was saying might be true, emptiness bloomed.

There hadn't been a mistake. They had been hit by a bus while crossing the street to the farmer's market. Her father was dead and her mother died in the hospital the next day. Emily wasn't prepared to confront the infinity of her parents' absence. Grasping for a way to corral the gaping hole inside her, Emily refused to admit she had no other relatives living in the United States, refused to return to Seoul to live with her aunt, refused to allow the hovering adults who weren't her parents to hijack her future.

Instead, Emily sat down in the middle of the garage. Surrounded by her mother's tools, she had closed her eyes and imagined that the invisible systems that governed the outside world could be taken apart, rendered comprehensible, and put back together just like the telescope. She read all the paperwork, reviewed the accounts, called in favors, and played the lawyers and the insurance people and the police and the psychologists and the school administrators and the distant relatives and the family friends and everyone else against each other, constructing a self-reinforcing bureaucratic fiction to obscure the fact that she was a bereaved teenager living alone.

Independence transformed from reaction to compulsion. Once the lies built up momentum, there was no going back. Money was a problem. She couldn't pay the bills with the legit part-time jobs available to her as a student, so she sold pills for Dane, quickly surpassed him, and leapfrogged up the supply chain until she was setting up major distribution transactions.

At that level, the business wasn't about drugs per se but rather the buying and selling of anything both valuable and shady. It might be details of a biotech company's new breakthrough molecule, an introduction to an accountant skilled at offshoring capital, dirt on a mayoral candidate, a coveted invitation to Wysteria's next house party, or the guarantee that Port of Long Beach drones wouldn't surveil Berth G215 between 3:00 and 5:00 a.m. The specifics were fungible. This was the realm of organized crime, and the Angeleno gangs liked Emily. As a smart, socially adept teenage girl, she was the perfect combination of competent and unthreatening, able to traverse the complex political geography of warring factions and broker otherwise impossible deals.

Soon, Emily had more money than she knew what to do with, and she spent it on the only thing she really cared about: her friends. She had a way of becoming a confidant without meaning to. Merely by finding people interesting, she earned their trust. Whatever Emily earned, she protected. So, when Florence received a death threat after posting footage exposing a secret white-supremacist rally, Emily made the problem go away. And when she found out that Javier's junkie mom had absconded to Houston, she'd rescued Javier and Rosa and invited them to live with her. Before long, she had a house full of brilliant misfits.

The more Emily's influence grew, the more legitimate her operation became. It wasn't about drugs or even trade secrets anymore. It was about favors, and she had accrued quite a tab from a long list of powerful people. The better she got at manipulating the system, the more broken she realized it was. By the time she graduated high school, she had begun to direct her influence toward repairing some of the rips in the social fabric through which her wards had fallen. Having won her independence, that became her mission.

An owl hooted in the distance, reeling her back in from reverie. Her body was stiff and sore. Grass scratched at her jacket.

Society was just another telescope. The feed was too. After taking them apart, Emily had left Javier to pick up the pieces.

CHAPTER 19

The sun burned away the morning fog until the last remaining tufts formed a fluffy patchwork above the gray-green surface of the San Francisco Bay. From this vantage in the hills, Berkeley spread out below them in a colorful grid, the campanile rising up from the leafy university campus. Emily wondered whether gangs fought turf wars over these idyllic blocks like they had in LA before the fires or whether she was just a relic from a darker age.

However the world might have changed, her presence here confirmed it hadn't entirely thrown off the shadow of violence. Javier walked beside her, his nervous energy palpable and incongruous in this quiet residential neighborhood full of period-revival homes.

Ping. Another notification in her feed. Lowell again.

I'm hosting a party next week up in the mountains. I can have a plane pick you up on Camiguin. What'll it take to convince you to come?

Emily hadn't expected Lowell to go full crush. Maybe she had overplayed the seductress bit. Now that Rosa was safe, Emily could always take Lowell up on his booty call and smother the old dirty bastard in his sleep. But she didn't have time for distractions right now. She dismissed the message unanswered.

On the flight down from Washington, Emily had tried to find a way to bridge the vertiginous gap that separated her and Javier, but he had remained immersed in his feed.

There is no justice, just us. Watching his fingers dance in the air, she thought about how the only honor to be found was the kind you fashioned for yourself. When politics was poisoned by corruption, nothing was more important than the promises you made to your friends.

This cute little neighborhood was the last place on earth she wanted to be, a picturesque hell. She couldn't be here, couldn't face these people, couldn't risk hurting them again. But she also couldn't desert Javier, couldn't be the person to walk out on him yet again. Every path, every thought turned back on itself.

"This is it," said Javier.

Emily looked up at the charming cottage with the neatly tended garden. So this was where Dag had spent the intervening years. A wave of dizziness washed over her and she caught herself on the railing as they stepped up to the door.

They stood there for an awkward moment.

"Are you going to knock?" she asked.

Impossibly, Javier seemed even more anxious than she was. He probably wasn't keen on showing up at Dag's home with the woman who had threatened to dox Dag's mentor. Whatever this was, it wasn't a friendly social call. But Javier grimaced and rapped his knuckles on the door.

The door opened, and Emily saw Dag face-to-face for the first time in thirteen years. He had put on weight, his face a little fuller and his body a little thicker. But his hair was still artfully mussed up, and his short beard had a little amber mixed into the brown. He wore a white linen shirt over khakis and where once she had seen hunger and ambition in his clear blue eyes, Emily detected an unfamiliar glimmer of contentment.

"Come on in," he said, and Emily flashed back to the hotel room where she had fantasized about riding Dag instead of Lowell. She hoped the disconcerting heat in her belly didn't reach her cheeks.

Emily and Javier removed their shoes and followed Dag through the house. The living room had been converted into an art studio, and there was a half-finished sketch on the large drafting table, a portrait of two barefoot girls wading into a stream.

"How are the twins?" Javier's tone sounded casual, but Emily could feel the strain underneath it.

"A handful, as ever," said Dag. "Layla is obsessed with architecture, which I didn't know was on the menu for third graders. She's always building these crazy models. And Drew is a social butterfly. I'm pretty sure she already has more friends than I've ever had put together. It's staggering how different they are. Age and DNA are apparently the only thing they share."

"It's beautiful," said Emily, nodding to the picture. "They're beautiful."

"Thanks," said Dag. "I love 'em to death."

Stairs led up on the right, but Dag took them straight through to the kitchen. In addition to a number of original drawings, there was a faded photo of a Greek coastal village and a couple of smeared finger paintings. She smelled caramelized onions. Bananas, mangosteens, and avocados were piled high in a bowl, and cast-iron cookware hung from hooks above the tile counter.

The whole home felt lived-in, and Emily had a strong sense of déjà vu. It was as if walking through the house was a physical manifestation of cracking Dag's feed so many years before. Both were filled with thousands of traces that reflected his habits, preferences, and identity. They told his story. She imagined taking apart every millimeter of this house with a full forensics team and using the results to reconstruct that story and shape its future chapters, just as they'd done with his feed.

Who are you? That was the question Emily had posed to Dag as he peeled away the layers, getting closer and closer to the truth of their careful manipulations. Did all the little clues people left in their wake sum up the lives they led? Did that sum encompass their identities, or was there some ineffable kernel in the leftovers, forever inaccessible? When all was said and done, who really was the man leading them through the back door of the cottage?

Javier followed Dag, and Emily was suddenly aware of being on the verge of something. A migraine blazed and withdrew in the space of a single breath. She was caught between her fear of burning up on reentry into these people's lives and the undeniable necessity of protecting them.

Shaking her head, Emily stepped out the back door and into a jungle.

Branches knit into a thick canopy overhead, the light that filtered through it soft and golden. Vines crawled and dangled everywhere. There were ferns big enough to hide a velociraptor and flowers of every hue and intensity. Her feed tagged the exotic varietals, supplying name, genus, and distinguishing characteristics. The air was humid and rich with overlapping scents of jasmine, citrus, and compost. Leaves whispered, water dripped, and Emily wondered whether, like Alice, she had just stepped through the looking glass.

But it wasn't a jungle.

It was a greenhouse, built directly off the back of the cottage so that the two combined were a single symbiotic structure. It might not be an alternate dimension, but it was a world away from Berkeley. In fact, it felt a lot like the rainforest hugging the slopes of Camiguin's volcanoes.

Emily hurried after Dag and Javier along the path that wound through the lush vegetation. After a few tight bends, they emerged into a clearing, a coffee table at its center. A woman stood to greet them. She had curly, brown hair, was neither tall nor short, beautiful nor unattractive. More than anything, she was unassuming, forgettable. But

Emily remembered her from long-ago forays into Dag's feed and from the rare but more recent Commonwealth press releases that referenced their chief intelligence officer.

"Holy shit," said Diana, eyes widening as she saw Emily. "You look like you got stuck in a BDSM dungeon and forgot the safe word." She raised a finger. "I *always* tell Dag to remember the safe word. If I'm ever forced to give one of those godawful commencement speeches that Javier is so fond of, that will be the kernel of divine wisdom I offer to the assembled throng of bored, horny graduates. *Remember the safe word.*"

"If she attacks you," said Dag, "the safe word is *zeppelin*."

"Baby, that's classified," said Diana.

"You two get settled in," said Dag, rolling his eyes. "I'll fetch the coffee."

CHAPTER 20

"Come on, Javier," said Diana. "You know we can't do that."

"Look," said Javier. "You guys understand what's at stake here." His leg was bouncing under the coffee table. Was this pitch, rather than her presence, what lay at the root of his obvious anxiety? "I've been working on this initiative for years, and it's got barely enough momentum to actually work. We're talking progressive wealth redistribution on a global scale. A real solution to inequality is within our reach. No civilization has ever been able to do this before. It'll raise hundreds of millions of people out of poverty, even the playing field a bit, make this precarious new world order a little more stable. Now that you've heard what Lowell's up to, it's even more important to get this thing implemented."

"You must have anticipated there would be pushback," said Diana.

"*Pushback?*" said Javier. "I've been dealing with pushback since I proposed the damn thing years ago. Everyone fighting tooth and nail to prevent it, even those who stand to benefit. This isn't *pushback*. This is a conspiracy."

"If I were about to antagonize the superrich, conspiracy is precisely the kind of pushback I'd expect," said Diana. "People don't like other people redistributing their money, especially the kind of people who like money so much that they dedicate their lives to collecting it."

"They tried to kidnap my sister."

Dag and Diana glanced at each other.

"We agree with you," said Dag. "I've been pushing my contacts to support your initiative since the beginning. Diana's doing the same."

"Great," said Javier. "That's why I came to you first. Keep supporting it by keeping this between us."

Diana shook her head. "You know I can't do that."

"Yes, you can," said Javier, frustration rising in his voice. "What's the upshot of reporting this kidnapping attempt? Having you increase security on me and the other board members and our families, right? *Right?* Tell me I'm wrong."

Diana drained the dregs of her coffee and stared at Javier evenly.

"You're not wrong," she said. "And if Rosa was randomly targeted, then I might be able to keep it to myself for a while. But unless I misunderstood Emily's report, this is anything but random." She turned to Emily. "Why did Lowell order the kidnapping?"

"To create a point of leverage that would allow him to pressure Javier into delaying or calling off the new inequality program," said Emily, remembering baijiu overflowing the rim of the little cup, spreading across the table.

Javier shot Emily a wounded look, and she shrugged. What did he want her to say? She'd already told them everything except for her own personal history as a fighter.

Diana opened her hands. "Exactly. Lowell and his cohorts aren't trying to collect a ransom. This is a political play to manipulate Commonwealth, and you can't ask me to keep this intel from the board."

Javier clenched his fists. "Just hold off until the initiative passes."

"And when exactly will that be?"

"Work with me here, Diana."

"What do you think I'm doing right now?"

"You know these things take time."

"And you know I can't ignore this. What if Lowell has already found other points of leverage? What if other board members suspect they might be at risk but don't want to raise a fuss, or what if they're already compromised?"

"You heard Emily," said Javier. "Lowell already has agents inside Commonwealth."

"Of course he does," said Diana. "And counterintelligence is part of intelligence."

"So you're saying you know about every mole?"

"That's not why you want to keep this quiet," said Diana. "But I do agree that discretion is required. We'll call an emergency board meeting tomorrow night. But we'll do it off-site so we can limit our exposure. I'll invite only enough to have a quorum, not the entire board. We can limit it to just us, Rachel, Sofia, Liane, and Baihan."

"Tomorrow night?" Javier was incredulous. "Fuck you, Diana."

"Hey," said Dag. "There's no need for that in here. Calm down, both of you."

There was an awkward silence.

"If I may," said Emily. "Why is telling the board about this situation so problematic?"

This time it was Javier's turn to glance between Dag and Diana. His sigh bore a heavy burden. He looked down into the film of grounds at the bottom of his cup and then up at Emily.

"It's taken everything I have to get the initiative to the brink," he said. "And this revelation about Lowell could destroy everything."

"Couldn't it also inspire people to get behind it?" asked Emily. "Nothing unites people like a common enemy."

Javier shrugged.

Diana drummed her fingers on the table. "Everyone is at each other's throats," she said. "It's all very diplomatic in the worst possible way."

"Diplomats," said Dag, "are people who murder you politely."

CHAPTER 21

"I need to think," said Javier. "Let's walk."

So he and Emily waved off the car she had ordered via feed and set off down the street. The enterprising roots of gnarled oaks thrust up through the sidewalk, as if the concrete was but a minor distraction. Many of the houses were well kept, but there were a few brooding hulks covered in rotting shingles that looked ready to collapse into themselves. A vulture cruised overhead, spiraling up thermals and surveying the terrain below, sharp eyes ever on alert for carrion.

A strange kind of jealousy fermented inside Emily. Having followed Dag's life inside and out for so many years, she had half suspected she might find herself unfairly resenting his marriage. But she wasn't envious of Diana's relationship with Dag. Instead, seeing the fullness of Dag's life highlighted the emptiness of her own. He had a wife, two children, an artistic passion, a cottage on a hill. She had . . . ghosts.

The thought carried a bitter aftertaste. How could she begrudge someone who had suffered as Dag had, often at her own hand, whatever happiness he had managed to win? It was a small miracle the vulture didn't spy out the corruption in her soul.

They passed large outcrops of rock and descended pedestrian stairs sweet with the smell of honeysuckle. A drop of sweat trickled down her spine. The darkness of Javier's silent brooding was out of place in the afternoon sunshine. His gaze was turned inward, his expression dour under the dappled light.

"My dad told me this fairytale when I was little," said Emily, remembering how his stories had been the soundtrack to her stargazing, polished by retelling until they were smooth pebbles in her heart. "There was a little girl who grew up in an ancient kingdom. It was a beautiful place, full of snow-capped mountains, dense forests, and fertile soil. The king was a good man who treated his subjects with kindness and respect. The little girl was the daughter of a carpenter, but she would always escape her father's lessons to play at swords in the woods."

How odd, that after so many years the stories stayed with her, never fading. "One day, an old knight was passing through and saw the girl slashing and stabbing at imaginary foes with a willow switch. The old knight took pity on the girl, perhaps because he had no children of his own, and sponsored her training in arms up at the castle. The carpenter didn't like the sound of that, but the girl insisted, and finally her father agreed. Nine years later, the girl was a knight and was admitted into the seven-member royal guard, sworn to protect the king and each other at all costs."

As the story gained momentum, Emily recognized her father's phrasing and inflections bleeding into her own speech. "On her first anniversary as a royal guard, a dragon descended on the kingdom. It was huge and black and furious, and fire gushed from its mouth as if it had swallowed a sun. Once it had gobbled up the goats and cows and sheep, it began to feast on the villagers. In a single breath, it burned down buildings her father had spent years constructing. The king ordered his archers to shoot the beast out of the sky, but their arrows bounced off its scales. Then, the king sent his soldiers to seek out the dragon's lair, but none of them returned. Desperate, the king finally sent his royal guard."

As a child, eye pressed to the telescope, Emily had imagined how it might feel to receive such a royal mandate, to know that the world depended on you. "Together, they trekked into the mountains, following the trail of scorched earth. Up past the tree line, the high country was rocky and rugged, all sheer cliffs and barren expanses of granite. At last they reached a cave that looked like a dark wound in the side of the mountain. Bones of all shapes and sizes were scattered around the entrance, and smoke trickled out in wispy tendrils."

As she spoke, Emily wondered how a dragon might ravage the hills she and Javier were strolling through, how the oily eucalyptus would explode and the bay would go up in steam and the terrified residents would cry out in disbelief at myth made real. The residents of this fairytale kingdom had never believed in dragons until one had arrived. And Emily's own hometown of Los Angeles had been reduced to smoking rubble. What was a dragon anyway except for danger that defied comprehension?

"The battle lasted seven days. It was a blur of sweat and blood and fire, an extended siege in which the guards and monster pulled out all the stops and, having tried everything in the book, invented entirely new tactics. Finally, all were spent. The dragon collapsed onto the rocks and the knights beside it. But the knight who was the daughter of a carpenter pushed herself to her feet one more time and drew her sword. She stumbled up to the massive head that was the size of a horse cart, planning to stab the beast in its only unarmored spot: its eyeball. She reached her target. The sclera was orange instead of white, and the ovoid pupil was big enough for a child to squeeze through. But in that giant alien eye, she saw not hate, but precisely the same fear and exhaustion she herself felt. So she sheathed her blade and whispered something into the dragon's ear. And the great beast blinked and then rose up on its haunches and launched itself into the sky, flying off over the mountains, never to return."

That was the best part. She had always secretly wished the story ended there. But as Rizal would say, *The show must go on.* "As they stumbled back to the castle, the other guards demanded to know what she had told the dragon, but she refused to share her secret. Bloody, worn out, and reeking of sulfur, they reached the throne room, only to discover that the king had been murdered by his younger brother in their absence. The guardsmen drew their swords one final time, killing the traitor and then each other. For while they had saved the kingdom, they had broken their vow to protect the king."

They crested a small rise, and the view opened up. The fog was gone now, and the bay glittered under the afternoon sun. Even at this distance they could see the rainbow of color formed by the flowering vines that climbed the suspension cables of the Bay Bridge, transforming the famous spans into the world's largest hanging garden. Across the water in San Francisco, the impossibly tall graphene skyscrapers of Commonwealth's American headquarters jutted up into the infinite blue like slender daggers. The breeze carried the taste of brine. This was where the feed had been born, the headwater of the digital river through which they swam.

"That," said Javier, "is a seriously fucked-up story."

"I remember reading some article that counted the acts of violence in children's stories," said Emily. "Rape, murder, abuse, decapitation, maiming—it's all in there. Hansel and Gretel is about cannibalism. Funny how we're more honest with our kids than we think we are." She imagined the teh tarik arcing from cup to cup without a single stray drop. "The thing I took from that particular story was how we have to be *perfect*. We can't settle for saving the king *or* the kingdom. We have to save both, or lose everything."

A plane lifted off from the Oakland airport, angling up into the sky as drones made way for it in an endless feed-choreographed dance. The seagulls lacked access to the flight plan, but those the jet engines didn't scare away, the algorithms made sure to dodge. This was a kingdom where the very thing that made it so beautifully efficient was also the thing that made it vulnerable. Power gave you leverage and made you a target at the same time.

"You know I've always loved Disney feed dramas," said Javier, and his voice was sad instead of hostile. "My favorites were always the ones about best friends. But just like with your fairytale, I never liked the endings. Somehow the best friend always wound up dead or betraying the hero. The sidekick was more narrative device than person, a mere container for whatever lesson the protagonist had to learn. That's bullshit. The sidekick is the hero of their own story. Isn't it honorable to help friends achieve their dreams? To support the causes of people you love? To care about something, someone, other than yourself? Sidekicks should be celebrated. Why are they the ones who always have to get shafted?"

Javier sighed. "I've just never wanted to be alone, you know? And that's what leadership is, almost by definition. It's taking a step forward when everyone hangs back, raising your hand when others balk. And when people follow, take your lead, it's intoxicating and isolating in equal measure. Every objective you achieve becomes yet another layer of lacquer on the mask that separates you from everyone else, that warps their perception of you and your perception of yourself. When I look in the mirror now, I can't figure out where the mask ends and my real face begins. Thank the gods I have Markus to keep me grounded, because that uncertainty is just another wedge that pries relationships apart, that formalizes what should be easy and codifies what should be implicit. The way people look at me now . . ." His narrow shoulders slumped. "There is nothing on earth more terrifying than adoration."

A single red balloon drifted up from some backyard birthday party far below them, nudged this way and that by the wind, trailing a ribbon. Shocked and scared at her own audacity, Emily reached out and took Javier's hand. He didn't flinch.

CHAPTER 22

As the car whisked them through the empty streets of San Francisco, Emily reviewed the results of her research on the members of the Commonwealth inner circle that would be her audience this evening. She browsed through the vast mosaic of bios, photos, video clips, profiles, résumés, interviews, and notes, trying to relax her focus and let her attention feel its way through the morass. Intricate rhymes fizzed over heavy beats, the music lubricating her intuition. The data available on the public feed was a far cry from what she'd once been able to tap with Javier's exploit, but it still provided useful context, clues that hinted at what made these people tick.

Beside her, Javier's long fingers fidgeted in his lap as he stared out at the harsh fluorescent cones of streetlights flickering by. The motley crew populating Emily's feed were his colleagues, his fellow players in whatever enigmatic games determined the course of Rachel Leibovitz's accidental empire.

Or maybe not so accidental, knowing Rachel.

The car pulled to a smooth stop in what appeared to be an industrial district.

They disembarked. Before them rose an enormous warehouse, a hulking, black mass like a hole torn from the night. Emily thought of the dragon's cave in her father's story. Two bouncers who would have fit in at Rizal's flanked the entrance, and a single oil lamp illuminated wrought-iron letters mounted above the bronze-bound oak doors.

ANALOG

So this was it. This was the place where Dag had revealed Javier's exploit to Rachel and ended the Island's clandestine efforts to make the world a better place. This was the place that had inspired Rizal and his fellow fight-club proprietors to go feedless. In a world of constant connection, this infamous club was a shadow node, a void that shaped everything around it.

The expressionless bouncers opened the door for them, and Emily and Javier stepped into a small anteroom.

"Welcome to Analog. My name is Nell."

Nell stood at a wooden podium. Red satin curtains rippled gently behind her. Strikingly beautiful in a way that would delight glamour aficionados, she wore knee-high suede boots and a conservative black dress with an innovative cut that revealed glimpses of flawless dark skin. There was a tiny retro air-force insignia pinned on her left breast. Her pale-gray eyes sparkled with sardonic humor and made Emily feel that she was the sole focus of Nell's attention.

"It's good to see you, Mr. Flores."

"You too, Nell," said Javier.

Nell consulted a paper list, but Emily was certain she didn't need the guidance. "And it looks like this is your first time with us, Ms. Kim. It's always a pleasure bringing new friends into the Analog family. Now, while I'd love to chat, I know you both have business to attend to. They should be ready for you in there."

Nell pulled aside the curtain for them. "Ms. Kim, newcomers often find Analog . . . disconcerting. Just take a deep breath and feel things out."

"Thanks," said Emily. "I'll be fine."

Stepping through the red satin, they emerged into a cavernous space lit by flickering oil lamps hanging on slender chains from the high ceiling. A long wooden bar ran down the left side of the room, shelves upon shelves of liquor rising up behind it. The opposite wall was covered in thick tapestries depicting royal boar hunts and fortresses under siege. Bow-tied bartenders muddled herbs and polished glasses. At the far end of the hall was a hearth large enough that their car could have driven through it. The whole place smelled of smoke and oiled leather.

But the pop and hiss of the roaring fire could not mask the deeper silence. Emily closed her eyes for a moment. Eric B. and Rakim's incandescent anthem "Paid in Full" had cut off midhook. All the notes she had assembled had vanished. The sum total of human knowledge, the hub of human communication, and the engine that drove human civilization were suddenly beyond her reach. She couldn't access the records of their ride, her inbox of unread messages, or even the local time.

The feed was gone. The umbilical cord that connected her to the digital fountainhead had been severed. There were no more murmurings from the endless news cycle, no more prompts delivered just in time to smooth the bumps of life, no more small reminders that she was never truly alone, that she was but a part of a beautiful, terrible, boundless whole. It was as if she were stargazing and between one blink and the next, an impenetrable fog had covered the sky, obscuring the cosmos.

Blood roared in her ears and adrenaline flooded through her veins. Her muscles flexed, her mind loosened, and she found herself waiting for Rizal to announce her to the assembled throng, to call her to the ring. Emily had never been to Analog before, but this feeling of profound disconnection was anything but new to her. The Camiguin fight club was feedless, and she had conditioned herself to associate this uncoupling with imminent violence, with the conviction that she would kill or be killed, with the desperate compulsion to face her own extinction.

A hand touched her arm, and it took every ounce of Emily's will not to murder its owner on the spot.

"It can take some getting used to, but I think you'll come to appreciate it," said Nell.

After she had quelled the urge to retaliate with extreme prejudice, Emily found herself absurdly grateful for the intercession. This was *not* Camiguin. This was San Francisco, and she was standing in a social club, not a fight club. She relaxed her muscles, remembered Nell's advice, and took a deep breath. The melancholy notes of a lone oud fell on her ears like raindrops. The gentle pressure of Nell's touch was an ecstatic connection, two spacecraft docking after an interstellar voyage. The sharp whiff of paraffin reminded Emily that there might be a reality outside her own. Whatever battle awaited her here, it would not be fought with fists.

She opened her eyes.

So, this was Analog. In which booth had Dag handed over their exploit to Rachel all those years ago? Where had Lynn Chevalier pinned the exposé of the century on Vince Lepardis? What vintage of bourbon had Malignant Kernel been drinking before their epic breakup brawl? It was here that Cory Doctorow had assembled the core group of activists that would reform global copyright laws. Mara Winkel herself had visited here before laying bare Wall Street's most ambitious money-laundering operation and putting an ice ax through the eye socket of its mastermind on national television. This place attracted intrigue like a magnet, and every rumor of infamy further stoked its reputation. Spies, celebrities, entrepreneurs, artists, scientists, politicians, and journalists made pilgrimages to this feedless shrine to dream and scheme and gossip. The arc of history refracted through Analog like sunlight through honey.

And there, at its center, around the circular table in the middle of the floor that had been cleared of all other furniture, sat the council that would determine their fates.

CHAPTER 23

Her presentation complete, Emily reappraised the faces around the table. This was the convocation Javier had wanted so badly to avoid.

Diana spoke first. "I've ramped up security on the entire board to three degrees of separation. That means heavy algorithmic filtering of every signal and expert review of all red flags. We're doing randomly assigned physical security audits as well, and each of you will be leaving here with a bodyguard."

"No need for that," said Baihan. His voice carried the strange inflections of a Mandarin speaker who had learned English from a South African. "I already have a full team."

"I realize that," said Diana. "But we're assigning one anyway. Please consider it a gesture of good faith from Commonwealth."

Baihan looked like he was about to object again, but Liane spoke first.

"I work from our San Francisco offices," she said. "Surely, there's no need—"

"Everyone will leave here with a bodyguard," said Diana firmly. "I know it's annoying. Your objections are noted, but we can't afford to take any chances until we have the situation under control."

"Annoying?" Sofia's singsong Italian accent accentuated her ironic tone. "Is that what this is, Diana? Or do you just want an excuse to peg one of your spooks on each of us?"

Sofia was beautiful in a hard way. Commonwealth's heir apparent had dark hair that was pulled back in a tight ponytail and she wore a Bhaskara Markoff suit that accentuated her lean muscles and total absence of body fat. Her cheekbones could have been chiseled from marble, and although she looked like she might have just collected successive golds in Olympic track and field events, Sofia's real expertise was network engineering. After escaping the dissolution of the European Union, Sofia had managed to obtain one of the rare American refugee visas. She and her family had started a new life here in the Bay Area, and Sofia had built a long career at Commonwealth, a career that would culminate when she took over as Rachel's successor.

"My people go through the heaviest vetting of any Commonwealth employees," said Diana. "It's an even more thorough process than our internal security teams. If Lowell does have inside people, they're not in the intelligence division."

"If I were after secrets, the intelligence division is precisely where I'd want to place a mole," said Sofia, her voice as flinty as her survivor's eyes.

There was subtext here, illegible but apparent, and Emily wondered what clandestine history the two women shared. Sofia had started as an entry-level engineer and earned every step up Commonwealth's ladder with brilliance and tireless dedication. Diana had left a career in the American intelligence community to freelance for clients like Dag before Rachel had named her Commonwealth's chief intelligence officer when the company declared independence. Did this friction reflect a cultural gap between the engineering corps that had built the feed and the political types who had gained sway as the company matured? Was it a power struggle between internal factions? Or was it personal?

"Look," said Baihan. "Bodyguards aren't the real issue here."

"That's right," said Liane. "The real issue is how we get ahead of this. Lowell has us on the defensive. We need to figure out what's next if we want to avoid more disasters. This was a near miss, and we won't get lucky again. I'll have my people interface with national attorneys general, review the best fit between our internal justice system and its territorial complements, and start laying the groundwork for either prosecution or retribution."

Liane was Commonwealth's general counsel. When Commonwealth apotheosized from company to sovereign power, she had gone from lawyer to chief justice. With few legal precedents at her disposal, she had pioneered the rules, processes, and systems the new paradigm required. Now she negotiated treaties as well as contracts.

"No," said Baihan, his tone mild. "That's not it either. This isn't about whose people are most trustworthy, gauging the appropriate security measures, or even competitive intelligence."

Baihan's late boss, Eddie Hsu, had been the choreographer behind Taiwan's geopolitical ascension. Eschewing official titles, Hsu had worked behind the scenes to relocate the UN headquarters to Taipei and reinvent the island nation as the clearinghouse of a new world order. Investing a significant portion of Taiwan's prodigious sovereign wealth fund had earned him a seat on this board, and when Commonwealth became autonomous, he became the primary arbiter of its favor among the world's nations. Baihan had been Hsu's consigliere for years and when the old man passed, his apprentice took over.

Baihan smoothed his tie. "We're talking about logistics and details. The real question here isn't when, how, or what. The real question is *why?* Why did this situation develop in the first place?" He raised an eyebrow at Emily, and she noticed a small scar on his temple. "If we can believe what Ms. Kim here has to say, and we must remember that we have nothing but circumstantial evidence besides her word that any of this is true, despite the fact that her story implicates many well-respected principals, then we must wonder what drove these notables to risk their fortunes and reputations on such a gambit."

Emily bristled. She didn't want to be here any more than they wanted her here. But she was trapped between the certain knowledge that her presence would do nothing but hurt the people she loved and the fact that she could not abandon Javier yet again. And so here she sat, enduring the stares of these masters of the feed who politely ignored her injuries and bandages as they harnessed her story to their own ends.

"They made it pretty clear," said Emily. "Their goal is to keep Commonwealth from laying its hands on those fortunes."

"Indeed." Baihan offered her an easy smile. "And can we blame them? Or, if we do blame them, can we really claim surprise? How many wars have started because aristocrats wanted to keep their assets from the mob? How many governments have toppled because they turned their most powerful citizens into enemies of the state?"

Baihan turned to Rachel, who had been sitting quietly through-out the entire meeting. Commonwealth's matriarch was shriveled and insubstantial. Emily imagined that her intravenous lines were the only thing keeping the breeze from carrying her away like an autumn leaf. But she sat ramrod straight in her wheelchair, an obnoxiously handsome nurse at her side.

"Forgive me for my bluntness, Rachel," said Baihan. "But we can-not afford the luxury of rose-tinted glasses. We are embarking on a delicate moment in Commonwealth's own history. Someday soon, Sofia will take the reins." Was that the slightest hint of sarcasm? "With so many balls in the air, we must make every effort to ensure the transition goes smoothly. It is not the right time to antagonize powerful incum-bents. First, let us stay the course. Later, we can adjust it."

"Later," said Javier sharply. "Later, later, later. There is never going to be a perfect time to make the change the world needs. There will always be reasons for delay. I'll win a sumo championship before oligarchs happily open their purses. It's *always* going to be later. Meanwhile, global wealth inequality is worsening in a world where the feed has made everything global. Baihan alludes to history. Well, how many empires have fallen because the nobility hoarded everything for themselves, sparking popular rebellion? We jet around in private planes while residents of Sofia's own hometown of Alba lack access to basic sanitation and millions of migrants flee floods, droughts, and rising sea levels. On a borderless planet stitched together by feed, nothing conceals the fundamental unfairness of some people owning almost everything while everyone else fights for the scraps. We're all in the same sandbox now. Envy corrodes. Inaction makes our new paradigm *less* secure. This isn't just a moral imperative—it's self-preservation. If we want the feed to endure, if we want to make good on our promises of a better future for everyone, then we must pass this initiative as soon as possible. Earning the hatred of Lowell and his cohorts is an indicator of success, not a reason to drop the ball. There is no *later*. Transition is precisely the time to act."

Sofia snorted. "Ah, yes. Javier has arrived on his moral high horse once again, calling on us to solve the world's problems. Is that not the height of arrogance, believing ourselves to be saviors? I will not argue that including the carbon tax in our terms of service was a failure. Even declaring sovereignty had its perks. But all these political entanglements have enormous downsides and put our mission of building and maintaining the world's information infrastructure at terrible risk. The feed's greatest achievement is that it has become a utility, a basic human right. By leveraging our stewardship to further our own political ends, however noble they might be, we hold humanity hostage. We are not players—we are the playing field itself, and neutrality is the most sacred boon we can offer."

"Political entanglements?" Javier was incensed. "What is the point of doing anything at all if not to make the world a better place? The feed's success isn't measured in ubiquity, but in whether and how it improves people's lives. Neutrality is just another way of saying cowardice. You

want the height of arrogance? How about claiming that *anyone* can be fair and objective. Playing fields make a lovely metaphor until the referee makes a disputed call."

As the debate raged on, Emily wondered at the unified front Commonwealth presented to the outside world while its leadership team was so clearly at odds with itself. Were all exemplars of progress so bitterly conflicted? *Diplomats are people who murder you politely.* Before Lowell's gambit, this council had tentatively signed off on Javier's initiative. Now that was all going up in flames. It was precisely this conflagration that Javier had hoped to avoid by backchanneling to Diana, and yet it was clear she could never have kept it to herself without making herself a target of backlash.

Emily tried to untangle a few stray threads of the complex web of influence crisscrossing the table. Sofia would want to solidify her own base to ensure a smooth transition when she took over as chairwoman. Diana would not want to risk her network of operatives or the pipeline of secrets they supplied. Emily had a hard time believing that Diana would want to supplant Sofia and rule directly, but there was clearly a fault line of some kind buried there. Baihan controlled many of Commonwealth's key relationships with heads of state and might be looking to expand his purview, or even contest Sofia's position. Liane seemed to want the impossible: a continuation of the status quo. Lowell, the elephant in the room, had his own plans for manipulating succession. And Javier . . . With his big ideas and public profile, Emily could see how Sofia might fear a coup from his camp. It was incredible that these leaders with all their conflicting interests had been willing to forgive Javier's involvement with the hack all those years ago. Perhaps it hadn't been forgiveness so much as savvy—maybe they preferred to keep their enemies close. Black-hat hackers often turned white hat, after all.

It was odd to be back in the middle of things, like a frozen asteroid on a wide orbit finally arcing into the inner solar system. Emily had started on the outer edges of fringe, clawed her way to the center of world affairs, exiled herself, and been thrust right back into the mix. The room spun ever so slowly around her and she couldn't decide whether it was existential disorientation or the lingering aftereffects of concussion.

She had taken Javier's hand, and he hadn't pulled away. As he made his passionate case, she admired the brilliant boy who'd become her closest friend and confidant. *I don't give a shit about your precious honor.* Was there even an infinitesimal sliver of a chance that there could be a life here for her to return to? Was that a glimmer of light at the end of the tunnel or a mirage that led to further damnation? Was it worse to abandon your friends or your word? Could you even have one without the other?

Emily had no answers, but she yearned to aid Javier's cause, to defeat Lowell's coercion, to convince these power brokers that profit and scale and technical wizardry were secondary, just more arrows in the quiver for the only fight that really mattered, minimizing human suffering and maximizing human potential. Ultimately, that was what all those late-night debates around the fire on the Island had boiled down to. The problem was as simple as it was difficult. Even so, Emily felt strangely detached. Compared to the blood and sweat and visceral fear of the ring, this intellectual melee was abstract and ephemeral.

"Stop."

Rachel's voice was soft but carried the undeniable clarity of command. A smooth pink scar bisected one milky sightless eye. Her other eye blazed purple as it raked across the assembled courtiers. Thousands of wrinkles turned her face into a detailed topographic map, and Emily had the uncanny sense that if she could only orient herself within its anatomical geography, the secrets of the universe would be revealed.

Rachel coughed into a handkerchief, and even as the nurse made it disappear, they all saw the crimson stain on the white cotton. A century was a long time to spend on this earth, even for an empire builder. In her presence, they all seemed to be little more than bickering children.

"You have found a new peg for old arguments," she said. "Rhetoric will not suffice. We need more data."

CHAPTER 24

"Can I talk to you for a minute?" Diana touched Emily's elbow.

"Sure."

As the others collected their things and broke off into side conversations, Diana led Emily to the roaring hearth at the far end of the hall. Three vizslas were curled up in front of the fire, two lean young pups and one graying old dog with cataracts. Diana knelt to greet them, and Emily followed her lead. The short amber fur was soft, and the dogs reveled in the attention, lapping at the petting hands.

Instead of taking the chairs, Emily and Diana rocked back onto the thick carpet, letting the dogs rest their heads on their laps. Diana gave Emily an appraising look that Emily returned. This was the woman who had helped Dag track down Emily and discover Javier's exploit. She had succeeded not only in winning Dag's heart but in becoming Commonwealth's spymaster.

"So whaddaya think?" Diana raised her eyebrows. "Did the super-secret council impress you with its supreme wisdom and peerless decisiveness? Were you awestruck into eternal devotion?"

Emily guffawed before she could help herself.

"Right?" said Diana. "I mean the *egos* on these people. Sometimes I think a generously rolled joint and a good fuck should replace the aperitifs and small talk. It could really grease the wheels. I mean, I'm

as guilty as the next gal of thinking I'm the shit, mostly because I *am*
the shit, but it doesn't mean I need to wax lyrical every chance I get."

"I guess it takes a certain kind of person to actually win a spot on
Commonwealth's board," said Emily.

"Sure, selection bias and all that jazz," said Diana. "Dag told me
that in ancient Athens, government officials were chosen by lot and not
election. Apparently Athenians threw serious shade on elections because
only candidates who want to win end up winning and, having won,
go full Machiavelli. We fine folks"—she tossed her head to indicate
the group behind them—"aren't even elected, so I tell Dag he should
cut us some slack." She winked. "But then again, you don't really need
a lesson in power corrupting, or in Dag's personal interests, do you? I
mean, you're the expert."

"Do you prefer the view from Langley or San Francisco?" asked
Emily. "Or maybe it was more fun to run black ops for the highest
bidder? Surely a woman with as many secrets as you can share at least
a few."

Diana's laugh was a bright tinkle against the crackling thunder of
the fire. "See, Phil?" She rubbed the dog's belly and he kicked his leg in
hedonic pleasure. "I *knew* I would like her." She looked back at Emily,
brown eyes sparkling. "I hated you at first, you know. Dag was obsessed,
obsessed. You had cracked his feed, spent years tweaking his standard of
beauty to match your own damn face just to create an edge. I mean,
that's seriously fucked up, dude. But I gotta say that it was refreshing
once I actually found out what you were using that prime-time exploit
for. You guys were arguably more effective at advancing the ball on
social change than all the charities of the world put together, and *certainly* more than Washington. Plus, as a total nerd for secrets, y'all had
a *gold mine*. Root access to the feed? I get wet just thinking about it.
Good guys doing bad things for good reasons. Ends justifying means
justifying ends, your scheme was a philosophy professor's worst nightmare. And then zap, Dag blows your operation, and you disappear off

the face of the earth. I mean, Javier doesn't know where you are, and not even my own spooks can find you. That's some A-plus hide-and-seek shit. Now you're back with a whole new bag of tricks that are throwing everyone into a serious tizzy. Brava, brava." She golf-clapped. "You, Ms. Kim, are a conundrum."

"If I ever decide to live a more public life," said Emily, "remind me to have you write my bio."

"Yuck," said Diana. "A public life? Gods forbid! The feed doesn't need more self-aggrandizing loudmouths. If there's one thing this age has a surfeit of, it's narcissists. Can you imagine how hard my job would be if people didn't go around blabbering about themselves all day long? Don't ruin this enigmatic thing you have going."

"Speaking of enigmatic things, what's going on between you and Sofia?"

"Oho, we go way back." Diana's sober glance belied her facetious tone. She paused, as if considering something, then said, "I helped her and her family get their American visas when they fled Italy."

Emily did the math. That had been during Diana's tenure at the three-letter agencies. "So the asset is finally bucking the case officer?"

Diana's smile was melancholic. "Bucked. Some wounds take a long time to heal, as it appears you're well aware."

Emily pushed her glasses up her nose and stared into the fire. Niko, previous challengers who had fallen in the ring, friends from the streets of LA, her mother and father . . . the dead peered back through the flames, trying to snatch glimpses of the world they'd left behind forever.

"Does he have a chance?" Emily's voice dropped and softened.

Diana scratched Phil behind the ear and the dog arched his neck and lolled his tongue. She was silent for so long that Emily started to think she might not have heard the question.

"I honestly don't know," Diana said at last. "It was a hard road getting enough soft commitments to pass this kind of an initiative in the first place. Commonwealth is the first organization in history with enough information and clout to actually implement a truly global wealth-redistribution scheme. It would be a first-of-its-kind experiment and many, many powerful people don't want to see that experiment happen. It's not just Lowell. Every person around that table has supporters lobbying them to call it off. Javier already has all his cards on the table, and this complication could very well be the straw that breaks the camel's back. I don't like it. I mean, he's right. Money is just one form of power, and the more centralized power becomes, the nastier the fallout when the pendulum swings back. Civilizations used to be isolated, parallel experiments. If Rome fell, Beijing might still thrive. The feed wove everything together, and now this is the only civilization we've got, which means disaster will be universally disastrous. But you're not the kind of person who likes to see the world through rose-tinted glasses, and the reality of the situation is that it'll be much easier for everyone to defer this kind of political hot potato. After it's been delayed once, well, you know how these things go."

"You said Javier has already played his hand. What about you? Do you have any cards left?"

Diana just looked at her.

"What?" asked Emily.

Diana quirked her mouth into a lopsided smile.

"Me," said Emily.

"Who are you?" Diana waggled her fingers and spoke the words with a theatrical flourish.

Emily started.

"Dag gave me root access to his feed way back when he was trying to figure out how exactly you were mindfucking him. So I got to see the message you left him in Room 412. Just the right kind of sphinxlike question to send someone down the rabbit hole of existential paranoia, only to discover how justified that paranoia really was. It reminded me of all the games they had us play back on the Farm during training. They felt petty to us high-minded rookies, but eventually you realize that parlor games are great training for real-world espionage precisely because real-world espionage is just a giant parlor game. You would have loved it."

A glowing log crumbled to embers with a gust of sparks. The heat beat against them in waves. It was a pyre. Humans downed trees for the simple pleasure of burning their corpses. Every hearth was a place of sacrifice.

"Is that what this is to you?" asked Emily. "A game?"

"And *that*," said Diana with a wink, "is why you would have passed every test but failed out of the Farm. The agency was big on patriotism and institutional loyalty. But they discouraged personal loyalty at all costs. It fucked me up for a long time. I could cultivate assets like a mofo, but couldn't build a real friendship for the life of me. When relationships become tools, your humanity starts to leak away. I've tried to relearn it with Dag and the twins. How to be myself. How to be open. How to be vulnerable." Diana sighed. "It's the hardest thing I've ever done, and I still suck at it. You, though. You take things seriously. You take people seriously. You're a manipulative bitch of the first order, and yet you have real friends to whom you're truly loyal. I mean, you violated your promises to them *once*, and it broke you. Wherever you've been . . ." Diana nodded to indicate Emily's scars. "Let's just say I'm not going to be asking you for holiday recommendations."

Emily touched the yellowing bruises at her neck self-consciously. "What exactly are you asking me for? Why are we here?"

Diana bit her lip. "Has Lowell made you?"

Sex, violence—all you need is drugs and rock and roll, and you've got the whole package, Pixie. "I . . . I don't know," said Emily. "I'm fairly certain we crossed paths accidentally. He wouldn't have wanted me to be able to ID his collaborators or overhear their plans if he knew who I really was." She remembered the singing cicadas, the sodden sheets, the thick funk of sex. "I guess it's possible the whole thing was engineered for my benefit—you yourself have pulled off some elaborate ruses—but

I don't see a payoff that'd be worth the risk." The false courier leered at her from behind the curtain of flame, cleaver still lodged in his neck. "The kidnappers would have no way to recognize me, so that's probably a low-risk vector. To a certain extent, it depends how much effort we assume Lowell's expending. If he has goons poking through my apartment, they'll notice I'm not there, which could lead to more questions with more difficult answers." Decision trees grew in her mind, branches forking through probability space. "On balance, I'd guess no."

Diana nodded, and Emily could sense the hunger just below the surface. "Do you have a way back in?"

I'm hosting a party next week up in the mountains. I can have a plane pick you up on Camiguin. What'll it take to convince you to come?

"I do," said Emily reluctantly.

"Look." Diana spread her hands. "I don't know what your plans are. Hell, we met for the first time yesterday. Speaking as a person who prides herself on her ability to sniff out secrets, I must say you did a bang-up job on the disappearing act way back when. And if we are to believe the story you're selling, you came out of hiding for one reason: to protect your friends." She rubbed Phil's head with her knuckles. "So maybe you're hoping to pull the same trick and vanish again. But I can tell you one thing for sure, Lowell's not gonna stop just because you screwed up a kidnapping. He's the kind of guy who always has contingencies, always finds new angles. So if you really want to protect your friends, and if you want to give Javier the kind of boost he so desperately needs to make good on his pet project, then you'll go back in and get us what we need to bring Lowell down."

Knowing people better than they knew themselves had once been Emily's forte.

"You're pitching me," she said.

"And you're gonna say yes, baby," said Diana. "Am I right or am I right?"

CHAPTER 25

Emily caught a glimpse of herself in the greenroom's cracked mirror. Although her aching body was a testament, it was hard to believe it had only been a few days since she fought Niko. It was here that she'd prepared for the fight. It was here that'd she huddled in its aftermath. After accepting Lowell's invitation, it was to here that she'd returned in order to keep up appearances.

Excellent. You will not be disappointed. Be at the airport at 7 p.m. local time the day after tomorrow. Come as you were.

Tearing her eyes away from the smudged glass, Emily continued to pack up her glitter, makeup, and body paint. She had already dropped by the apartment to pick up an extra leotard. Nothing had appeared out of place, though she hadn't made a habit of setting traps for intruders. In fact, she herself had felt like an intruder. A tourist visiting a scene from someone else's life.

The door opened behind her, and she saw Rizal's shocked face in the mirror. Damn. She'd been hoping to slip in and out without running into him.

"Pixie—" he said. "I—You're okay. Where have you—"

Yet more demands for impossible explanations. What drugs would he think she was on if she actually told him what had happened over the past few days?

"Hi, Riz." She tried an apologetic smile, remembered the berserk roar of the crowd. "Sorry I went dark. Niko really threw me for a loop, you know?"

He grimaced and shook his head.

"I get it," he said. "Sometimes it's just another fight, and sometimes it gets inside your head. Doesn't matter how many times you do it or how jaded you think you get. Demons are vermin. They don't try to breach your walls, they live inside them." He took a tentative step into the room. "Look, Pixie, that's why I've been on your ass to consider getting out of the game. It's silly, I know. What's more stupid than trying to convince your most consistent fighter to retire? But you've done me good, and I'm gonna return it in kind even if you don't listen. Niko was your eleventh. One of these days you're going to be the one leaving in a body bag."

That's the plan. She almost said it out loud but caught herself just in time. Death wishes weren't things to broadcast to the world. And was it even still true? So many unbelievable things had happened in the past few days—was it possible that the story she'd been telling herself all along was wrong? Did the future contain a place for her after all, or was an unmarked grave the best she could hope for?

"Hold on," said Rizal, frowning. "Are you packing your things? What's going on?"

Emily turned on the stool to face him. Even when she stopped, the room kept spinning. For a Copernican moment, she imagined that she was in fact still, and the planet itself had inexplicably begun to rotate on a new axis. Rizal could never understand Pixie because he didn't know Emily. Javier, Rosa, and the rest could never understand Emily because they didn't know Pixie. She had transformed herself into Janus, but didn't know what it meant to be two people, to live two lives both impoverished and enriched by each other, to bridge the gap opening in her soul.

"I'm going away for a while," she said, willing the room to stop spinning. "I'm not sure when I'll be back, but it shouldn't be too long."

Rizal raised his palms in a placating gesture. "Pixie, I'm sorry. I don't mean to come on too strong. I'm not trying to tell you what to do. I'm just trying to be a good friend. I hope I'm not scaring you off to find a new club to fight in."

Emily swallowed. Ever since they'd met, she'd pushed Rizal away, kept their relationship to the bare professional minimum. Yet he'd made the extra effort to train her up despite her age and inexperience. He'd given her a chance in the ring when other owners would have scoffed. He'd nursed her back to health after narrow victories and even offered to make her a partner in the club itself, offering her a way out that few fighters could even dream of. Whether or not she admitted it, he had proven himself to be a truer friend than she deserved.

She crossed the distance between them in two quick strides and wrapped him in a tight hug. *When relationships become tools, your humanity starts to leak away.* He tensed, then patted her uncertainly on the back. He smelled of sweat and the vinegar solution he used to wipe down the bar.

"Riz," she said into his armpit, "I don't say this enough, but thanks for everything you've done for me."

"Okaaay," he said gruffly. "Now I'm *really* worried about you."

She pulled away and sucker punched him on the shoulder.

"Don't be," she said. "I've got some business to take care of. After that . . . Well, I dunno, but I'll be in touch."

He scratched his chin. "You've always got a place here, you know. I wasn't kidding about helping to run this joint. With this offer on the club, we'll have more cash on hand. Nothing would please me more than having a manager who can tell the difference between an invoice and their own asshole."

Emily scooped up her bag.

"Thanks," she said. "But I'm not your gal. I find my own asshole endlessly fascinating."

He snorted, and she threw him a salute as she left the greenroom.

Emily kicked up fresh sawdust as she walked through the club proper. It felt small and banal without the crowd. The empty ring, locus of so much blood and glory, just looked sad and lonely. The bar was scuffed but clean. She wondered whether Analog's bouncers had ever had to dispose of a body like their equivalents here on Camiguin. Maybe some of what had drawn her to Rizal was how honest he was about dishonesty. The fight club was a black-market institution, but he ran it in an honorable way. If Emily had learned anything growing up, it was that the only true honor to be found was among thieves. Everyone else could safely pay it lip service while taking advantage of every loophole they could squeeze through.

She knelt, scooped up a handful of sawdust, and blew it into the air, watching the particles whirl and settle like so many galaxies. Then Emily rose to her feet, opened the door, and climbed the steps into the sweltering heat of a Camiguin afternoon.

CHAPTER 26

Emily finished applying her makeup on the helicopter. Run-DMC *oonce-oonced* in her feed, drowning out the roar of the rotors. What would she really find at the end of this journey? How would she wring the information they needed from Lowell? Was this stupid, brave, both, neither? Would she ever see Rosa or Javier again? If she did, how could she reengage in their lives without hurting them again? She had run away to protect them from herself but, in running, had done them a deeper violence.

Just like when she was preparing for the ring, Emily poured all her fears into the fractals she was drawing on her skin. They seemed to grow of their own accord, these runes born of anxiety. They spiraled up her forearms, wrapped themselves around her chest, and turned her entire body into a glittering mural of primary colors. As she worked, time and space and thought all slid together to become a single flow state that moved beyond consciousness into pure existence.

Finally, she cocked her head at the travel vanity.

Emily closed her eyes, and Pixie opened them.

Perfect.

Packing away her things, she turned her attention to the world beyond the cockpit's soap-bubble canopy. The Sawtooth Mountains rose below, snowcapped peaks reaching for the impossibly blue dome of sky. Jagged ridges surrounded the natural amphitheaters of glacier-cut cirques and brilliant aquamarine lakes polka-dotted the pine-covered slopes. The epic geography called to mind the implacable machinations of vast tectonic plates beneath the planet's skin, the invisible forces shaping the very land unwary animals walked. Like stargazing, apprehending such vast wilderness defied the limited container of the human mind, leaving Emily awestruck even as she considered the very real dangers that awaited her.

Surely, this was precisely the effect Lowell intended. Natural splendor would lend gravity to his hustling, and a sense of wonder could be molded into its opposite, self-importance. When you made it your business to manipulate world affairs, you needed an impressive place to host the power brokers you hoped to woo.

The sun dipped below the western horizon, painting the clouds purple and the snowfields gold. Summoning her courage and her feed, Emily killed the music and made a call. This made her more nervous than the mission itself, but she couldn't keep running away forever. Two faces materialized in front of her.

"You caught us prepping dinner," said Javier.

"Holy crap!" said Rosa. "Is that a mask?"

Emily grinned. "You like?"

"Um . . . striking," said Javier.

"It's a costume party," said Emily. "This is part of my ensemble."

"It must be quite an ensemble," said Rosa.

"I expect it to be quite a party, knowing Lowell," said Emily.

"Maybe we can host an exhibition in Addis when this is over," said Rosa. "You can be the star." The words were lighthearted, but her tone was taut.

"I'll be okay, sweetheart," said Emily, trying to imbue her own words with a confidence she didn't entirely feel.

"Look," said Javier, all business. "I'm still not comfortable with this. Diana didn't consult me on the operation before suggesting it. She's good at convincing people to do dangerous things. But it's not too late to call it off."

"She didn't consult you because she knew you'd say no," said Emily. "And I'm pretty good at convincing people to do dangerous things too. Diana's a force I can reckon with just fine, thank you."

"Em," said Rosa. "I know you're trying to help. But is this truly necessary?"

"I'm pretty sure I can handle a bunch of weirdos drinking fancy cocktails," said Emily. "And Diana already has an extraction team in place just in case I need backup. Lowell is a motherfucker. I don't want him running wild with you in his sights, and I'm the person with the best chance of scoring inside intel on his plan B. If we don't get his cabal under control, the progressive-membership initiative won't stand a chance. It's so much easier to defer than to take action, and they're busy manufacturing violent excuses for delay."

The skin around Javier's eyes tightened. "Don't put this on me," he snapped. "I'm not asking you to die for the sake of my proposal."

"Nobody is going to die," said Emily. "Unless it's from a heart attack after overeating hors d'oeuvres."

"I think what Javi is trying to say," said Rosa, throwing him a sidelong glance, "is that we don't want to lose you again."

Javier looked down at his hands. The darkening mountains beyond the feed flash flooded Emily with vertigo. She wasn't worthy of these people, friends who would forgive so much after so long.

"You guys are just plain terrible at pep talks," said Emily. "Promise me you'll never try coaching."

"Promise us you'll be careful," said Rosa, narrowing her eyes.

"Sometimes the safest path is straight into the dragon's lair," said Emily.

"That's *not* an answer," said Javier tightly.

"I promise," said Emily. "Now get back to your dinner. I've got a boss battle to fight."

She killed the connection, spun the music, and jacked up the volume.

The chopper cut through a pass, enormous walls of black granite rising up on either side, the roar of the engine echoing down into the invisible depths. It was claustrophobic, and Emily waited for a gust of wind to dash the fragile machine against one of the walls. She would tumble down amid the shattered wreckage, vultures picking through her charred remains come morning.

Then she was out the other side, and the landscape opened up. A dome of stars covered a ring of peaks surrounding an alpine lake. The chopper descended, trees writhing on the slope below, and then it was skimming across the surface of the water, kicking up curtains of spray. A hot-pink laser traced a thick vertical line from the far shore into the outer atmosphere. As she got closer, Emily could see that it emanated from the parapet of a sprawling wood-and-stone mansion. More palace than house, it sported so many wings, floors, verandas, outbuildings, and courtyards that the operant philosophy of its owner could only be to maximize ostentation. Besides the laser, the only exterior illumination came from hundreds of small fires that flickered and gyrated bizarrely throughout the grounds.

The Ranch. Lowell's exclusive personal resort. This was where he had laid the plans to win his concessions from the Arctic Council and helped Dag kill his first stag. Emily remembered playing voyeur in Dag's feed as he'd forced down the buttery venison, then returned year after year to cavort with senators and captains of industry before ultimately finding his conscience and betraying Lowell. Taipei might be the central gravity well of official power, but the Ranch was where the elite came to loosen their ties and their morals. People had been murdered for invites, a fact that Lowell made sure nobody entirely forgot. That he had extended one to Pixie meant Emily had really gotten inside his head or, more to the point, his balls.

And then the chopper cleared the shore and dropped smoothly onto the lawn. Emily unclipped her harness. This was really happening. She touched her glasses for luck, steeled herself, and opened the door. A fathomless bass beat churned her internal organs, and she silenced the competing music in her feed. She held up a hand to her forehead to block the chopper's downdraft as she stepped down onto the lawn. As soon as she disembarked, the engine whined, and it leapt back into the air as if scalded, accelerating off over the lake.

A few meters away, tall, imperious, and impeccably outfitted as the Norse goddess who was her namesake, stood Freja. The wind whipped at her robes but she ignored it completely, staring at Emily with the same mute disapproval she'd displayed in the fight club's VIP room.

"Welcome to the Ranch," she said in her precise Danish accent. Her expression soured. "Lowell specifically requested that I tell you that this is 'the party to end all parties.'" She shook her head. "He says it every time."

CHAPTER 27

Emily followed Freja up the winding path to the mansion. Lowell's right-hand woman was quite dismissive of her nominal master. Was the friction simply a harmless part of their dynamic, or could it be exploited? As his unofficial general manager, Freja knew the details of Lowell's operations even better than he did. Although he had ordered the kidnapping, she was doubtless the one who had actually hired the Addis contractors. It would be a coup if Freja could be flipped, and Emily made a mental note to mention it in the debrief with Diana.

As they climbed through tiered gardens, Emily discovered the source of the uncanny flames she'd glimpsed from the chopper. Hundreds of naked fire dancers leapt, swayed, and twirled, their skin slick with sweat and their eyes reflecting the burning poi, staffs, nunchaku, wands, hoops, fans, and batons that they wielded with eerie grace. They were scattered across the entire property, illuminating every path, clearing, and balcony with hypnotic patterns of flame that etched blurry afterimages onto the eye of the beholder.

And beholders there were: guests dressed as pirates, geishas, princes, tigers, ninjas, priests, jesters, nomads—a bespoke menagerie of excess. They drank, laughed, gossiped, flirted, danced, and pleasured each other. Everyone and everything was dominated by the thunderous rhythm emanating from the wide balcony above the main entrance to the mansion. It was there, at the base of the laser that strained to touch the stars, that the DJ presided over the bacchanal like the exultant demigod of music that sounded like robots having nonconsensual sex.

Emily had been to a lot of parties, but never anything quite like this.

Freja led her straight up the stairs toward the wide entrance, and Emily thought her eardrums might burst as they passed directly beneath the DJ and through the open doors.

"Pixie!"

A figure stood on the threshold, arms raised. Emily froze for a moment, questioning her sanity. The figure wore nothing but a G-string, and every centimeter of its body was covered in precisely the same kind of glitter fractals that she had adorned herself with on the ride in. It was like staring through a peephole into an alternate reality where she was an aging, overweight man. But presumably her doppel-gänger wouldn't be able to reach through the multiverse to smack her ass, which is exactly what Lowell Harding did.

"You asked for a sacrifice," he yelled into her ear. "And I figured my dignity might be a worthy offering."

Emily pinched his Adam's apple between her thumb and forefinger. When he instinctively tried to swallow she pinched harder, locking it in place. Standing on her tiptoes to reach his ear, she yelled back, "If you ever touch me without permission again, I will kill you where you stand."

His pupils dilated and he nodded incrementally, careful to keep his neck still.

This transcontinental booty call had nothing to do with Emily's prowess in the bedroom. For men like Lowell, it was never about the sex. He could, and did, hire courtesans with unmatched technical skills. No, for Lowell, it was always about power. He had dedicated his life to chasing it, to play not just games, but the greatest game of all. Hence all the pomp. This spectacle was a way to make his chosen few feel special, demonstrate his magnanimity, and create a world with him at its center. And for someone who reveled in gaining power over others, the prospect of prostrate powerlessness was tantalizing. With her domineering attitude and violent competence, Pixie was Lowell's perfect foil. All the better because he felt sure he could crush her easily if he ever wished to. That dynamic was what created the tension that set his loins aflame, that turned him to putty in Emily's hands. The thing that disturbed Emily the most was how obvious all this was to her. It took one to know one.

Emily released him.

"This is quite a production," she said.

"I promised you that you wouldn't be disappointed," he said, recovering his composure. "Now let me show you around."

Freja shook her head disgustedly, and Lowell gave her a two-finger salute as she strode off into the crowd.

When Emily stepped across the threshold to join him in the entrance hall, the noise level dropped from deafening to just loud.

"What can I get you?" Lowell asked with a flourish. "Bar on the right, pharmacy on the left. We've got anything you could possibly want, and if we don't happen to carry the intoxicant you desire, I will move heaven and earth to get it for you. You did cross the Pacific to attend, after all."

Opposing bars lined the vast atrium, one stocked with liquor and the other with pill bottles of every size and color. Attendants poured drinks and handed out tablets like candy. An ancient oak grew in the middle of the space, strung with thousands of tiny lights that pulsed with the music, ordered sequences coruscating along the trunk and branches before their shape or meaning could be discerned. Guests poured in and out of the many hallways leading off the atrium, and backlit dancers threw giant shadows across the vaulted ceiling.

Dag had always hated attending these parties, and Lowell had loved to tease him about it every chance he got. For someone who had once frequented the world's corridors of power, Dag was in many ways a total homebody. It was hard for Emily to quell her jealousy for his apparent domestic contentment. She was here under orders from his wife to play double agent against his old boss. Forget alternate realities, this one was weird enough.

"I'll take a Casa Dragones," she said, immediately chastising herself for what could be a tell.

"Ahh." Lowell grinned wolfishly. "A tequila girl. I knew you were my soulmate."

"Don't get your hopes up."

"Joven blend, neat," said the bartender as he poured the platinum liquid into slender-bowled tequila glasses. "Full body, vanilla and pear, well balanced, hazelnut in the finish. Fifteen degrees Celsius."

Lowell raised his glass.

"To my dignity," he said.

"May it rest in peace," said Emily.

They toasted and sipped.

"Fucking ambrosia," said Lowell.

The sweetness of roasted agave transported Emily back to the first time she had met Dag in person thirteen years ago. They sipped this very tequila on the balcony of the hotel bar, looking out over the glimmering sprawl of Mexico City. Both of them made every effort at nonchalance, though each had their own reasons for mutual fixation. She had been so full of purpose then, so sure of herself. Where had that confidence gone? When was the last time the world made sense, that events conformed to her plans? And yet, here she was seducing a different, blunter man with different, blunter methods for different, blunter reasons. Yes, she wanted Javier's grand vision to succeed, but her own vision had narrowed, like adjusting the eyepiece of her telescope to focus on a specific cluster. More than anything she just wanted to defend Javier, Rosa, Dag, and the rest from the predations of men like the one who now led her on a grand tour of his private carnival.

Each parlor was dedicated to a specific game. The chess gallery was packed but silent except for the thump of distant music and the sharp click of players making moves. The beer-pong tournament was raucous, and Emily noticed a few bouncers on hand to break up the inevitable fights. Two teams dressed in frilly Revolutionary War garb slid curling stones down a full rink, while onlookers slurped vodka shots off an ice luge. Competitors in the Starcraft lounge marshaled their digital minions on vintage '90s computers and supervised apocalyptic clashes over an antique feedless local area network.

Everywhere they went, people came up to Lowell. Some appeared to be old friends, others petitioners hoping to impress their host. Lowell was beneficent but concise with each and every one, always finding a way to make a joke, move on quickly, and refocus on Emily, who received quite a few jealous looks from those who sought the great man's attention. For her part, Emily surreptitiously recorded each face in her feed, noting the details of their appeals. You never knew what unassuming tidbit of information might later turn out to be the critical clue revealing a vast but latent web of associative connections.

"I think that's about enough of that," said Lowell, as they exited the ax-throwing arcade.

"I dunno," said Emily. "I can see you as a lumberjack."

"One of the great tragedies of my life is that I've never been able to pull off a mustache." He smirked. "Come on. Time for the real fun to begin."

Lowell took Emily's hand and pulled her into a side kitchen where a lone cook was prepping caviar canapés.

"How's it hangin', Chibundi?" asked Lowell, popping a canapé into his mouth as they passed.

"Never better, Mr. Harding," said the cook.

They passed Chibundi and approached the walk-in freezer at the far end of the kitchen. Lowell's fractals shimmered under the bright lights. Emily hoped against hope that he didn't have some weird fetish for ultralow-temperature sex. It was unpleasant enough fucking him under normal circumstances.

He pulled open the stainless-steel door with a wet sucking sound. Mist curled out around the edges, and Emily was suddenly terrified that a frosty quickie was far from the worst thing that might lie beyond. Maybe unbeknownst to her, Lowell was a hobbyist serial killer and Chibundi would assist him in carving her up with medical precision, keeping her conscious as long as possible while they incorporated her flesh into the night's menu, turning clueless guests into cannibals, per-haps saving a token finger as a prize, mounting it on a rack of pinkies in the freezer that was really a grisly trophy room.

No. She had to calm down. This was dangerous enough as it was. There was too much on the line to torpedo the mission by freaking out. If disaster struck, she could always simply call in Diana's emergency backup via feed.

Emily tamped down her burgeoning dread and stepped through after Lowell.

The freezer was dark, but it wasn't cold.

The door hissed shut behind them.

Panic blossoming, Emily reached for her feed, but it wasn't there.

CHAPTER 28

Lights snapped on.

It wasn't a freezer, nor the torture chamber Emily had feared.

They stood at the top of a stairway.

"This is where the *real* party starts," said Lowell. "I mean, I love a rave as much as anyone, but sometimes, it just isn't intimate enough." He began to descend, trailing fingers along the stone walls. "This was mind-bogglingly expensive to install. But the best things in life are priceless, right?"

Emily leaned against the wall to steady herself. The rough travertine blocks were cool against her palm. The bass thump of the music had disappeared when the door closed, but the deeper silence of her absent feed was the disorienting part. The faces she'd captured, the notes she'd taken, even the map that had kept her oriented in the vast mansion, all were gone. So was her lifeline to the outside world, her only way to call for rescue.

Lowell glanced back over his shoulder and wiggled his eyebrows. "I probably should have warned you we were going feedless, but I didn't want to ruin the surprise. Just like Rizal's, right? You'll be right at home. I love this feeling. It's like canceling all your appointments, dosing yourself with something fun, and stranding yourself on a deserted island. Hah. Disconnection as dissociative. Plus, everything's just more *sensual*."

Emily could turn back, manufacture some excuse to stay in the main house, maybe drag Lowell to the middle of the dance floor. But her mission was to unlock his secrets, and this might well be where he hid them. Whatever was down here, Diana certainly didn't know about it yet.

"It's like one percent of what combat feels like," said Emily. "When I'm fighting, everything else just sort of fades away into the background. Wiping away the feed feels sort of similar."

"Ever fucked someone in a place like this?" he asked.

"Ever killed someone in a place like this?" Emily responded.

"Zing," said Lowell. "This is why I love having you around."

Emily followed him down the stairs. They descended in a wide spiral and the air took on a subterranean coolness and density, the special atmosphere of caves and tombs. Their steps echoed oddly and intermingled with sounds of conversation filtering up from below.

Then they passed through an archway and the space opened up into a small amphitheater. This had originally been a natural cavern, a little geological pocket, and the ceiling was rough, sharply angled bedrock. The steps continued past three tiers of stone benches to a circular sandy floor at the center of the room where twenty or so people were chatting and milling about. Water tumbled down from a narrow gap in the far wall and ran in a landscaped stream through the center of the floor to disappear beneath the nearest seats. Servers dressed in elaborate seventeenth-century French gowns and doublets replaced empty glasses with fresh drinks and handed out gourmet finger food. Armed guards in tuxedos and silver-filigree masquerade masks stood at attention around the edges of the circle.

Freja's carefully neutral gaze rose to meet them as Lowell and Emily reached the sand. In the raiment of an ancient goddess, Freja appeared strangely at home in this sacrosanct grotto, as if being cut off from the feed didn't impede her ability to invoke her peers in Asgard.

"The man himself!" The speaker wore a theatrical-quality Batman outfit, complete with mask and flowing cape. "For fuck's sake, could you be any later to your own party?"

"Uh-oh," said Lowell. "Are we going to have to put Jason on liquor watch already? The night is young, good sir. Don't waste it by blacking out. We have much to discuss and more to enjoy."

Lowell snapped his fingers, and the serving staff trouped upstairs.

Jason. Emily did a double take. This huge, slouching Batman was the whiny hedge-fund prodigy from Rizal's VIP room. Emily's eyes flickered around the room. Yes. The cowboy was Singaporean sovereign wealth fund manager Lex Tan. The sleek cyborg was Dutch prince Barend Laurentien. The jaguar whose costume looked like it had been fashioned from a real pelt was heiress Midori Kawakami. The matador was Kenyan robber baron Barasa Lelei. And although Emily couldn't identify Nisanur Demir's feathery costume, the Turkish tycoon looked like she had slipped out of an avian nightmare. Emily's heart hammered in her chest. It was a different VIP room, but this was a reunion of everyone who had been there the night she'd killed Niko, the night that had dragged Emily back out of her ferocious hibernation.

A fifth of total global assets. It was surreal to think that seven costumed people in this little room buried under a mountain in Idaho controlled as much wealth as half of the world's total population. Next in line for prodigious inheritances, Midori and Barend had done nothing whatsoever to earn their share. Barasa and Jason had been born into rich families and had managed to multiply their fortunes. Nisanur's parents had been professors at Bilkent University and were constantly surprised at but supportive of their daughter's entrepreneurial endeavors. Lowell was the only self-made billionaire here, but after the collapse of his fossil fuel empire, his was by far the smallest fortune in the room. This whole mess was his play to level back up into the big leagues.

The feed had accelerated the global economy, created a single global currency, and opened borders not just for people but for capital.

Governments lost their onetime monopoly on fiscal and monetary policy, and became less and less able to control tax evasion and capital flight even as Commonwealth found it easier and easier to track and tabulate every transaction. The feed offered countless benefits to all—it was a modern miracle—but it amplified winner-take-all economics, and these people were some of the biggest winners. If Emily included Rachel, Baihan, and the others in attendance at Analog a few nights ago, the net worth of the dozen or so people on that list would dwarf the aggregate wealth of the vast majority of everyone on Earth.

It was so unfair as to be simply ridiculous, strange and sad in a way that was somehow all too human. It wasn't about the money. These people had left behind any limits on personal consumption long ago. At this scale, wealth was simply a proxy for power, fungible for its political, social, and other equivalents. Emily had always understood the fire in Javier's belly when it came to this issue, the moral logic for instituting a progressive feed membership system that would be the first step in a long journey toward making civilization more equitable, ensuring wealth was something to be earned through valuable work, not granted by the lottery of birth. But standing here in the presence of these petty titans, feeling the sand shift under her feet, that intellectual understanding cemented into a visceral feeling in her gut, an aversion to the self-evident tragicomedy of the status quo. Had he been here beside her, Dag would have pointed out that this was precisely how human societies had operated throughout history, that modern humans had simply renamed what had once been termed nobility to make ourselves feel better. And Emily would have responded that such a precedent was all the more reason to fight for something better.

"This isn't a game," snapped Jason. "There's far too much on the line."

"Games with far too much on the line are the only ones worth playing," said Lowell. "If this is more than you can stomach, there are tables with lower stakes upstairs."

"Fuck you."

"Pixie's more my type," said Lowell with a lewd wink. "Plus, I hear bats carry some nasty venereal diseases."

"My family office never received payment for the kintsugi," said Midori. "Does that mean the operation was successful?"

So that's where the delivery had originated.

"From what I hear from my people in Addis, there was quite a kerfuffle at a prominent apartment building not far from the Commonwealth embassy," said Barasa. "The police reports described a simple burglary, but I hear there may have been a body bag carried out through the back alley later that night. Rosa Flores hasn't been seen in the gallery since."

So Barasa had informers in Addis who had either found witnesses or been near the scene themselves. Definitely a highlight for Emily's debrief.

"You *killed* her?" asked Barend, staring at Lowell incredulously. "Jesus Christ, get me the hell out of here already. What a bunch of amateurs."

"I want to make it extremely clear that we can have absolutely no exposure on this," said Lex, frowning. "No one can know about our involvement, no matter the circumstances."

Lex was especially concerned with blowback, another tidbit that could be useful to Diana if they needed to outmaneuver him.

"My dear Lex," said Lowell. "There can be no exposure because none of you is involved in anything. You're simply attending the party to end all parties"—Freja winced—"along with many other notables, I might add. Who could possibly fault you for that?"

"Common-fucking-wealth," said Jason in a tone that made Emily wonder where he might have built luxury bunkers for himself to wait out the apocalypse.

"Who, even if they were willing to violate the sanctity of their precious feed, which would be a PR nightmare for them and a boon for us, would see exactly nothing because just like this conversation, this lovely little home addition never happened," said Lowell. "Relax, loosen up, enjoy each other's company."

Jason looked like he was about to fall on Lowell with his gauntleted fists, but Nisanur held up a hand.

"Lowell," she said with the slightest hint of a smile. "We are all so very delighted to attend your soirée. And I'm *sure* you can understand how eager we are to hear the update you must be dying to share. Freja has refused all our entreaties for information. Candidly, I don't think she wants to steal your thunder. But now that we are finally graced with your presence, would you care to enlighten us?"

"Ahh," said Lowell, bending over to plant a kiss on Nisanur's hand and meeting her condescension with magnanimity. "I knew that there must be *someone* with manners in this band of rapscallions. Welcome one and all to my humble abode. I hope you find the refreshments refreshing and the hospitality hospitable. If you ever find yourself at a loss for carnal delight, don't you dare hesitate to raise your hand. Here at the Ranch, *we* are the animals."

Freja narrowed her eyes.

"Aaaaand of course you want to hear the update," said Lowell, plucking a fresh tequila off a passing tray and taking a swig. "I have good news, and bad news. If I ever write a business book, it's going to be titled *Shit Sandwiches Taste Like Shit.* Y'all have too much experience to want to be coddled, so I'll give the bad news to you straight. The kidnapping was a bust."

Midori blew air out through her nose. Jason shook his head in disgust. The rest took the news without affect. Emily followed Lowell's lead and snagged a tequila for herself. She needed something to do with her hands while she ignored the disdainful looks from the assembled crowd that saw Pixie for exactly what she was: a vain indulgence.

"Who could have guessed that an art dealer could have bested seasoned pros, right? Barasa is correct. One of our contractors left in a body bag. The other survived but sustained severe injuries. The upshot is that we don't have Rosa. Without her, we don't have leverage over Javier. Without leverage over Javier, well, even Jason is bright enough to fill in the blanks."

"Jason and I don't see eye to eye on a lot of things," said Barend coolly. "But he isn't the only one who's concerned. We aren't going to stand around and let Commonwealth hijack our capital just because you can't execute a basic op. I should have had our family do this in-house. We have people with actual experience."

Barasa turned down his lips in an inverse smile. "Forgive me, but do you mean experience sparking international scandals? Chile? Nepal? Geneva? Unless I'm wildly misinformed, the House of Orange has a . . . checkered history running covert-action projects."

Jason snorted. Emily made a mental note to have Diana cross-check for rumors of botched operations in those locales and link them to the Dutch royals.

"Right," said Barend. "Ever wonder what operations you might *not* have heard about? Or whether having a reputation for sloppiness might cause others to underestimate your capabilities? Your approach seems to be to not even bother to try anything clandestine out of sheer incompetence. That matador costume is apt—you're a bull in a geopolitical china shop."

"The matador *kills* the bull," said Barasa. "But maybe you need your intelligence officers to clear that one up for you."

"Hey." Lowell raised a hand to stop Barend's response. "Cool it, all of you. Do you remember what I said on Camiguin?" He looked around the room, making eye contact with each of them. "I told you that my goal with this project is to earn your trust. Rachel is dying. Change is coming. Sabotaging Javier's plan is only step one. Now, does failure earn anyone's trust? I don't think so. Trust is based on one thing and one thing only." He raised an index finger. "Results."

Lowell paused, letting tension build as the burble of the stream filled the space. Emily was as on edge as the rest of them. Any clues to

Lowell's next moves would be the intel jackpot they'd need to subvert his operation.

"Which brings us to the first bit of good news," he said with a wide grin. "And our guest of honor."

At that precise moment, something cold and hard touched the back of Emily's head. She froze, quelling her immediate instinct to duck and disarm. Scenarios trampled through her mind like a herd of bison, but no matter what variables she considered, she couldn't outmaneuver a point-blank bullet.

"Don't even try," said a voice from behind her. "We're the real deal, not Addis thugs. Do anything except for exactly what I tell you to do, and you get a soft point to the skull. Not even the baddest martial arts motherfucker can out-ninja a gun, and even if you somehow pull some voodoo shit on me, my colleagues have multiple lines of fire on you. This is the part where if I were an amateur, I'd say something like *capisce*. But I'm not an amateur, am I?"

Silence. All eyes were locked on her with rapt attention. Emily had expected a violent death, but never summary execution.

"Good girl. All right, I'm going to step back, and you're going to get down on your knees and put your hands behind your head. Easy, now. That's it."

Emily followed the instructions slowly and carefully. The sand was cool and coarse. Her mind was strangely empty.

"Ladies and gentlemen," said Lowell. "I give you . . . *Pixie*."

Rizal would have envied Lowell's dramatic flair.

CHAPTER 29

Lowell rubbed his hands together, and tiny pieces of glitter sparkled as they wafted away.

"Pixie, it turns out, is a woman of *many* talents." Lowell was playing the storyteller, drumming up his act. "Performing a coup de grâce with a champagne flute was just the flashy opening act. She's also adept at spilling baijiu, fucking like a demon, murdering security contractors, and snitching. I mean, she even came here voluntarily hoping to dig up more dirt." He blew Emily a kiss. "She's the whole package, I'm telling you."

"You've got to be fucking kidding me," said Jason.

Lowell ignored him. "She nearly decapitated one of the contractors with a kitchen cleaver and gutted his partner with a chef's knife. The apartment looked like a scene straight out of those classic Tarantino films. Serious carnage. The surviving idiot used the sedative intended for Rosa to dull his own pain, and when he came out of it, he went into shock. We had to do a full interrogation just to work out what really happened, but he had managed to record a snippet in his feed, and boy was I surprised when our favorite Camiguin street fighter made a cameo. It took me a hot minute to recognize her without the makeup, but the way she aced those two dudes, who else could it be? So she snatches Rosa and manages to evade our dumbass support team. Freja's people are turning Camiguin upside down, and Pixie seems to have mysteriously disappeared. Doesn't visit her apartment, doesn't go to the gym, nothing. When we ask the fight-club owner, Rizal, about her, he gets all cagey. Meanwhile our analysts are reverse engineering feed transport data and give us a high-confidence estimate that Rosa and, now we're pretty darn sure, Pixie hop on a private plane to Javier's island off the coast of Washington State. Then—this is a little sketchier because Seattle's a hub—someone, probably Pixie and Javier, put some flowers in their hair and take a trip down to, yes, you guessed it, San Francisco to meet some gentle people there."

Lowell whistled the song's chorus, and Freja winced.

"But my *favorite* part has to be that this backstabbing little cunt of a forest nymph has cojones ginormous enough to play hard to get with me and then actually accept the invitation to join us here tonight." He raised both hands, fingers splayed. "Ahh, it's just so good. I wish I had thought to set us up with a live band down here so we could have a drumroll."

Lex's face was ashen. "But Pixie was there on Camiguin," he said with an air of dawning realization. Emily felt his horrified eyes on her. "She's seen our faces. Are you telling us that Commonwealth *knows* about our involvement?"

"You bet," said Lowell in a chipper voice. "But before you suffer a nervous breakdown, remember that this is good for us."

Barend rubbed his eyes as if he could wipe away this revelation. "You're insane," he said.

Lowell barked a laugh. "Well, I can't argue with you there. But those of you having panic attacks should be wondering why the smarter half of this prestigious company don't appear to be spiraling down into wormholes of self-pity."

Everyone looked at everyone else.

"Well?" asked Lowell.

Nisanur stroked her feathers. "My own people inside Commonwealth are reporting that the progressive-membership initiative has been delayed indefinitely. They don't know the details, but apparently there is friction on the board."

"Friction." Lowell let the word roll around in his mouth, relishing it. "My fellow collaborators, friction is exactly what we set out to create. That's the beauty of our position. We don't need decisive action in our favor, we just need to jam the gears. Having Rosa in hand would do just that, but it turns out that whispers of conspiracy can sow discord just as effectively. Nisanur, my dear, did your ever-so-well-informed contacts happen to mention anything about the state of Rachel's health?"

Nisanur shrugged. "She's dying. Hard to know when, but it's coming."

"Death comes for us all in the end," said Lowell. "And in Rachel's case, discord in her inner circle can be cultivated. When it's time for succession, those fault lines will crack Commonwealth apart at its foundations, and we'll be there to patch things up and take the reins. And with our capital and Commonwealth's infrastructure, who's going to stop us? That's the real prize. Not a temporary reprieve. A global empire. We don't play to draw, we play to *win*."

"But Commonwealth knows our identities," said Lex. "They can pursue retribution, legal action, who knows what else."

"So can we," said Lowell. "Our capital doesn't respect borders any more than the feed does. If they want to wrestle, let 'em get muddy."

"Fuck this," said Jason, throwing up his hands. "I'm out. This is a goddamn train wreck."

"I don't think you can back out now," said Midori thoughtfully. "None of us can. They know who we are and what we were planning. They're not going to forgive or forget. That means we're committed to this path, to each other." She looked up. "To Lowell."

Lowell bowed. "Lines in the sand, baby. I said my goal was to earn your trust. Would you really trust anyone who gave you a choice in the matter?"

Barend swore under his breath.

Barasa shrugged. "To be fair, he did promise results."

CHAPTER 30

"How about we consecrate this partnership with blood?" asked Lowell brightly. "Don't worry, not your own. The gods only know what hematological contagion we'd pick up from Jason. I'm talking about our guest of honor."

The weight of everyone's gaze brought Emily back to herself. Grains of sand pricked her knees. She was a spy turned sacrificial lamb. Or an unsuspecting double agent? She almost laughed. She'd managed to rescue Rosa and play right into Lowell's hands at the same time.

Friction.

She remembered the fraught debate in Analog. Whoever Nisanur's spies were, their intel was good. By sharing her story, Emily had doomed Javier's initiative and underwritten Lowell's ascension. She couldn't have left Rosa unprotected. She couldn't have avoided telling Javier the truth. She couldn't have avoided winding up in this hellish cavern.

Death comes for us all in the end.

So this was how death would come for her. A 9 mm to the back of the head. Blood leaking out onto the sand. Body cremated and disposed of with grim professionalism. She could almost see the glint on the reaper's scythe. This had been what she had wanted, what she had chased all those years on Camiguin. Too ashamed to face her friends, too cowardly for suicide, she'd stepped into the ring again and again, circling closer and closer to the light at the end of the tunnel. She had sought to wash away her sins with pain, but death was the only cure for her self-hatred. That's why she always kept her memento mori close at hand. She saw the world through lenses that were proof of her mortality, a hair's breadth from sweet relief.

"Pixie, Pixie, Pixie," said Lowell. "I really wish we had gotten to know each other better. You're definitely my kind o' gal. A total mind-fuck. You asked for a sacrifice and, to be perfectly honest, I never had much dignity to lose in the first place, so I figured I'd just make one of you instead. Oh, and you're absolutely right about the fact that the more you have to lose, the better it feels to win. I'm feeling like hot shit at the moment."

Now that she knelt on the threshold, Emily no longer wanted to face what lay beyond. A month ago, a year ago, a decade ago, with nothing to live for but abnegation, she would have welcomed oblivion. But now . . . The weight of Rosa's head on her shoulder as the stars wheeled above them. The dry warmth of Javier's hand. The quiet glow of Dag's contentment. The bewildered look on Rizal's face. Even Nell's reassuring touch. These bittersweet threads bound her to the living, bound her to life itself.

For the first time in thirteen years, Emily did not want to die.

"Please," she said, her voice raw and husky. "Please."

It was all she could manage.

Lowell sucked his teeth.

"*Eeesh,*" he said, grimacing. "Begging, really? Honestly, I really didn't see that one coming. It doesn't suit you. Maybe you're not my type after all. Damn shame."

Emily shifted her gaze to the tuxedoed guards, but the eyes staring down the matte-black barrels were hard and unforgiving jewels mounted in silver filigree. The stream babbled. The cave smelled of minerals and primeval stone. She was a flame rekindled, only to be snuffed back out.

"Unwittingly or not, Pixie here has done us all a favor," said Lowell. "And this is a party, after all. So I'm going to let her go out with more of a bang than a bang. It's only fair, and it's a hell of a lot more fun." He waggled a finger. "Let no one call me ungrateful."

Lowell clapped three times, and one of the security goons took off up the stairs.

"Ten years ago, something odd happened on one of my Arctic oil platforms," said Lowell. "This was after my fall from grace, after Commonwealth destroyed my fossil fuels business. As Midori alluded to on Camiguin, my net worth was shedding digits like a sick dog, and I was doing what I could to pick up the scraps. One of those scraps was an ex-lobbyist of mine who'd betrayed me and helped Rachel screw me over. I had him detained, and we were holding him on one of those abandoned oil platforms for safekeeping. Nobody's around to ask questions in that frigid wasteland, right? Well, apparently someone was. Long story short, they drugged the guards and made off with my lobbyist. And when I say drugged, I mean *drugged*. No, not poison. This was a high-dose psychedelic aerosol. Probably quite a lot of fun under the right circumstances. But these were not the right circumstances. Suddenly the only people running around on the rig were a bunch of assault rifle–toting paranoid ex–special forces motherfuckers tripping balls harder than any human has tripped before. The feed footage is . . . out of this world. Let's just say that if we ever wanted to produce a true-crime horror serial, we'd have prime source material. Only one of these unwilling psychonauts made it out alive, and he's never been the same since."

Lowell's face brightened. "Ahh, speak of the devil, and I mean that quite literally. Vasilios, how kind of you to join us this fine evening."

CHAPTER 31

Vasilios. Emily's mind raced. She recognized the name from somewhere, but where? It had been on Camiguin, maybe even in the fight club. That was it—Rizal had been chattering about a fighter on the international circuit. People called him the Greek, and he'd earned a vicious reputation. Emily hadn't paid much attention. She didn't follow the rankings because she didn't care about her own. She never traveled to fight. She was in hiding—fame was the last thing she wanted. That was why she only fought the low-level grunts like Niko who made their way to Rizal's. Emily's distaste for celebrity was probably how she'd survived as long as she had given her relative age and inexperience.

Vasilios was different, a fighter on another level entirely. He had fans, glory, an agent. Real money rode on his matches. Real law enforcement tried to shut down his fights and usually failed because of generous bribes carefully applied by promoters. That he had special forces on his résumé might help explain Vasilios's meteoric rise through the brackets.

"If we could all take our places," said Lowell.

Lowell, Freja, Nisanur, and the rest sat on the second tier of stone benches running around the perimeter of the room. The tuxedoed enforcers retreated to stand on the floor directly in front of the lowest benches, clearing the central ring of sand. They didn't holster their weapons, but they did lower them to their sides.

The silence stretched like a rubber band. Emily was aware of her own breathing, the strange fact that she was still alive and that base terror could still manifest. Her stomach twisted. Her pulse was arrhythmic. Bile seared the back of her throat.

Slowly, half expecting the goons to pack her full of lead, she released her hands from the back of her head. Nobody objected. Nobody moved. Reaching down, she scooped up a handful of sand and rubbed it between her palms. Then, rolling back onto her heels, she rose to her feet and turned around.

Vasilios stood on the last step, as still and erect as a mast. His golden hair was tied back in a ponytail. His face was classically handsome but smooth, too smooth, as if he had arrived straight from a plastic-surgery theater. His eyes were chips of jade and there was something deeply unnerving about his gaze, as if the dragon from her father's fairytale lurked in its green depths.

He grinned when their eyes met, wide and toothy. Then he descended the final step onto the sand and shrugged off what looked like a short kimono. *Shitagi*. The word sprang into Emily's mind, a relic of Rosa's long obsession with samurai serials. Underneath, Vasilios wore nothing but a *fundoshi*, the long piece of white linen wound around his slender hips, tucked between his legs, and knotted at the back. *Samurai diaper.* Rosa had hated it when Emily called it that. Vasilios was not a big man, but his body was lean and muscled and he moved with an athlete's grace. His skin was hairless and as glossy as his face, with pink patches that looked like they might have been grafted on recently.

Reaching to the small of his back, Vasilios brought something around in front of him, a stick that he gripped with both fists. Then he pulled his fists apart and it wasn't a stick but a short blade that he unsheathed, a *wakizashi*, the katana's little sister. The curved steel glinted, displaying the grain of thousands of expert folds.

151

Lowell applauded in delight. "I'm trying to remember that night at Rizal's," he said. "But the champagne was flowing, so I just hope I get this right." His voice dropped to an affected baritone. *"May fortune favor the bold."*

Emily pushed her lucky glasses up her nose.

Pitting her against the Greek was already hopeless. Giving him a blade and leaving her unarmed made it ridiculous. But this wasn't a fight. This was a baroque execution.

She remembered her mother's reassuring instructions as they disassembled and reassembled the telescope, the murmur of her father's stories under the stars. There was the unmooring shock of their deaths and the fierce joy of claiming her own independence. Then channeling that zeal into protecting others, and an unexpected softening as those others became a family she would do anything to defend. Fission. Her crusade and her honor diverging, splitting her apart and her new family with it. Darkness. The agony of protracted self-flagellation, turning her crusade inward, laying siege to her own soul. And then that most unexpected of prospects, the sliver of a chance of a new beginning. If this was where that new beginning would meet its premature end, Emily would hold nothing back. If this was to be a show, let it be a *show*.

Cycling through her mental record collection, Emily selected Afrika Bambaataa's "Planet Rock." She didn't need the feed for a song she knew by heart. Bambaataa had introduced the Roland 808 drum machine to hip-hop, and this particular rhythm was a lazy river in the heat of summer. The synth spiced everything up, dropping a kaleidoscopic lens over the entire piece. Staccato lyrical chants exploded over a groundbreaking mashup of electro, R&B, techno, and favela funk that inspired and prefigured decades of subsequent musical evolution. This was music to face the music to.

Emily let the beats cascade through her body, relinquishing conscious control. She began to step, to move, to dance, enhancing the childlike liberty of her untethered movements.

That inhuman grin was still plastered on Vasilios's face. He side-stepped to match her, relaxed and unhurried. His cheeks flushed to a rosy pink. This was his element.

They circled each other, the damp air electric.

And then he struck. The attack came impossibly fast, a high kick that Emily only just managed to duck under. Too late, she realized the kick was a feint, and could do nothing as the wakizashi snaked in to taste first blood.

Circling again.

Blood dribbled down Emily's deltoid, but the cut was extremely shallow, barely skin deep.

Another strike, a triple feint, and this time he drew a fiery line across her left breast. But something was off. He was too good. She hadn't been fast enough—he could have sunk the blade into her heart.

Circling.

Emily came at him with a low kick as he was stepping across the stream, hoping that she might catch him off balance. But he turned his leg to deflect the kick off his calf, and steel flashed.

Only then, panting as they resumed their circling and reaching up to touch the superficial wound on her cheek, did Emily understand. Vasilios wasn't fighting her at all. He was *playing* with her. He was ex–special forces. His name sat at the top of the global fight-club rankings. She was a civilian who had trained under a mediocre martial artist late in life, fought nobodies in a backwater ring. Emily was hopelessly out-matched, and Vasilios wanted to sate himself on her death, revel in her suffering with predatory glee.

It was the same power trip that petty bureaucrats savored when they raised impediment after impediment to her teenage autonomy. It was the apathy that drove so many people to disenfranchise themselves through cynicism. It was the self-conscious free riding with which Lowell and his cohorts in this room had forged their dominions. It was the cat toying with the mouse just for the hell of it. More so even than the prospect of her own death, it was the one thing Emily could not abide.

She had to find a chink in Vasilios's armor. She had to make him, them, pay.

Or die trying.

Thoughts churned, far outstripping Bambaataa's lazy beat. The ex-lobbyist Lowell referenced while announcing Vasilios had to be Dag, but Emily had no idea what he was referring to. Lowell had said this took place ten years ago, after Emily had arrived on Camiguin. Apparently she had missed a lot. But she *had* been inside Dag's feed when he visited Lowell and Freja on an Arctic oil platform years before that, when he was their partner, not their prisoner.

"Eternal twilight," she called out in a singsong voice following the beats of her mental soundtrack. "Purple and orange and green, the fiery ball of the sun skimming along the horizon like a child skipping a stone across a pond, but never sinking, never dropping below the endless gray-blue of the ocean."

Dag had struggled to come to terms with how they were hijacking the feed. Even just the possibility of a breach was a lot to take in. *There are two broad families of martial arts,* she had explained to Dag. *Hard forms, like karate, use direct strikes and meet force with force. You might aim to break an opponent's arm with a block. Soft forms are all about using the minimum force possible to deflect an opponent's attack to their disadvantage. Instead of blocking, you might redirect a kick to throw your opponent off balance. In the fight over ideas, we use the softest of soft forms. We plant seeds and nurture them to maturity. We encourage potential opponents to take our side of their own volition.* In the past thirteen years, Emily had reverted to a hard form. But there was no way she could beat Vasilios at his own game.

He came at her and Emily threw herself to the side, landing hard in the sand and popping back up. Blood oozed from a fresh cut on her thigh.

"You know it's going to be freezing," she continued. "A cold that makes your bones ache, that leaches all vestiges of hope. But they don't tell you about the humidity, how the air is thick and viscous, how moving through it is like pressing yourself through solid ice, how the wind cuts like a knife. *That* knife." She pointed to the wakizashi. "And how, staring out over that slate sea, watching the dirty bergs float on groundswell and cargo haulers traverse this remotest of shipping lanes, that it's beautiful in a rugged, alien way, that its sheer natural savagery illuminates your own fragile humanity."

Another strike. Another dodge. A burning trace across her shoulders.

Emily remembered waking Dag up in the middle of the night with mugs of steaming cocoa—hopefully she had added sufficient quantities of marshmallows that time—and dragging him out to stare up at the cosmos. *Even actors have a choice,* she had told him. *Once you know there's a script, you can choose your own inflections. You can learn to improvise. You can make the play better. Understanding how things came to be frees us to imagine new possibilities. That's part of what our whole effort here is all about. Ultimately, the only power we have is to choose how we see the world.*

"And rising from that hostile sea like a leviathan, aviation lights blinking and paint peeling, is a miracle of engineering, a symbol of our endeavor to conquer an environment that once confined us: an oil platform," she said. "The helipad, the cargo elevators, the cabins and stairwells and control rooms, the endless branching corridors, turning back in on themselves like an industrial labyrinth."

Vasilios wasn't smiling anymore.

A blur of slices. Emily leapt back, hitting the chest of one of the tuxedoed guards who grunted and shoved her back into the ring, blood pouring from a crosshatch of slashes across her torso, mixing with the glitter, turning her into a sparkling wax candle that dripped crimson.

She would only have one chance. Making her gambit too early would mean certain death.

"And there's this odd thing about labyrinths that we all know deep in our hearts, even if we pretend not to," she said. "There is always *something* living in the center. We reach a dead end, but there's a whiff of sulfur. We turn a corner to see a monster, only to realize that it's our reflection. We open a door, and the walls are covered in gore." Emily wiped her hands across the cuts, smeared the blood across her face, and then licked each finger one at a time, pretending to savor the sharp tang of iron. "We can run, we can hide, but we can never, ever escape."

The wakizashi spiraled in, her naked skin a canvas for its violent calligraphy.

Identity was narrative, and if you were careful, you could unravel the threads and knit them back together in a new pattern. Emily couldn't face Vasilios without Pixie. Pixie couldn't face Vasilios without Emily. Vasilios couldn't beat her if she could find herself in him.

"Look at me, Vasilios," Emily screamed, forcing herself to meet his emerald gaze. "I know what's in the center of things, I know *who* is in the center of things, I know the Minotaur waiting in your labyrinth. If I were real, how could I possibly know his name, the one you were tasked to protect, the one who disappeared into thin air, the reason you are here at the end of the world, at the end of time? Dag Calhoun. *Dag Calhoun.*" She stepped toward him, conjuring the memory of every bad trip she'd ever had, summoning the ecstasy and the agony of every existential crisis, invoking the wondrous terror of infinity. She opened her eyes wide, contorted her face, and stuck out her tongue in her best demonic impression. "Tell me! How could I possibly know that? *How could I possibly know his name?* You pathetic little maggot. *Don't you get it?* Fighting on a global circuit? Shadowy visitations on sleepless nights? A cave under a mansion in the mountains? *None of this is real.* The past ten years never happened. *You. Are. Still. On. The. Rig.* And no matter

how hard you try, you can't kill me. You *are* me. I *am* you. We *are* each other, you dumb fuck. Killing me is killing yourself."

Vasilios's eyes glitched. An inarticulate roar tore itself from his throat, and he charged. This time, his attack had no grace. It was raw, desperate, fueled by incandescent rage.

Emily broke her rhythm, forcing herself to move faster than she ever had. She mirrored Vasilios, charging directly toward him instead of the sidesteps, ducks, and dodges she'd survived with so far. As the blade came hissing down in a vicious overhead cut, she threw herself at him, getting inside the arc of the wakizashi, snatching her lucky glasses off and snapping the right temple from the frame.

Getting this close was suicide. He could wrap her in his arms and crush her in a deadly embrace from which there would be no escape. But then his glistening chest hit her like a freight train, she stabbed the temple into his pec, and the auto-injector released. His arms came down to trap her and he squeezed the breath from her lungs, laughing madly, a man believing himself the victor, thinking he might just have rediscovered sanity. It took three heartbeats for the fast-acting neuro-toxin to cross the blood-brain barrier. Only then did his muscles seize.

If there was one thing Emily had learned, it was that luck was something you made for yourself.

CHAPTER 32

Emily heaved, kicking up sand as she thrust forward. Foam oozed onto her head from Vasilios's mouth as his body twitched against her. Time was short. It would only take them a few seconds to figure out that something was wrong.

But Vasilios was heavy with ropy muscle, and Emily almost lost her footing in the sand. She howled at the top of her lungs as her vision narrowed. She was Sisyphus pushing a boulder up a hill forever. She was Atlas holding the world on his shoulders. She was Pixie and she was Emily Kim, and if Vasilios hadn't been able to kill her, she wasn't going to let his corpse finish the job.

Like a rugby player rucking over a loose ball, Emily threw herself and Vasilios into one of the guards standing around the edge of the ring. As before, the guard tried to shove them both back onto the sand but wasn't prepared for the deadweight of Vasilios's shuddering body. As they both went down, Emily slid out from Vasilios's embrace and snatched the wakizashi from his spasming fingers.

Frozen in disbelief, Lowell was seated on the second tier of benches, less than a meter away. The rest of the guards had no clear line of fire.

Emily leapt.

In a split second, she was behind him, locking her legs around his waist, pressing the razor-sharp blade to his throat, and bringing her lips to his ear. "I warned you"—she whispered—"to keep your ghosts at bay."

A moment of perfect silence. Even her imaginary soundtrack had ceased.

"Do you want to die today?" she asked.

His entire body was trembling so badly his teeth chattered and his fat jiggled. The masqueraders had every gun trained on them. The other guests were sliding along the benches to the far side of the room. Vasilios's corpse was convulsing on the blood-soaked sand.

"I asked you a question," she said. "You've got a nice thing going here. Big house. Pretty ladies. A gang of megalomaniacal friends. Whatever special level of hell you've earned a ticket to probably won't stack up. But who am I to say?"

Lowell gurgled, and Emily felt his Adam's apple bob under the wakizashi.

"I'm going to ask you one more time because it's really best to be sure about these things," she said. "Normally, certain death is rather, well, certain. What you just witnessed is the exception that proves the rule. So, Mr. Harding, do you want to die today?"

"No," said Lowell. "Please, no."

"Ahh," said Emily. "I remember you saying something rather unkind about begging for mercy earlier this evening. But you know what? Fuck it. I'm willing to give the Golden Rule a shot and treat others how I want to be treated."

Lowell let out a muffled sob. Tears ran down his cheeks and splattered onto the blade, rinsing away her blood.

"There, there," said Emily. "I'm working with you. We're on the same page now, buddy. You don't want to die today, and I'm willing to consider the possibility of not opening your throat. That, as the therapist you so badly need would say, is progress. But if we're going to get through this, we're going to have to do it together. Think you can handle that?"

He nodded awkwardly, trying to keep his neck perfectly still.

"What a trooper! I knew you had it in you. Lowell Harding knows how to pivot when the winds of change blow. You've never been one to go to the wall for anything or anyone except yourself." She cinched her legs tighter. "Now stand."

"What?"

"*Stand.*"

Leaning forward to support her weight, Lowell rose shakily to his feet.

Emily raised her voice to address the room. "My dear masqueraders, please drop your fucking weapons."

They hesitated, and she pulled the blade a little tighter, drawing blood.

"Do what she says," shrieked Lowell.

The guns hit the sand with muted thumps.

"A little slow on the uptake," said Emily. "But you got there eventually. I'd give it a C plus, but hey, that's still passing." She adjusted herself slightly to secure her piggyback position. "Now we've got a party raging upstairs, and you seem like just the kind of dickwads who enjoy crowd control more than dancing, so I'm going to give you the opportunity to shine. You're going to go up those stairs with Mr. Harding here right behind you, and then you're going to cut us a path through the shenanigans, straight out the front door, and down to the dock. Capisce, assholes?"

They exchanged looks.

"Do it!" said Lowell.

Vasilios gave one final gurgle. His face stretched into a horrific asymmetrical grimace, his back locked in an arch, and his extremities twisted at unnatural angles. The temple from Emily's lucky glasses stuck out of his chest like an arrow's fletching.

The chief masquerader nodded and led his compatriots up the spiral staircase.

"Move," said Emily, and Lowell followed.

Lowell struggled as he carried Emily up the stairs. His breath came in sharp pants, and his body was so slick with his sweat and her blood that Emily had to constantly calibrate her grip. She counted the turns, keeping a close eye on the back of the masqueraders ahead and throwing occasional glances over her shoulder to make sure nobody was following, but these guests were not about to risk their necks for Lowell. They'd wait below until they were certain the action had resolved itself.

An unexpected wave of gratitude washed over Emily. Whether or not she made it out alive, there were people in this world she was willing to risk everything for, and who might just do the same for her. She might not have much else, but what more could you ask for?

"I—I think I'm gonna faint," gasped Lowell, reaching a hand out to lean against the stone wall.

"Deep breaths," said Emily. Between the blood loss and the combat hangover, her head was spinning too. "That's it. You can do this."

And then they came around the final curve, and the lead masquerader opened the stainless-steel door. His compatriots marched out and then Lowell stumbled through the faux mist and into the kitchen and they were shoving Chibundi out of the way and the feed came flooding back in all its overwhelming glory, the gentle touch of a digital deity that Emily had never thought she'd feel again, and Emily was broadcasting *"Zeppelin zeppelin zeppelin"* on the emergency channel.

"Extraction team is eleven minutes out," Diana's calm efficiency almost drove Emily to tears. No questions. No bullshit. "Haruki's running point. We're tracking your position. Hang in there."

The masqueraders fanned out into the ax-throwing arcade, cutting through the crowd in a wedge, Lowell staggering in their wake. The jostled guests stared and pointed, not knowing what to make of the bloody demon riding on the back of their illustrious host and holding a knife to his throat, glitter sparkling off the few sections of her skin that Vasilios hadn't shredded, their fractals blending into each other so that

Emily and Lowell might be a single nightmare creature, Frankenstein's monster escaping from the mad scientist's dungeon laboratory. As they moved from gallery to gallery, guests began to follow them, astronauts and witches and zombies whispering and rubbernecking and desperate to know whether this was part of some grand plan, an unexpected twist in the night's entertainment that would soon become legend in the tight-knit community of global socialites.

"It won't work, you know," said Lowell between heavy breaths.

"What?" His jerky steps were making Emily seasick.

"Whatever it is you're hoping to accomplish," said Lowell. "Fix inequality. Eliminate waste. End corruption. Heal every social ill. Turn the world into a techno-utopia. Commonwealth has a savior complex, but you arrogant pricks can't seem to wrap your oh-so-smart heads around the fact that you're your own worst enemy."

"I'm not really in the mood for riddles," said Emily. "And if I were you, I'd try to keep the woman with the wakizashi in a positive state of mind."

They entered the main atrium, and the lights strobing up and down the tree left hazy trails in Emily's vision. The masqueraders marched straight down the middle between the opposing alcohol and narcotics bars. Guests peered over balconies, stoked the rumor mill, and joined the mass of people following in their wake.

"You think that if you manage to stop us and institute progressive membership that it'll be some kind of endgame," said Lowell. "Another step toward Rachel's grand vision, or the board's or whatever. But those people in the cave, the ones you're so eager to thwart, they're the least of your problems. Nation, profession, religion . . . the feed undermines so many institutions at once, so many traditional sources of identity, that you've earned enemies on all sides. Government officials who see their authority corroding, cultural minorities who want to protect their children from the influence of the global feed, there were so many groups I could have organized to oppose Commonwealth, so many groups that are *organizing themselves* to oppose Commonwealth. I just picked rich people because it was easy. Small head count, simple pitch serving their self-interest, a strong sense of urgency because of Javier's pending proposal."

Bass thrummed through them as they passed beneath the DJ's balcony and emerged onto the grounds. There were screams from the ecstatic revelers that the masqueraders pushed roughly out of the way, opening a path through the middle of the dance floor.

Lowell had to shout to be heard as they descended the steps lit by fire dancers. "The feed connected everyone. Then Commonwealth leveraged its utility to disenfranchise everyone. Now just a handful of people hold the keys to all of civilization, and everyone else fucking hates you for it, especially folks who used to hold keys of their own. Everything you do wins you enemies. Rachel hates politics. I get it, a lot of entrepreneurs do. She wants results. She wants to optimize metrics and achieve milestones. Well, you know what's efficient? Dictatorship. But what used to be a feature is now a bug. Rachel hates politics so much that she accidentally turned the world into an autocracy."

"Whereas you're happy to kidnap innocents to seize power on behalf of your oligarch pals," said Emily. "If you're hoping to flip me, this isn't much of a pitch."

Wood creaked underfoot as Lowell took his first step onto the dock. The masqueraders formed a line blocking the hundreds of onlookers filling the grounds from following them out over the water. "I hope you enjoy your little moment," he said. "Because Rachel is nearing the end of her reign. You can kill me. You can expose those assholes downstairs. You can implement your stupid plan. You can win every battle, and you'll still lose the war. That's the thing about being queen. The bigger your realm, the bigger the bull's-eye on your back. This empire is so flimsy, it'll shake itself apart without my help."

"Incoming," advised Diana via Emily's feed.

Suddenly hundreds of lights began pouring through the mountain passes on the far side of the lake. An alarm went off up in the mansion, its high-pitched wail slicing through the pounding music as security drones streaked up from launchpads hidden in the surrounding forest. Emily realized that the lights racing across the water toward them must be Commonwealth drones. The two fleets met above the middle of the lake, corkscrewing into impossibly fast dogfights, raking each other with projective and missile fire, loosing chaff to stave off the inevitable, and erupting into successive fireballs in spectacular fashion, the detonations and sonic booms echoing off the surrounding mountains. Debris crashed into the lake, throwing up clouds of smoke and steam. New squadrons entered the fray in tight formation. The aerial battle turned the entire valley into a vast fireworks display, and the DJ, thinking this must be a climax to the night's festivities, maxed out the volume, filling every interstitial moment between explosions with thumping beats and looping melody. The crowd of onlookers filled the grounds beneath the colossal pink laser, writhing and cheering and pumping fists in awestruck wonder.

Something nudged Emily's foot.

"Are you *turned on* right now?" she asked in disbelief.

"Well, if you're not going to kill me," said Lowell, "I thought you might be down to fuck. All this excitement has me riled up."

Then downdraft blasted over them, and Lowell stumbled before regaining his balance, the wind excruciating against Emily's open wounds. Her head spun, and darkness encroached on her peripheral vision. A large chopper was descending, kicking up ripples across the water. It touched down lightly on the dock between them and the shore, its rotors carrying most of its weight. Four men in full combat gear spilled out and charged toward them. The one in the lead threw Emily a casual salute.

"Ms. Kim," he said. "I'm Haruki Abe, director of field ops. It's time to get you out of here."

"Mr. Harding is coming with us," she said. "Do me a favor. Kick him in the balls"—Haruki promptly sent a boot into Lowell's crotch—"and cuff him."

Releasing her grip, Emily slid from Lowell's back and onto the dock as he crumpled to curl up in fetal position next to her. Haruki and his team had to carry them both to the chopper as the audience applauded and the sky burned.

CHAPTER 33

Emily stepped out of the elevator and into a sculpture garden. Paths curved between installations, connecting seating areas where Commonwealth employees chatted and worked, submerged in their feeds. Moss grew on one side of a stone whale breaching through gravel. A group of visiting students wandered through a driftwood maze. There was even a life-size bear made from thousands of fused antique American pennies. The air smelled fresh and clean, no hint of the recycled staleness typical of skyscrapers this size.

This was her first time inside a Commonwealth building. The organization behind the feed was something she had always viewed from the outside, depending on Javier for gossip on the all-too-fallible stewards of the world's information infrastructure.

Years ago, Emily had tended the garden outside of the big house up on the Island. She'd always eschewed gloves, preferring to feel the moist earth on her hands even if it got under her fingernails. Reading up on horticulture, Emily had been surprised to discover that the biggest living thing was not the now-extinct blue whale but a mushroom whose underground tendrils spread through a patch of soil four kilometers wide. That mycelium, the single-celled filaments that formed vast three-dimensional networks underground, connected trees in a complex, redundant, and scalable network, a biological feed that conveyed nutrients and information between root systems, stitching forests into integrated, resilient arboreal superorganisms. Now she stood in a node of the digital mycelium that stitched together humanity into something similar, and no gloves could have kept her from getting her hands dirty.

Buoyed by painkillers, Emily made her way along the path leading to the conference room. Bandages covered most of her body, making her movements feel awkward and stiff. Even through the mental cotton candy of the drugs, she could feel the deep ache in her joints. Two fights in one week was far too much, especially when one of them was involuntary.

The real miracle was that she had survived at all.

May fortune favor the bold. She shook her head, hoping that whatever cell they were holding Lowell in was small and uncomfortable. She could still hear the burble of the subterranean stream, still taste the thick mineral air, still see Vasilios's grotesque corpse when she closed her eyes.

She reached up to push her lucky glasses up her nose, but they weren't there. While she liked their aesthetic, she'd never needed them to correct her vision. Their secret venom had always been a last-ditch defense, but more than anything they had been a reminder of impermanence, the transient nature of life on this strange little planet tucked into a random solar system in the corner of a backwater galaxy in an expanding universe. Maintaining respect for mortality had always helped her stick to her guns in trying times, but now that the glasses had proven their luck, maybe she didn't need replacements to see the world through that particular lens.

"Em!"

Javier ran toward her up the path, gangly limbs flying and eyes wide. Despite the gray in his hair and the limp in his gait, something about his unselfconscious charge resurrected the boy who had become her brother. He wrapped his long arms around her, then immediately let go as he felt the bandages beneath her clothes and heard her involuntary gasp.

"Oh no," he said. "I'm so sorry."

"It's okay." She grimaced, but it was the sweetest pain she'd ever felt. "The docs assure me I'll heal up. A hug isn't going to do me in."

He bit his lip.

"Look, Em . . ." Lines creased his forehead as he grasped for words. "I—I'm sorry. I've been a jerk. When you left, it—it made me feel like I was a little kid again, that my mom was ditching us for the hundredth time. But you weren't my mom, and I wasn't a little kid. I keep blaming you for leaving me in charge, but I was the one who decided to take over. I don't know what you've been through over the years, but you have every right to your privacy. I've just *missed* you so much. When Lowell took you through that door and you went dark . . . Diana had to kick me out of the command center. I just couldn't bear to lose you again."

"Sounds like Rosa's gotten to you." Emily laughed, emotion welling up.

"She's always been smarter than me," said Javier ruefully.

"Same here," said Emily. "I don't know what we did right with her, but she's a hell of a person."

"Seriously."

"Javi"—now it was Emily's turn to struggle for words—"I'm the jerk. I'm the one who left with no explanation. I'm the one who privileged my sense of honor over our friendship. I was being selfish, wallowing in my broken pride. Seeing you again just makes me realize how sorry I am, and how lucky."

Javier wiped his eyes with his black leather sleeve.

"They're waiting for you in there," he said.

"Then let's do this thing before my painkillers wear off."

CHAPTER 34

Seagulls glided in a ragged line toward the Golden Gate Bridge, trimming their wings to ride the incoming marine breeze. Alcatraz sat barren and defiant in the wind-blown surf, the prison-turned-museum waiting for the day when rising sea levels submerged the rocky island. Fog had built up against the Marin Headlands, the white mass poised like a tsunami, ready to sweep away the entire Bay Area.

In contrast, the waters of the Strait of Juan de Fuca were darker, stormier, hinting at a power humming beneath the waves that was somehow more diffuse this far south. The Island was a beacon, an oasis amid the rise and fall of swell, old-growth forest covering loamy soil, blackberry bushes the size of houses that yielded their exquisite fruit to those willing to brave the thorns. They had made it their home. With Southern California reduced to ash and rubble, it was the only home they had. Maybe, just maybe, it was a home to which Emily might return.

"The attorney general is pulling his hair out," said Liane. "We've had calls from the governor, both senators from Idaho, the FBI, the Pentagon, the president's chief of staff, even the FAA. Lowell's own attorneys are raising hell. It's a hot mess."

The simmering anger in Liane's words called Emily's attention to the world inside the wall-to-wall windows. They sat around a solid-glass conference table. The bouquet of white lilies at its center appeared to levitate in midair because the table and the crystal vase were transparent. Beads of condensation clung to the pitcher of ice water. The expressions around the table ranged from stern to furious.

"You heard Ms. Kim's testimony," said Diana, and Emily was touched by the woman's unerring confidence in her, the conviction with which she'd ordered the evacuation. Emily hadn't known Diana long enough to claim to understand her, but she'd learned enough to reveal the inadequacy of her preconceptions about the spymaster. "Emily was there on our orders. We did what we had to in order to get her out alive. Lowell is in our custody and this building is an embassy, our sovereign soil. Let them whine. The FBI can't just roll in to claim him. We have breathing room, and we've shown any other schemers that we're ready to take necessary action."

"She was there on *your* orders, you mean," said Liane. Desperation undergirded her tone. How would Emily feel in her place, saddled with the creation and administration of a brand-new legal system, establishing precedent in disaster after disaster, all too aware of the unintended consequences each decision would set off? "Orders that resulted in starting a goddamn shooting war in the Rocky Mountains. Half the attendees at that godforsaken party broadcast the whole thing via feed. Do you have any idea of the concessions we'll have to make in Washington?"

"Other governments will demand reciprocity," said Baihan. He was cool and collected, and Emily had the sense that he was assessing the positions of all the players, seeking opportunities for advantage, architecting his next move. Emily smiled despite herself. Canny old Hsu would have been proud. "The UN Security Council is drafting a resolution. Amsterdam and Tokyo have both been harassing my people."

"Diana, I think it's time for you to take a leave of absence," said Sofia with grim satisfaction. "You were trying to do your best in a tough spot, but the situation is untenable."

Some wounds take a long time to heal. And some reopen again and again. Sofia had been Diana's agent inside Commonwealth for years, the price of her loyalty the visas Diana had secured for her family. But released from the yoke, she must chafe at having to work with her former case officer, must want to oust Diana as soon as Rachel handed over Commonwealth's reins. Maybe this was her opportunity to strike, or at least to lay the groundwork for a fall from grace.

Diana guffawed. "Looking for a scapegoat, sweetie? You know what's *untenable*? What Emily confirmed at Lowell's shindig. We've got a Dutch prince, a Japanese heiress, a hedge-fund hotshot, and a bunch of other high-net-worth VIPs conspiring to meddle in Commonwealth governance and happy to attack us and our families in the process."

Emily could almost smell Rosa, that unique olfactory fingerprint laced with traces of makrut lime. Then Dag's half-finished sketch of their twin girls flashed in Emily's mind's eye. They all had people they loved, and in the wrong hands, that love could be a weapon. "We have their mastermind in custody. If that's the kind of *situation* you want to smooth over, then maybe we've got the wrong successor queued up to captain this particular ship."

Rachel raised a hand that was little more than skin and bone. The room fell silent, but the glares could melt steel. This woman had built a juggernaut, acquiring startup after startup, sinking competitor after competitor, recruiting genius after genius to assemble the miracle that was the feed. It was hard to picture Rachel in the prime of her youth, but could she ever have imagined what Commonwealth might one day become? She really had made a dent in the universe, making good on the famously unbridled ambitions of Silicon Valley. She had started out as an entrepreneur and had become a monarch.

"Personal attacks will get us nowhere," said Rachel, her purple eye blazing. "The only question that matters is what comes next."

That's the thing about being queen. The bigger your realm, the bigger the bull's-eye on your back. Lowell was right about one thing at least: The fate of Javier's proposal had never depended on earning unanimous support from the people around this table. At the end of the day, they were advisers, not deciders. There was only one vote that really mattered, and Rachel Leibovitz was the hardest of nuts to crack.

"This conspiracy is a symptom of inequality," said Javier. "Lowell and his cohorts are able to kidnap, murder, and manipulate at will because their wealth makes them nearly untouchable. Allowing that much capital to accrue to so few people puts the entire system at risk. Poverty is one problem the progressive-membership initiative will help address, but that's not all. By charging more to those with more and funding the feed with the proceeds, we'll be creating the level playing field that Sofia is so keen on." He pressed his hands together, summoning all the poise and charisma he'd polished in countless commencements, keynotes, and public appeals. "Let's get real. Our current fee structure is *regressive*. By charging all individuals the same fee, we force the poor to pony up a much higher percentage of their income than the rich. That's not just unfair, that's wrong. We're making the world worse, not better, and we're endangering the future of the feed at the same time. It must change. We should prosecute Lowell, expose his collaborators, and demonstrate that their meddling has done nothing but strengthen our resolve."

It took everything Emily had not to squeeze Javier's knee under the glass table. Pride swelled within her. He wasn't the person she'd thought he might become. He was someone better in every way, someone more unique, more himself. The digital ghosts she'd spent years chasing from hibernation on Camiguin were still alive, still real, and, against all odds, *did not hate her*. It was her own selfishness that had imprisoned her, her overwhelming sense of shame. *I just couldn't bear to lose you again*, Javier had said to her a few minutes ago. *I've just missed you so much.* Emily's heart was still melting, crying out, *Me too*. Again, Emily felt the weight of Rosa's head on her shoulder, saw the stars wheeling above them. These people were too good for her, too kind, too courageous, too brilliant. But somehow they cared about her, wanted her in their lives, overlooked the flaws she judged so harshly.

Down in that cavern, Emily had realized she wanted to live. Now she saw *how* she wanted to live. She would earn back the friendships she'd abandoned, prove herself worthy of the open arms Javier and Rosa were extending. She had brought in Lowell, helping to stave off the worst. It was time to seal the deal. If she could convince Rachel to do the right thing, to make a stand against the scourge of inequality just as she'd made a stand against climate change, Emily could take her rightful place among the people she loved.

"So," said Sofia. "Just to summarize, you're saying that we should fight this fire with gasoline."

Javier clenched his fists. "I'm saying that if we don't do something, who will?"

"And why do you get to decide on all the 'somethings' we should be doing?" asked Sofia. "Look, I hate Lowell as much as the next person. He's an asshole, and the crew he's assembled is a catalog of terrible human beings. Barend, Nisanur, Barasa, all of them have some serious human-rights violations on their résumés. But they're *reacting* to us. This wasn't a preemptive attack—this was a badly conceived, badly executed response to Javier's proposal. We've declared ourselves sovereign and crippled national governments. We've taxed carbon, unified currency, and opened borders. These are good things, and I applaud the passion with which Javier champions them. But we're moving too fast. The world can't handle it. This is what happens. We're in a moment of transition. If we want to make changes that last, if we want the feed to survive, we have to hit the brakes. We should let this storm blow over. Then, once everything has settled down, we can come back to this and see if there's a way we can work our way toward a solution."

Unconditional compassion washed over Emily, lubricated by the saccharine buzz of the painkillers. Sofia didn't really oppose this plan. She was just scared. As Rachel's appointed successor, more than anything, Sofia just wanted the transition to go smoothly. She was smart and knew that they were approaching a turning point, that this was just the calm before the storm. Like a squirrel hoarding nuts for winter, she wanted to store every ounce of strength, every iota of political capital and public goodwill, for the battle on the horizon.

Emily knew the feeling, and knew how deceptive it could be. It was precisely this logic that gnawed away the potential of the visionary, that turned dreams to rust. What better argument for inaction than the promise of future action? What better defenders of the status quo than well-meaning leaders who hedged? A quote floated up from a half-forgotten high-school history class. *Change will not come if we wait for some other person or some other time. We are the ones we've been waiting for. We are the change that we seek.*

Javier made to speak, but Emily put a restraining hand on his arm.

She stood, calling on the fierce grit that had carried her through years in the ring, digging deep for the easy confidence she'd once possessed.

"Have you ever watched that classic science-fiction film *The Matrix?*" she asked. "I remember loving that movie when I was a kid, even though the special effects were absolute trash. The campy slow-mo won me over, dodging bullets and kicking ass. But what stuck with me afterward was the idea that the world we perceive isn't real—just a membrane concealing a deeper reality. I began to see things everywhere that I thought were real but were really made up. Teachers told us that our grades mattered, but really they were just an inaccurate and ineffective bureaucratic sorting mechanism. We weren't allowed to vote until we were eighteen, but the distinction between child and adult was totally arbitrary, just a number that someone decided on one day. We called politicians leaders when they were often the most corrupt, vain, and impotent people around. Suddenly, everywhere I looked, I saw facts revealed to be fiction."

Reaching out, Emily plucked a lily from the vase, turning the flower in her hands with exaggerated care. "That's the *real* power of the feed," she said. "It's the red pill. The feed has ripped the veil from so many of the fantasies we once thought were natural laws. Nations are just a collective fiction, an awkward mashup of anecdotes, anthems, and historical circumstance that we use to draft a social contract. I was born in what was once Los Angeles, but I am only American to the extent that I believe I am. The nation state is a relatively recent invention, and when you declared Commonwealth sovereign, you demonstrated that institutional innovation has no more of an endpoint than its technological equivalent. When you mandated open borders, you showed how little those lines in the sand really meant, how the colors we add to maps are a conceit. When you created a unified global currency, you proved money to be a figment of our imaginations. The only value money has is the value we believe it has. That's why I can buy fresh produce with a few ephemeral electrons, credits adjusted and cleared through the feed. But the problem with nations, money, religion, and other human constructs is that they're *convincing*. If they weren't, they wouldn't work. Sometimes they work too well. Sometimes we drink our own Kool-Aid. We lose track of first principles."

She returned the lily to the vase. "That's what is happening here. Lowell and his pals want to protect their private property. But private property isn't an actual thing, like granite or gravity. It's just something we all agree to, like not cutting in line. We agree to private property because inequality is *useful*. Wealth gives us a way to reward valuable work and trade with each other, benefiting everyone. But taken too far, inequality is deadly. We're motivated by *relative*—not absolute—wealth, so when a tiny minority seizes almost all the money, discontent snowballs. The result is social unrest, not economic dynamism. And social unrest is something that Commonwealth's new world order cannot afford, particularly at a 'moment of transition.'"

They were almost there, Emily could feel it. Rachel's stare bored into her, as intense as the laser at the Ranch. The room was listening with surprise and rapt attention, even Sofia. "The feed is the single most important piece of global infrastructure, interdependent and reciprocal with everything else. It's the engine that drives civilization, and you are its stewards. It has blessed you with freedom and cursed you with responsibility." This was the brink. They just needed one last push. "And it shouldn't take Diana and Dag trading knowledge of Javier and my backdoor to get you to do the right thing, like it did with the carbon tax. People like Lowell might only make good decisions under duress, but you can do the right thing for the right reason right here, right now. Implement Javier's proposal. Build a future we want to live in."

Emily collapsed into her chair, spent. With a little luck, it would be enough.

There was a moment of silence.

"Hold the fuck on." Sofia kicked back her chair and stood up. "What are you talking about? A *backdoor* into the feed? *Trading* it for the carbon tax?"

Emily's breath caught in her throat.

Baihan frowned. "Rachel, what is she—"

"So this is why I had to rewrite the terms of service on a goddamn moment's notice?" demanded Liane. "We were blackmailed into making climate change policy?"

"Oooohhhh," said Baihan, shaking his head. "Any breach of feed security should have been disclosed to every signatory to Commonwealth's agreements. This invalidates every treaty, and as a special adviser to the UN Security Council I can tell you right now that we will take steps to—"

"Oh, hell no, asshole," snapped Liane. "You're not reneging on *years* of fucking work. Whatever this is, it's not yours to leverage into some kind of hostile takeover."

Baihan smiled coldly. "It sounds like Commonwealth is already the victim of a hostile takeover. Of course—"

"Don't make me bring up Bangladesh," said Diana. "Seriously, Baihan, don't make me do it. I don't want to, but I will."

Color drained from his face. "Bitch—"

"The fuck happened in Bangladesh?" asked Liane, looking back and forth between them.

Sofia reached out, lifted the vase, and smashed it down onto the table. The vessel shattered on impact, sending water and flowers everywhere.

"Explain," she said in a low voice that promised murder.

"I think what Emily is trying to—" said Diana.

"Oh no you fucking *don't*," raged Sofia. "Javier and this—" She stared at Emily in disbelief. "This—whoever she really is, had some kind of backdoor to the feed? And you and Dag *knew*?"

"That doesn't carry a lot of moral authority coming from someone who was the highest-placed agent embedded in Commonwealth," snapped Diana with the hopeless air of someone making a last-ditch attempt to defuse a bomb.

Sofia's mouth fell open. "I reported to *you*, bitch."

"You did *what*?" asked Liane.

"I'm calling security," said Baihan.

"Shut up, all of you!"

It was the nurse. The avalanche shuddered to a sudden halt.

Rachel was twitching in her chair. The right side of her face was slack, and spittle fell from her lip. Her one good eye was dull, staring into the middle distance.

"She's having a seizure," said the nurse, checking her pulse and referencing diagnostics in his feed. "You"—he pointed to Liane at random—"call the emergency response. Tell them we need the helicopter. We have to get her to the ICU ASAP. You"—he pointed at

Diana—"come here and help me keep her steady. You"—Sofia—"get us an elevator and make sure nothing's blocking our path."

Emily turned to Javier. He was staring at her, lips slightly parted, shaking his head in abject disbelief. He looked like he would shatter if she so much as touched him. She had only seen him like that once before.

Her eyes wandered, searching the room for a hint that all was not lost. But all she found was shock, betrayal, and an emergency medical intervention.

Even the window was blank.

The fog had rolled in, occluding the view.

CHAPTER 35

Emily fled.

Faces flew by, phantoms peering at her in surprise over their cappuccinos. Abstract shapes reared up around her. The paths converged and diverged, their lazy curves designed for meanders, not sprints. She vaulted over the breaching whale, shearing moss off the cool rock, kicking up gravel as she stuck the landing and continued her mad dash through lounge areas and conversation nooks to the central elevator bank. She wanted one of those chameleon jumpsuits that rendered you all but invisible. She wanted these people, these engineers and scientists and marketers and whoever else, to look somewhere else, anywhere else. She wanted to get out of this building, this spear thrust into the sky like a thorn in God's side.

An elevator door was opening just as Emily reached the bank. She shouldered through the people waiting to board. They went from indignant to disturbed as soon as they saw her, not a single one venturing to join her as she directed the elevator to the ground floor. Ignoring their stares, she queued up Grandmaster Flash and let the music take her.

The doors slid shut too slowly, eyelids closing in an impossibly long blink. Her entire body throbbed. If only she could tear away these bandages and slough off her shredded skin. She imagined herself emerging into the lobby naked and flayed, bare muscles and tendons exposed to the air, an anatomical model brought to hideous life.

They knew.

The elevator began its descent and she was weightless, wishing that it would fall faster and faster until it hit terminal velocity, that she would plunge to her death floating light as a feather.

They all *must* know. It was thirteen years ago. Javier had been a key architect of feed security. Together, he and Emily had used the backdoor he'd installed for himself. With Diana's help, Dag had unearthed that backdoor and offered it to Rachel in exchange for the carbon tax. Javier had returned to join Commonwealth's board. Diana had signed up as their chief intelligence officer. Even Dag had consulted on a number of key projects. They had worked directly with Rachel for years, participating in every major Commonwealth decision. Of course Rachel and the rest of the board knew about the long-extinct exploit and who was involved. That Javier and Diana participated in Commonwealth management at such a high level was a testament to Rachel's long view. She and the board saw how valuable it was to access insights from people who had outwitted their supposedly inviolable system. Black hats turned white hat all the time.

They knew. How could they not?

The walls of the elevator closed in around Emily. Her breath came in ragged gasps. Why was the building so damn tall? This was taking too long. Maybe Diana's spooks had hijacked the elevator and were sending it to a deep sub-basement not listed on any architectural plans, a shadowy skunkworks stocked with experimental truth serums, padded cells, and mad scientists for whom Emily would be just another guinea pig.

They hadn't known.

Rachel Leibovitz, supreme overlord of information flows, hadn't known the secret history of three of her closest advisers. She hadn't known that Javier authored the single largest breach in feed history. She hadn't known that Diana played a key role in uncovering said breach.

She hadn't even known that Sofia had been Diana's mole for most of her career, starting on Sofia's first day as a Commonwealth trainee.

After what had been either an eternity or a few scant minutes, the elevator came to a stop. Emily's joints compressed, gravity reminding her of its inexorable pull, that she could never be truly free of anything.

At any hour of any day, Rachel could have granted herself root access to the feed. She'd built it, after all. She could have snuck peeks into the digital lives of anyone she'd wanted, played voyeur on billions. She could have tapped this infinite library for inspiration, incriminating evidence, or even to shape the psychology of world leaders, just as Emily and Javier had. At the very least, Rachel could have used this latent superpower to vet those she charged with running Commonwealth and steering its path into the future.

The doors opened, and Emily stepped into a lobby that was also an indoor forest, live redwood trees reaching up into mist that obscured the unreasonably high ceiling, the cathedral space paying homage to the combined power of nature and human engineering.

Rachel had never used the key to her own kingdom. It had sat there in its plush box gathering dust all these years, its seductive promise unrequited but for Emily and Javier's original heist. Rachel must have been an angel or a demon to have disregarded its pull. Emily remembered the force behind her violet gaze, how the seizure had robbed it of its strength. No. Rachel was all too human. It was just in this world of backroom deals and endless intrigue, she had decided to employ that most subtle and counterintuitive of strategies: integrity.

Emily burst out of the doors and onto the street. The fog was thick and soupy, reducing visibility to no more than a few meters. The effect was uncanny, as if the entire universe had shrunk down into a woolly bubble. Emily accelerated into a run, trying to reach the edge of the bubble, the boundary of the universe itself, the asymptote of blindness.

Trust was the one thing the feed needed to survive. It was the active ingredient, the catalyst that had precipitated Commonwealth's unprecedented ubiquity. Only by inspiring and sustaining faith in its inviolability could the feed sate its insatiable appetite for information and connection. Rachel never broke her own rules because she knew that nothing was worth more than her word, that her dreams rested on her honor. Emily saw herself in Rachel, and hated both Rachel and herself for it.

Block after block flew by in a blurred fugue, dog walkers and shops and bicycles and pigeons and lonely-looking park benches. Emily was tunneling into this cursed city, letting cars swerve around her as she dashed across busy streets, ignoring the protestations of fellow pedestrians.

Her feed pinged.

Javier.

Emily swiped it away.

Ping.

Javier again.

This time, she blocked him entirely.

Ping.

Diana.

Swipe.

Ping.

Block.

The goddamn feed was *everywhere*. It piloted the cars that refused to hit her, ferried the messages she didn't want to read, and powered the streetlights that glowed like bioluminescent fish in the fog. It was always there in the background, a genie ready to grant any wish, a speakeasy where global conversation hummed like an antique diesel generator. The world was a junkie and Commonwealth was its dealer, supplanting bankers, heads of state, and everyone else whose product was less potent. It knew the contents of every scientific paper ever published, and it knew you better than you knew yourself. It was closing in on Emily like the walls of the elevator, and she wanted to get *out*.

Block. Block. Block. Block. Block.

Emily shut her feed off from everyone and everything. Consigned herself to digital solitary confinement. She dismissed it entirely, closing every window through which Rachel's brainchild shone down on her, save for the music whose beats were her lifeline. She wanted out. *Out.* But there was no such thing as out. The only true exit was the one she had sought in the ring.

"Ma'am?"

An enormous man in a suit held out a meaty arm to stop her from barreling into him. Emily reeled. Her lungs burned. Her legs were numb. Wait, had she seen this giant before? Was this yet another loop? Could she be wandering her own version of the corridors that had trapped Vasilios? Her sanity was fraying.

"Hey, Gerald," said the giant to his besuited partner, "can you just give the boss lady a quick heads-up?"

Sweat stung Emily's eyes. Her train of thought jumped the rails. Give who a heads-up?

"All right, ma'am," said the giant in a gentle tone that was at odds with his imposing physique. "Come right this way. We'll get you sorted."

She had to stop herself from spinning away and dislocating his shoulder when he put a massive hand on her upper back and guided her through a door.

"Ms. Kim," said a gorgeous apparition, another déjà vu–inspiring member of this fever dream's cast. "Welcome back. This is a little unusual, but we'll put you down as a guest of the house."

CHAPTER 36

Red satin parting in front of her. Oil lamps smoldering. Golden hunting dogs lounging in front of a roaring fire. The low buzz of conversation punctuated by laughter. Monumental tapestries depicting scenes from her father's fairytales. Glasses clinking. The languid chords of live blues guitar covering a deeper silence, the feed in abeyance.

Analog.

Nell guided Emily to the bar, made sure she was steady on her stool, raised a manicured finger.

"Virginia, can we get a mineral water over here?"

"And a whiskey," said Emily. "Three fingers. Neat."

Virginia looked at Nell, who raised her eyebrows.

Emily pulled up her sleeve, displaying the bandages beneath. "My meds are wearing off."

Nell shrugged. Virginia delivered both drinks.

Emily sipped the water. She hadn't even realized how parched her throat was.

"I have to get back to the door," said Nell. "But let us know if you need anything. Anything at all, okay? We can call the house doctor if you'd like."

"Thanks," said Emily. "But I'm good. This is good. Really." She tapped the side of the whiskey glass and forced a smile. "Just the prescription I need."

Nell looked at her for a long moment and Emily was afraid she might decide to babysit, but she turned on her heel and strode back to the anteroom.

Emily slugged the whiskey.

Feedlessness was an indescribable relief, like ears finally equalizing to a painful change in air pressure. She was here at this bar on this stool in this body with this aftertaste of single malt searing her throat. It jacked up her senses, cleared her head, primed her for Camiguin-conditioned combat.

You've always got a place here, you know. I wasn't kidding about helping to run this joint. She shouldn't have been so dismissive of Rizal's offer. She was a fool. She had managed to convince herself that she had changed, that she *could* change. She had waltzed back into her old life and it had taken less than two weeks for her to push things too far, to find a new way to stab her friends in the back.

Virginia poured her another drink.

Emily had become enamored with herself. She remembered the cool greenery of Addis, her tantalizing first steps into Rosa's apartment, Otto nestled in tousled sheets. It was supposed to be an emergency rescue mission. That was all. Once Rosa was safe, Emily would fade into the background. But no. She had to let Javier convince her to share her story. She had to let Diana convince her to double down. She remembered watching that red balloon floating up into the sky over the Berkeley hills and reaching out to take Javier's hand. She had to let the big hearts of her too-generous friends convince her she was worthy of their love, that she was capable of redemption.

She downed the whiskey.

How could Emily deny the simple fact that she did nothing but sow pain? Actions spoke louder than words. As soon as she saw the sliver of a chance of forgiveness, what did she do? She pushed harder. She let her drive get in the way of her common sense. It wasn't enough to have her friends back. She had to change the world too. So she jumped in with an argument that wasn't hers to make and ripped the scab off a wound that had never truly healed. By revealing her friends' secrets she had doomed their dreams and doubtless ousted them from their privileged positions. And why should it stop at turmoil within Commonwealth? If Lowell was to be believed, she might even have sparked a war. Maybe this catastrophe was really just the calm before the storm.

Emily called for another whiskey.

"Time to slow down, sister," said Virginia, adjusting her bow tie.

"Nah," said Emily, trying her best to suppress her surging buzz and summon a roguish grin. "Don't worry about me. I'm a heavyweight. Can't even taste it until the third dram."

Virginia looked at her sidelong, but poured another.

Despite Rizal's offer, Emily couldn't return to Camiguin. Diana knew that was where Emily had flown in order to catch Lowell's ride without arousing suspicion. Freja and the rest of the cabal knew everything about her shadow life, and Lowell had bought the damn fight club. It wasn't a big island. Emily would be easy to find. An overwhelming nostalgia for her shabby studio apartment washed over her. She had hated the place until circumstance forbade reclaiming it. She couldn't return to Emily's old life and she couldn't return to Pixie's, so she'd need to find a new rock to hide under.

The prospect was exhausting. She wanted to scream. She wanted to cry. She wanted to wither away and die. Emily let out an anguished giggle. Maybe she could just go curl up next to those dogs by the fire and never wake up. The world would be better off without her.

Glancing over at the hearth, she was reminded of the legendary Southern California wildfire. The feed footage was riveting disaster porn. Flames turning all the colors of the rainbow as they gorged on chemical plants, smoke clogging the skies of the entire Southwest, steel skeletons of downtown buildings glowing as they shed apartments and offices, desperate refugees seeking sanctuary wherever they could find it. Emily identified the location of her childhood home by its GPS coordinates, but the satellite stream revealed it to be just another indistinguishable scar in the mountains of ash.

Emily had spent her entire life fleeing wreckage. Why stop now?

She drained the glass, immediately regretted slamming it back on the bar.

A hand touched her arm without warning.

Emily spun on the stool, kicking her legs off the bar and whipping her torso around to add juice to the punch, lashing out with all her anger and shame, realizing her error too late to soften the blow.

Nell stumbled back, clutching her broken nose. Blood poured between her fingers, bright red under the warm light of the oil lamps. Emily had a flash of absurd satisfaction at sticking it to the proprietor of this elite club that had turned disconnection into privilege, before dismissing the uncharitable thought. Who was she to judge Nell, who had shown Emily nothing but respect? Who was she to judge anyone but herself? Drunk on self-righteousness, Emily had hijacked people's lives by cracking their feeds. She had murdered people in the ring in a failed attempt to escape her own guilt. She had lost both her honor and her friends, not once, but twice. Breaking Nell's nose was just another stone to add to the wrong side of the scale.

Virginia swore. The dogs barked. The room swam.

Too much whiskey.

Too much everything.

When the giants came for her, Emily didn't resist, only babbled incoherent apologies.

CHAPTER 37

The stars danced. They jumped and twirled and zigzagged across the sky, crackling green and orange and purple and all the colors of Tokyo nightlife. They smelled like kettle corn and sang a cappella and nothing could be more beautiful.

Emily twisted the knob, zooming in. But instead of bringing the stars into focus, she was launched into them. Gas giants flared and belched. Icy asteroids made pilgrimages across vast expanses of nothingness. Nebulas hung luminous and thick as aurorae borealis. Moons raced circles around the planets that held them hostage. Red dwarfs smoldered. Black holes sucked at the fabric of space-time. Galaxies folded in on themselves like celestial origami.

It was all so . . . big. The sheer scale was impossible to fathom, as if some cosmic deity was pouring an ocean into the teacup of her mind. It was exquisite and fearsome, this overflowing of so much more than she could ever contain. She was sucking for air in the face of an impossibly strong wind.

"Once upon a time . . ."

"Come on, *appa*," she said. "I've heard this one before."

"It gets better every time."

She peeled her eye away from the rubber eyepiece with a sucking sound.

Sand underfoot, scratching between her toes. She was standing in the cave underneath Lowell's mansion, alone in the middle of the room. The stream was dry, the water-polished rocks in its bed gleaming dully.

It was quiet at first, uncannily so. Then something teased at the very edge of her hearing, but no matter how she strained her ears, she couldn't identify it. She knelt and rubbed a handful of sand between her palms. Was that a gasp? A grunt? She went to push her lucky glasses up her nose, but they weren't there. She looked around, but there was nobody. Just the empty stone benches and rough rock walls.

That was definitely another gasp. And a grunt. And a scream. And laughs and moans and shrieks and whimpers and sighs and squeals and the wet slaps of flesh on flesh. She could smell sweat and maple syrup and roasted jalapeño and cum. The air was viscous, and she could feel the Earth's molten core churning beneath her feet.

The cave was still empty, but the sounds were getting louder and louder, more and more graphic, until they were so loud they were splitting her head in half and she was covering her ears and screaming but couldn't hear herself over the din. It was torture until she decided it was lovely and then it was fine but she still couldn't figure out where it was coming from.

She walked across the sand, and the grains her feet disturbed floated away as if her touch granted a temporary suspension of the laws of physics. Pain flared as her shin ran into the edge of the first tier of stone benches. She climbed, but even though there were only three tiers, they rose up before her like alpine massifs and she had to scale each bench as if it were a cliff, stretching to grasp slippery handholds.

When she reached the top, she looked back to see the view from the mountainous peak, but she was still in the cave and had summited nothing but three knee-high benches.

The sounds were louder, though, a cataract of ecstatic howls rattling her bones and echoing inside her skull and lighting a fire in her belly.

She raised a hand and touched the rough wall of the cave. Dust came away on her fingers. She touched the wall again, rubbed her hand across it. It was like wiping condensation off a mirror, except it revealed not her own reflection but the long curve of a naked hip painted on the rock beneath. She rubbed back the other way and there was the calf, the delicate ankle. Then both her hands were on the wall and she was scrubbing madly, dashing around the wall to reach every surface, filling the air with choking dust, all to unveil a single massive cave painting, a painting that moved, dozens and dozens of people in the throes of desperate, indiscriminate lovemaking.

The closer she looked, the more detailed they became until she recognized Dag and Rizal and Freja and Barend and Rachel and Dane and Frances and Ferdinand and Nisanur and Ms. Randolph and Javier and Diana and Lowell and Florence and Niko and Carolyn and Midori and Liane and Baihan and Vasilios and Jason and the courier kidnappers and her mother and father and the fire dancers and everyone she had ever known, ever met, ever glimpsed and then they weren't a painting at all but an orgy of teeming, heaving flesh that filled the cave and she was one of them and she was all of them and she was none of them and she blinked and she was alone.

No, not alone.

There was Rosa. Clothed, thankfully, and sitting cross-legged in the sand.

Silence at maximum volume.

Emily leapt, flying through the air until she considered the implausibility of the maneuver and fell to the sand at the speed of thought.

Rosa's eyes were closed and her hands rested on her knees.

Emily knelt in front of her.

"There's so much I want to tell you," said Rosa, and her voice was the growl of a jungle cat, but Emily could understand every word.

Emily mirrored Rosa's cross-legged posture, and their knees touched.

The burble of water on rock.

Emily looked over and saw the stream was flowing again, but when she traced the water to its source, it sprang not from the bowels of the mountain but from her own tear ducts, pouring down her cheeks over her legs and onto the sand.

"You're such a crybaby," said Rosa, and her feline snarl was affectionate.

As Emily's tears gushed out faster and faster, the stream overflowed its banks and the water began saturating the sand.

"I can't stop." Emily laughed.

"You're such a crybaby," repeated Rosa.

The water level rose over their knees, waves bouncing off the stone benches.

"I can't stop." Emily wasn't laughing anymore.

"You're such a crybaby," said Rosa, and although her inflections hadn't changed at all, they were suddenly disturbing instead of tender.

Tears flowed and flowed and flowed and the water reached their chests. Emily wanted to move, but she was frozen in place.

"I can't stop," she said with growing horror.

"You're such a crybaby," growled Rosa.

And then the water surged over their heads and filled the entire cave, leaving no pocket of air behind. It tasted of caramel and thunderbolts. It didn't sting her eyes. She and Rosa floated, arms limp, lungs burning, bubbles streaming up from their faces.

They were drowning.

She looked around for the door. If they could make it to the spiral staircase, they could escape, find the space to breathe. But no matter how she searched, she could not find the exit—the cavern walls were unbroken, just a circle of rough, suffocating stone.

She completed her circle, trying to keep herself steady underwater, mind racing, seeking an answer to an impossible problem, reaching beyond the infinity that she had glimpsed through the telescope, and Rosa opened her eyes wide and instead of irises there were fractals sprouting out of her dilated pupils and the geometric shapes branched and multiplied, sending tendrils out onto Rosa's skin and then into the water, filling the cave like a three-dimensional self-replicating spiderweb woven not from silk but from shining strands of what gold dreams itself to be.

And then the intricate matrix grew into itself, tangling in ever-increasing density, and as all the empty spaces filled, the color deepened from gold to pink to the red of light shining through closed eyelids and Emily tasted bile and her eyes snapped open and she spat out the boozy vomit she had been choking on.

CHAPTER 38

Incredibly, there was a small trash bin within reach, and Emily managed to puke into it, spitting and gasping for breath as she barreled into consciousness. She was lying on a cot in a small room. There was a pitcher of water, a washcloth, and half a baguette on a side table. Thick candles caked in layer upon layer of baroque wax drippings threw flickering light over everything.

Emily sat up slowly.

Memories swam beneath the murky surface of her attention, but she bid them stay there a little longer. Instead, she dipped the washcloth in the pitcher and wiped her face and the back of her neck. It was a cool blessing, the air feeling fresh and clean against her wet skin. She drank directly from the pitcher, water dribbling down her chin. Her temples throbbed and her balance wavered, but she took a deep breath and steadied herself. Ripping off a piece of baguette, she chewed on the fresh sourdough, washing it down with more water. More bread, more water. The basic ingredients of life.

Rising to her feet, Emily felt insubstantial. Her body ached. Her stomach rumbled. Dark thoughts ascended into her mind like whales preparing to breach.

Movement. Movement was life.

She was a little wobbly on her feet, but she'd be okay.

She opened the door and stuck her head out. A hallway connecting to other hallways. Torches smoldering in wall brackets. Sounds of distant conversation, clattering dishes, movement. She began to explore, glancing into any open doors she passed. There was a supply closet, a suite of cubbies, and what looked like a lounge.

A waiter emerged from a side corridor holding a steaming tempura platter. Emily walked faster, following him. He pushed through a pair of batwing doors that swung back and forth on well-oiled hinges. She approached and peered beyond them.

Analog.

The crowd was thinner now. A few serious drinkers nursed cocktails at the bar and a couple of booths were occupied. Emily must be in the staff area. She had set off a grenade at the Commonwealth board meeting, ended up here, drank herself silly, and punched Nell in the face. Instead of tossing in a few punches of their own and then calling the cops, the bouncers had apparently deposited her in a spare room to sleep it off.

At the opposite end of the club, the red satin parted and Nell entered, a bandage over her nose. She was talking over her shoulder to someone coming in behind her. Fuck. Emily ducked back deeper into the hallway. Javier. Tall and gangly and worried. He and Nell conversed with quiet intensity, and she pointed back toward the batwings.

No. Not right now. Not ever.

Emily turned and ran. Her stomach sloshed and she almost threw up the baguette, so she slowed her sprint to a jog, passing the kitchen and the supply closet and the room they'd put her in. She made a turn, backtracked, tried again, pushed open a wide cargo door, and stepped out onto a loading dock.

Bass thrummed, synth bubbled, and lyrics piled on top of one another in a rapturous cascade. Emily sucked in a breath, looking up and back. She was standing in an alley behind Analog and the club's feedlessness was limited by the walls of the converted warehouse. She must have been listening to her playlist on her headlong flight through the streets of San Francisco, beats and rhymes directing her feet while her mind drowned in itself.

The feed flooded back in all its confusion and glory, and with it came the realization that her dreams of finding a new Camiguin in which to vanish were a shallow, drunken fantasy.

When Emily had fled thirteen years ago, the only people who knew to miss her were her friends. Now a shortlist of the most powerful people on the planet would stop at nothing to hunt her down. She would be a permanent fugitive, and there were few enough places like Analog in which she could avoid the sticky strands of the feed, any of which might be the stray thread they needed to unravel her identity and location. Lowell himself was in the process of monopolizing the network of feedless fight clubs. The disaster at the Ranch had turned Emily into an enigmatic feed celebrity. She had been spinning a broken record, her life repeating in a scratchy loop.

But the record spinning in her feed wasn't broken, and although she had heard Grandmaster Flash and the Furious Five's "The Message" a thousand times before, it rang true in an entirely new way. Melle Mel's rhymes were ornate and snarled, lyrics that played fast and loose with metaphor, confession, and simmering outrage. In that often-forgotten pre-internet era, the Bronx had been ravaged by poverty, ignored by the government, and plagued by austerity, violent crime, and police brutality. It was held hostage by a broken system. Flash himself scavenged parts from junkyards and abandoned cars to build his first stereo, and went on to invent new turntable techniques. But this anachronistic music that resonated with Emily so deeply, these poetic riffs that enflamed her revolutionary zeal, had been born from the ashes of the burning housing projects. Flash, Kool Herc, Bambaataa, and other early rappers hadn't just pioneered a new genre, they had given a voice to the voiceless. With everyone and everything against them they had spoken up, spoken out, and made music that inspired a generation. In a society that cast them as criminals and victims, they redefined themselves and created something fresh, something that mattered, something that lasted, something that did so much more than fight back, something that forged the world anew.

Emily hopped off the loading dock and lost herself in the cramped alleys of the industrial district, letting the music carry her. The night was cold and the only light came from city glow reflecting off the clouds overhead. It smelled of urine. Graffiti looped and swirled across the high walls, the shadows muting all color to shades of gray. The screeches of a catfight echoed off concrete. This was another one of those liminal zones, strange places that cropped up even in the grandest megalopolises, thresholds between new and old, light and dark, ecstasy and paranoia.

Emily's lips mouthed the verses falling through her head like sunshine through foliage. She moved in a half trot, half dance. Her headache flared, and she embraced the pain, riding it out of the maze of alleys and onto the street where the car she had summoned was waiting. She opened the door and slid inside, the chorus tearing itself from her throat as loud as she could possibly shout it.

Sometimes the only way out was in.

CHAPTER 39

Emily could see all of downtown San Francisco from this recessed stairwell. It was here in the Bay Area that the feed had been conceived, had grown from an embryonic startup into a global monopoly, cannibalizing so many of the institutions that had accelerated its meteoric rise. But the city was home to so much more than the graphene talons of Commonwealth's regional headquarters. Teachers and artists and firefighters and social workers and baristas and bodybuilders and poets and chefs and geeks and freaks lived in the shadow of the superstructures, more people than Emily could ever hope to meet, with more fears and dreams and ideas than anyone could capture. It was that richness, that vibrancy, those contradictions that had fueled Commonwealth's growth, a particularly nutritious culture that enabled cells to multiply until they dominated the petri dish.

Multiply they had. This skyline was mirrored in Addis, Taipei, Amsterdam, and all the other coequal, sovereign Commonwealth headquarters that had sprung up as if they shared a single giant root system that flourished in the planet's mantle. The feed had displaced so much, and yet every ending was a new beginning.

Emily could only hope that this particular new beginning didn't lead to a violent end. Even as Commonwealth was laying the foundations for a new world order, its brain trust was falling apart. For what felt like the thousandth time, she summoned her feed, but there was no news of Rachel's condition. Diana must have done a good job keeping the hospital visit under wraps.

Instead, the feed seethed with controversy over what had gone down in Idaho. Squadrons of drones exploded like fireworks on infinite loops. Rumors churned about the mysterious woman riding Lowell through the party with the wakizashi to his throat, drenched in blood and covered in glitter. Journalists demanded details about the reasons for the abduction and Lowell's current status. Socialite guests traded accounts, the gossip growing wilder with every telling. Senators called the dogfight an act of private war on American soil. White House officials issued contradictory proclamations, and foreign-policy experts debated the implications of Commonwealth's dramatic action. Conspiracy theorists delightedly used the event as a jumping-off point into all manner of paranoid fantasies. Pundits one-upped each other with outraged hot takes, and think tanks published white papers like Vegas dealers dishing out cards. *Zeppelin.* Emily's fingers clenched involuntarily. She had made it out alive, only to sabotage her own success.

Emily dismissed the feed, tried to slow her heart.

Let this not be a taste of what was to come.

Across the water, dawn stretched gray fingers over the hills behind Berkeley and Oakland, and Emily remembered Diana and Dag's verdant greenhouse. *You look like you got stuck in a BDSM dungeon and forgot the safe word.* Emily repressed a grin. She had remembered the safe word, but whatever she had looked like when she visited their cottage, she must look ten times worse now.

Forward. Only forward.

Emily hugged herself to ward off the chill. Lights illuminated the hanging gardens of the Bay Bridge. Bamboo leaves whispered above her. The concrete step dug into her ass. The back of her neck prickled, but there was no one else in sight, and she pushed the feeling away.

Always forward.

Two cars pulled up across the street. Three security guards emerged from one, and Rachel's husbands, Leon and Omar, and her nurse got out of the other. The nurse waved back the two older men, leaned down, and tenderly scooped Rachel up from the back seat. They climbed the stairs to the modest Edwardian sandwiched between a small apartment building and a pedestrian byway. The lights came on, and Emily could see the open-plan first floor through the bay windows. The nurse deposited Rachel in a wheelchair, hooked her up to IVs, and fussed over her. Omar knelt beside them, holding Rachel's hand, and Leon went to fetch water from the kitchen.

Relief flooded through Emily with anxiety following close in its wake. That Rachel was alive meant that there was still some possibility of righting the boat before it sank, and even the faintest glimmer of hope precluded the possibility of resignation, demanding action instead.

Emily hugged herself tighter, willing herself to be up to the task.

The scene inside the house was so intimate that Emily struggled to resolve its domesticity with the pivotal role Rachel had come to play in world affairs. This was a home, not an estate, and even in the aftermath of a medical emergency, it was obviously a familiar and comfortable place for Rachel and her family. Emily remembered her parents' garage, how her mom had kept her tools so clean and organized, the faint smell of oil and sawdust.

"Can I help you?"

A woman stood at the bottom of the narrow public stairway. Her tone was friendly, but her eyes were hard. Emily's stomach sank. It was one of the bodyguards.

Emily felt compelled to make excuses, to fabricate some flimsy story about how she climbed up Telegraph Hill every morning to watch the sunrise from Coit Tower, or that she was trying out a new fitness routine. But the woman had caught her sitting here staring through the gap in the bamboo straight into Rachel's living room and, despite Emily's lifelong habit of flaunting authority, there was no reason to lie.

"I'm here to see your boss," said Emily.

The bodyguard stared at her evenly. "Well, isn't that nice for you? Unfortunately, my boss is quite particular about her appointments, and about Peeping Toms."

"She'll want to see me," said Emily, hoping it was true.

"How about you take a walk with me," said the bodyguard. "I'll buy you a coffee down at Herbert's, and you can go on home. No need to make this harder than it needs to be."

Emily walked down the stairs and looked the woman straight in the eye.

"Tell her it's Emily Kim," she said.

The bodyguard held her gaze for a moment and then shrugged, withdrawing into her feed.

Emily glanced up at the house. Inside, Rachel frowned and said something. Leon stood up in disbelief. Omar stepped toward the windows. The nurse made a conciliatory gesture. Whatever conversation they were having turned into an argument, Leon throwing up his hands and Omar staring daggers down at Emily and her escort. Emily could imagine their consternation. The woman whose revelation had landed Rachel in the hospital wanted a second act a few scant hours later, this time right in the middle of their home. Rachel held up a thin hand, and both men marched upstairs, leaving her alone with the nurse.

The bodyguard cocked her head, listening to something in her feed.

"Fuckin' A," she said, surprised. "Never seen this happen with a stalker before." She extended a hand toward the house. "Ms. Kim, if you'll follow me."

CHAPTER 40

Emily sat on a low couch, unable to meet Rachel's eye as if their gazes were magnets repelling each other. The old woman was in her wheelchair, tubes and sensors connecting her frail body to a compact trolley of medical equipment. A cutting board with a knife, two blood oranges, and a small turquoise ceramic jar rested on the coffee table that separated them.

Books filled the shelves behind Rachel, spines creased and worn. William Gibson, Ada Palmer, Isaac Asimov, Samara Amupanda, Richard Feynman, Malka Older, Jorge Luis Borges, Olivia Fernel, and many more authors that Emily did not recognize. The floor-to-ceiling shelves covered the entire wall, wrapping around the back of the house to create a cozy, L-shaped library complete with reading nooks. Emily imagined Rachel curled up on one of the chairs, immersed in a novel. Rosa had once remarked to Emily that all of literature was just a single extended conversation, and Emily had responded that hip-hop was too. Perhaps *everything* was, at the end of the day. What inspiration did Rachel find in these dog-eared pages? What strange force drew the author of the feed to such an antique form of physical media? Emily wondered how large a record collection she might have if she replicated her feed playlist in vinyl.

Rachel's hands rested in her lap, gnarled fingers laced. The wrinkles on her face were as dense and intricate as the fractals Emily had so often painted on her own. Rachel's poise only jacked up Emily's own nervousness. This was a bad idea, a dangerous idea. Emily was as much a fool as the knight walking straight up to the dragon, only this wasn't a fairytale. If history was a guide, she would only make a bad situation worse. But how could she live with herself if she didn't try?

Emily steeled herself, conjuring the flow state she entered when stepping into the ring, and met Rachel's eye.

It was like sticking her head into a wind tunnel. Rachel's purple gaze stripped away Emily's preconceptions and self-deceptions like so much chaff, leaving her feeling naked and raw. In some unseen dimension, the air between them crackled and sparked with energy. As difficult as it had been to look into Rachel's eye, Emily found that it was now impossible to look away. The other woman had been so reliably prescient by being so ferociously present, and her palpable immediacy sharpened Emily's own focus on this place, this moment, this person.

Emily realized that in a strange way she and Rachel had been revolving around each other their entire lives. They hadn't met until last week, but each had exerted an invisible pull on the other, their dreams mutually empowering and constraining as if the ripples they set off in the fabric of the universe were inverse waves. What would Emily have achieved without subverting the feed? Where would Rachel be today if Commonwealth hadn't entered geopolitics with the carbon tax? Their masterpieces were codependent.

Emily remembered holding a socket wrench as her mom showed her how to fix her bike while savory smells emanated from the kitchen where her dad was preparing *gaeran tost-u*, her favorite breakfast. The world was a vast machine with cogs and axles and motors and maintenance requirements and out-of-date documentation. Emily had used that knowledge to find points of leverage. Rachel had decided to build a new engine, keeping the original one interoperable while she replaced part after part until the whole machine had transformed into something new and different. Both of them were trying to affect change, to steer society in the direction their personal codes demanded.

"I'm not here to apologize," said Emily. "Although I owe you an apology. And I'm not here to convince you to implement Javier's plan, although I think he's right."

She paused, forcing herself not to rush. "Have you ever tasted teh tarik? It's this delicious Malaysian milk tea. But what makes it special is how airy it is, almost like the steamed milk on a latte. Street vendors make it on every corner, but they don't have espresso machines. Instead, they throw the hot tea between two steel cups to froth it up." Emily mimed the motion with her hands, remembering taking the first creamy sip en route to fight Niko. "It's half food prep, half street performance, and some vendors are true showmen. They turn the whole process into a mesmerizing dance, throwing the tea from all heights and angles without ever spilling a single drop. They make juggling boiling liquid look easy. That's the thing that fascinates me about it, the perfection of their control."

Emily remembered the beige walls of the principal's office, his visceral discomfort at being forced to deliver the news of her parents' death. "It's not easy to admit, but control is something I've always aspired to," she said. "The pursuit of control gave me a mission, established a base for my independence. But it's more than that. It's like . . . If only I were in charge, I could make things better, protect people, unravel otherwise intractable problems. And I *did*. I built a home for people society had cast off, gave them a chance. And once Javi opened a backdoor into the feed, we scaled our efforts right along with Commonwealth. There was so much tragedy in the world that we could help avert, so much suffering we could assuage." She smiled sadly. "When you know you're right, there's no reason to solicit input from others. If they disagree, they're either ignorant, stupid, or malicious. And if you're in control, why would you ever let ignorance, stupidity, or maliciousness poison the well? I was so used to being in control, so convinced of my own righteousness, that it blinded me to the fact that sometimes efficiency and efficacy are not ends in themselves. I forgot that people don't just want solutions. We want to be heard. We want to *participate*. The lack of opportunities to participate in the system was what inspired me to subvert it in the first place."

And you never even thought to ask us first? You never considered whether a decision this important was one we would need to make together? Javier had asked her that right after Dag broke the news that Emily had blackmailed him to get her way. That was the worst moment of her entire life, the day Emily lost her friends, her old life, the day she fled to Camiguin. It was worse than the fights that had earned her these scars. Worse even than the day her parents died, when she had been too young to fully wrap her head around the implications.

Strange to hear a grander version of Javier's sentiment echoed by a man like Lowell. *The feed connected everyone. Then Commonwealth leveraged its utility to disenfranchise everyone. Now just a handful of people hold the keys to all of civilization, and everyone else fucking hates you for it.* Emily hadn't wanted to listen as she bled out under the exploding sky. She still didn't. But she also couldn't deny the kernel of truth in his words.

"You've changed the world many times over," said Emily. "You've built a new system from the bottom up. A long time ago, Commonwealth was a startup. Your insights and decisiveness transformed it into a mega-corporation and then an entirely new form of global sovereign entity. You always tried to minimize internal politics because you saw how it slowed everything down and diluted results. You stayed out of geopolitics too for as long as you could, until Dag forced you into it." Emily remembered the painful isolation of her years in exile. Yesterday's revelation hadn't just sent Rachel to the ICU, it had robbed her of her closest advisers and confidants, her chosen successor. *I've just never wanted to be alone, you know? And that's what leadership is, almost by definition.*

It's taking a step forward when everyone hangs back, raising your hand when others balk. If taking the helm had eaten away at Javier, how must Rachel feel right now? Emily had hijacked her life's work, undermined her council, and was asking her to take yet another leap of faith. But this woman had never been one to balk at difficult truths.

"The feed isn't just technology anymore, it's everything. And, being everything, it's subject to the same machinations as any other source of power, whether you like it or not. Sofia argued that infrastructure should be apolitical, that the feed should be neutral. But infrastructure is the foundation upon which we live our lives. Nothing could be more political. Ignoring that fact doesn't make Commonwealth neutral, it makes it autocratic by default."

Emily leaned forward. "The infighting among your lieutenants, this scheme of Lowell's, even our original hack, all of it is just the court politics that crop up in any autocracy. We are the moths to Commonwealth's candle flame. Can you imagine how history might be different if Augustus had reestablished the Roman Republic at the end of his reign? Or if George Washington decided not to hand off power to an elected successor? Dag could give you a thousand examples. One way or the other, it's no secret that big changes are coming. Succession is the fuel feeding this fire. As of yesterday, Sofia was in line to be the next chairwoman. I'm here to tell you how grave of a mistake that is, not because of Sofia—I'm sure she's brilliant and dedicated and up to the task. No. It's a mistake because you made her appointment *your* decision."

Emily's words found a rhythm, picked up enough momentum to carry a freestyle MC solo. "If you want your legacy to survive, you need to bring the same creativity and conviction to governing the feed that you did to building it." She thought of the protesters and counterprotesters that had delayed Javier's commencement speech, the raging preacher in the Addis market, the graffiti scrawled along the San Francisco alleyways, the blissed-out junkies on Camiguin, the billions

of people like Rizal with no real power but a surfeit of humanity. The
world was disoriented by accelerating change. Traditional sources of
identity were crumbling. The old rules no longer applied. Everyone was
struggling to make meaning out of madness. "You need to find a way
to make Commonwealth democratic, to give everyone a voice in the
future, even if it delays the arrival of that future or roughs it up a bit.
Sofia and Javier and Diana and Baihan and anyone on the feed should
have to present their competing visions on equal footing. As much as
I'd like to see him executed, we should release Lowell and invite him
and his little cabal. It'll take the teeth out of their coup d'état. In the
long run, the only way to defeat your opponents is to empower them.
Rachel, you made the feed. You can change the feed. It won't be perfect. The teh tarik will spill. Nobody will be in control. Early on, the
feed needed to be efficient to survive. Now it needs to be redundant,
multipolar, and resilient. By establishing a structure for everyone to
share power, to participate, you'll channel discontent into productive
contribution and perhaps convince future generations of Emilys and
Lowells and all the rest to lend a hand instead of fomenting revolution."

And then, like a record spinning to the end of its groove, she was
done.

The moment dilated.

Once upon a time . . . Appa's voice was just beyond the edge of hearing. The knight had defeated the dragon and then fell on her own sword
for failing to protect the king. Emily had always imagined the moral
to be that you had to be perfect, that you had to meet life's demands,
however unreasonable, with unfailing competence. But maybe the real
lesson lay in the power of whispers over blades, the danger of failing
to adapt and forgive, and the strange magic of recognizing yourself in
the alien other. Maybe the knight was the protagonist but not the hero.
Maybe, as they sat wrapped in fleece blankets gazing up at glittering
night sky, her dad had imagined Emily to be the hero, even though all
she did was listen.

Maybe listening was the most important thing of all.

Careful to not yank free her IV, Rachel leaned forward, picked up the knife, and cut the blood oranges into neat slices. Dark juice stained the wooden cutting board, and the bright smell of citrus filled the room. She opened the little turquoise jar and sprinkled a pinch of cinnamon over everything.

Then Rachel plucked up a single slice, indicated that Emily should do the same.

"After thirteen years of fruitless searching, I had nearly given up on ever having a chance to meet the mastermind who found a way to hack the feed," said Rachel. "And I must admit that while you're not at all what I imagined, you do not disappoint."

Rachel bit into the slice and then smiled, her lips parting to reveal nothing but pebbled orange skin.

CHAPTER 41

Bees ducked and wove through lavender, sipping nectar. The morning was hot, as if the sun was making up for time lost to yesterday's fog. The windows of the cottage were open to let in the breeze.

Emily stopped on the threshold, pastry box in hand. A part of her still wanted to turn around, summon a car, hop on whatever international flight was about to leave the Oakland airport, find a plastic surgeon who could make adjustments to aid in evading facial recognition, and spend whatever days were left to her chasing shadows. But ultimately, she would be running from herself. If she challenged others to face up to painful realities, she could hardly ignore her own.

She knocked.

Dag opened the door and looked her up and down.

"It sounds like you've had quite a few days," he said. "Seeing that footage of you at the Ranch brought back memories I'd rather forget, but I have to admit that you appeared to be partying harder than I ever did. I guess age hasn't mellowed Lowell."

"*Mellow* is not a word I would use to describe him," said Emily. "In Lowell's case, age seems to be distilling him into an even purer version of himself."

Dag half smiled. "That's a hard fate for any of us to escape."

Then two girls charged up behind him, all curly brown hair and elbows. They both stared at the label on the box Emily held.

"Fournée!" they squealed, clapping.

"Girls," said Diana sternly, arriving at the door.

"Sorry," said one.

"I'm Drew," said the other. "This is Layla. Can we have some, please?"

"Hey," said Diana.

"I *said* please," said Drew.

"It's okay," said Emily, laughing. "I come bearing gifts."

She opened the box, revealing a dozen fresh croissants. There was an intake of preadolescent breath.

"Wait," said Drew, leaning sideways to look past Emily. "Who is *that*?"

Emily looked over her shoulder, Dag and Diana following suit, but the front yard was empty except for the bees.

Emily looked back to discover the girls were gone, along with two croissants each. Footsteps pattered up the stairs, and they heard the receding sound of giggling and an ex-post-facto shout of "Thank you."

Diana sighed.

Dag gave Emily a shrug. "I told you they were a handful," he said.

"Let's go to the kitchen," said Diana. "The greenhouse is a sauna this morning."

They sat around the kitchen table. Emily transferred the croissants to a plate and Dag made coffee. Diana's eyes never left Emily. Finally, the French press was ready, and they settled in.

"Dag," said Emily. "I've never actually apologized for what I did to you, and while I know that an apology is next to nothing, I want you to know that I'm sorry. I justified everything with the false logic that I was nudging people, not hurting them, but at the end of the day, it was just thinly veiled manipulation, and all the more cruel for its subtlety. What I put you through . . . Nobody should have to suffer that. There's nothing I could ever do to make it up to you, but I see all the pain I caused you, and it breaks my heart."

Dag laughed, and Emily was once again struck by the extent of his ease, how his contentment clashed with the hunger and ambition that had nearly consumed the man he'd been.

"You were running quite a racket," he said. "But if it hadn't been for you, we'd probably still be living without any real action on climate change, I'd still be a lobbyist, and I would never have wound up with this crazy person." He nudged Diana. "So. Water under the bridge. But I appreciate the sentiment."

Emily tried to imagine what it might feel like to live with a touch so light that you could forgive someone who had mindfucked you for years, who had been drowning in guilt for over a decade.

"I'm more interested in your absolutely spectacular fuckups this week," said Diana. "First, I warn you to stay out of the limelight, and you ride Lowell straight out of the Ranch and into international stardom like a dominatrix on a sex pony. Then, you double down by evicting every skeleton from the collective closet of Commonwealth's board. You, Ms. Kim, are either a total fucking maniac or seriously out of practice at this whole intrigue thing."

Emily felt blood rushing to her cheeks. "I—I can't believe I'm saying this, but I actually thought that Rachel knew, that the board knew. It just seemed . . . It seemed impossible that you'd all worked together for so long with something like that under wraps."

"Remind me to keep your innocence in mind while the world burns," said Diana. "I mean, holy fuck, of all the things I expected from you, naivete was not one of them."

"I think it's as beautiful as it was stupid," said Dag. "I mean, Emily believed you guys worked well together *because* everyone knew, that by acknowledging and overcoming the adversity of the hack, you cemented the bonds that help you lead. Let's hope you're all able to summon that much perspective in dealing with the aftermath."

"I survived one war," said Diana darkly. "That was enough."

There was a beat where all their attention turned inward. Emily remembered the ashes to which her hometown had been reduced, and felt the undercurrent of divisiveness raging around the edges of her feed.

"Let's hope it doesn't come to that," said Dag.

Diana seemed to return to herself. Her eyes found Emily's. "So, what did you say to her?"

"Wait, what?" asked Emily, thrown off by the change of tack.

"You may be out of practice with clandestine ops," said Diana, "but I'm not. You don't think the chief intelligence officer of Commonwealth knows when some creep is scoping our chairwoman's house? Haruki set up a sniper's nest in Coit Tower. He had eyes on you the whole time. If you had so much as *touched* Rachel . . ."

"I—" Emily fumbled for words, retroactive fear flaring.

"Rachel sent out an all-staff notification that she'll be making an important announcement tomorrow," said Diana. "That's it, no other details. And she hasn't backchanneled to any of us, not even Sofia, who called me about it this morning. Our chairwoman-in-waiting is shitting her pants. I had to talk her down from the brink of a full-blown panic attack, which, to be fair, was an entirely sane reaction."

"I told Rachel," said Emily, "that if she wants the feed to survive, she has to find a way to make Commonwealth democratic. All this *intrigue* that I'm so out of practice at endangers the whole system. If she keeps running Commonwealth like it's still just a corporation and hands the torch to Sofia, I think the war you're worried about will be inevitable."

Diana stared at Emily for a long time, then grunted. "That sounds like an absolutely terrible idea," she said. "And what's worse is that I can't come up with a better one."

"Democracy can mean a lot of different things," said Dag thoughtfully.

Emily shrugged. "All I did was make my case. I don't even know if she listened."

"Oh, she listened," said Diana. "Rachel may not agree, but she always listens." She paused for a moment. "In happier news, Lowell is going to be a lot less of a problem from now on."

"Why?" asked Dag. "Aren't there platoons of attorneys demanding his release?"

"There are," said Diana. "But I heard something very interesting through the grapevine. It's not public yet, but Freja has officially taken over their entire organization and assets. She had her people reach out to my people to let Commonwealth know and make peace. She's doing the same with all their other partners." Diana's grin had more than a little in common with a shark's. "Apparently, she's been preparing this for years and was waiting for the right opportunity. Now she's hanging him out to dry. She had already seized control of every official account a long time ago, but Lowell didn't realize it because she ran all their day-to-day operations. Even the deed to the Ranch is in her name. So whenever we put him back on the street, Lowell's going to be just another private citizen."

"Holy shit," said Dag. "Good for Freja. The old man's going to go batshit."

"If anyone else were the victim, he'd be cheering her on and asking for an encore," said Emily. So she wasn't the only ghost he hadn't been able to hold at bay. She remembered Freja's tight sarcasm, how her accent colored her precise diction.

"*He had it coming* just doesn't quite capture the rapturous joy of seeing the anvil of justice fall from heaven to crush the right asshole," said Diana.

"Fingers crossed that *we* don't wind up getting what we surely deserve," said Dag.

Diana snorted. "You can say that again."

They sipped their coffee, thinking.

"There's one more thing," said Emily at last. She turned to Dag. "I was hoping to ask you for a favor."

CHAPTER 42

Javier reached out a hand as Emily stepped from the pontoon to the dock. Wind buffeted their hair as the engine of the seaplane ticked down. The ocean was a changeable gray, as if it couldn't decide on a mood. Kids laughed as they ran between classes up at the school. Gulls circled overhead and late afternoon light bathed the Island in a sympathetic glow.

"Did you ever imagine we'd wind up in a place like this?" asked Emily.

Javier turned to assess the view and the light kissed his face, softening his gaunt features, calling forth the boy from the man. Emily remembered the first time they had visited this remote location, chugging out on an old fishing boat to see the decrepit house and barn left behind by a family whose children had moved away to chase careers in the city. So much had changed since then. After thirteen years surveying his life from afar, Emily couldn't quite believe she was standing here on this dock with Javier. Likewise, she couldn't believe she had spent so long absent from his life. She had missed his wedding, hadn't even met Markus yet. Javier had matured, come into his own, and was now more of a leader than she'd ever been. And yet he was still the boy who had never ceased to amaze her, whose mind was a prism through which the universe shone. Pride and shame and nostalgia and relief and abject terror warred within her. There were so many ways in which she'd failed Javier, so much she wanted to give him, so much she didn't want to admit she needed from him.

"To tell you the truth," he said, "I had enough trouble imagining where we could get our hands on something to eat or how I'd be able to finish my homework. What's happened since then"—he shook his head—"sometimes I just don't know what to make of any of it. I'll wake up in the middle of the night and wonder whether it's all some sort of dream, but then morning comes, and I realize that reality is so much stranger than anything my subconscious could cook up."

They walked up the dock, wood creaking under their feet. When Emily had unblocked the contacts in her feed after leaving Rachel's house, messages had flooded in from Javier, Rosa, Diana, and even Dag. Instead of demanding answers for the avalanche she'd set off in the board room, they'd all been asking where she was, whether she was okay. In the midst of a crisis, Javier had tracked her all the way to Analog. Emily's obsession with honor, her desire for control, her striving toward perfection, all of these were just different shades of selfishness. Surrounded by friends who had become a family, a family whom she loved even when they fucked up, she had somehow persuaded herself that the unconditional love she extended was not reciprocal, had shut them out when she had needed them most, and they her.

"Speaking of," said Javier. "Have you gotten your dossier yet? Rachel being Rachel, she's not taking anything at face value and is going back to first principles. Apparently, Aristotle thought elections were anathema to democracy because they fall victim to the whole 'power corrupts' paradox. Instead, he believed the only way to incentivize leaders to be truly thoughtful and fair was by ensuring that they didn't know who was going to be in charge next. So Rachel has Sofia and me iterating through complex sortition models to figure out options for turning feed governance into jury duty on steroids. I'm sure she's parallel pathing researchers on a slew of representative structures as well. My team is working 24-7, and I still have no idea how we're supposed to have it ready for the constitutional convention, but I guess everyone else is in the same boat. Liane's recruiting pretty much every legal scholar alive. Baihan's stuck wrangling heads of state. Diana's spinning up a major security and counterintelligence op to make sure the convention itself doesn't get attacked or conned. Rachel even brought in Dag to consult on comparative historical case studies, which is how she stumbled on the whole Aristotle thing. So what does she have you doing?"

"She sent me a dossier, but I haven't opened it yet," said Emily.

Javier stopped and turned around. "You haven't even looked at it? Wasn't this whole thing your idea?"

Emily laughed. "Hardly," she said. "I might have given her a push, but the rest is all Rachel. She's a force of nature. That's beside the point, though. I'm going to read the dossier, but I needed to finish something more important first."

Javier narrowed his eyes. "Something more important than the future of Commonwealth?"

"Right," said Emily. She unslung her backpack and removed a brown parcel, handing it to Javier. He looked at the parcel, up at Emily, back at the parcel. Turning it over in his hands, he carefully removed the tape and unfolded the wrapping paper.

"It's everything I can remember since the day I left," she said. "Every single thing. This is why it took me a week to get up here. There's a lot . . . Well, there's a lot I'm not proud of. There's a lot that might change who you think I am. There's a lot that *did* change who I am."

Javier's slender fingers traced Dag's portrait of Emily on the cover. Her expression was thoughtful, melancholic. On the flight up, Emily had inscribed "From:" in glitter at the top. Javier flipped through the thick bundle of handwritten pages, seeing Emily's abysmal penmanship, glimpsing where tears had smudged the ink. Starting had been painful, like pulling splinters. But once the words began to flow, she hadn't been able to stop. In an anonymous hotel room surrounded by discarded takeout containers, she had written until her hand cramped and she passed out on the desk in the early hours of the morning, only to take up the thread when she emerged from the blank nothingness of exhausted sleep. Day after day after day, she milked every last drop she could from memory. In making her doubts, compulsions, and neuroses explicit, she had shed ballast and glimpsed freedom, emerging from the hotel room buoyant. Javier turned the homemade book over in his hands, and under a glitter "To:" saw the portrait of himself.

His big eyes found Emily. Dark brown struck through with gold. She worried she might drown in them, wished she could.

"This is just the start," she said. "I know you'll have a million questions. You deserve answers. You deserve the truth." She remembered the expression on his face when she'd bluffed her way into that Houston drug den to claim him and Rosa. Her voice broke. "Honestly, Javi, you deserve a much, much better sidekick than me."

Javier ran a hand through her hair and then leaned forward, pressing his forehead against hers.

"Em," he said. "You're not my sidekick. You're my sister."

CHAPTER 43

Javier led Emily into a bedroom in the main house and left her there to unpack. She didn't have much, so it didn't take long. Once her change of clothes was stashed away in a drawer, she unlatched the window and looked out at the purpling sky. The birds were out, ducking and weaving through the gathering dusk, their calls clattering into one another like wind chimes.

Sucking in a deep breath redolent of brine and soil, Emily summoned her feed and finally opened the dossier that had been waiting for her there.

Per your suggestion, wrote Rachel, *I have been investigating alternative governance structures for the feed. I'm sure you saw the announcement of the upcoming Commonwealth constitutional convention. What I did not mention in the press conference is that I need your help, and, given the passion with which you called on me to empower people to participate, I don't see a way for you to refuse such a request. As you are no doubt aware, we have many experts at our disposal. However, outside consultants lack an intimate familiarity with the mechanics of the feed, and my closest advisers have their own history and incentives within the Commonwealth organization. You are both an outsider and an insider of sorts. You are also, to my chagrin, an accomplished social hacker, and that's precisely the kind of person I need to vet the ways in which we might lose ourselves in this maze of institutional engineering.*

Can you prove yourself to be as effective a rule maker as a rule breaker? In the course of investigating some of the paths we may want to consider, I came across a twentieth-century political philosopher named John Rawls who wrote that "the fairest rules are those to which everyone would agree if they did not know how much power they would have." It is with this sentiment in mind that I ask you to tear apart everything we develop with the unwavering ferocity I glimpsed in our little chat over oranges. It's time to doff the black hat and don the white, to, as you so eloquently put it, "lend a hand instead of fomenting revolution." If the only way to defeat my opponents is to empower them, then consider yourself duly equipped.

The message was the prow of a cargo ship of information. There were comparisons of the relative strengths and weaknesses of various democratic structures, case studies of tabula rasa institutional formation, first-person accounts from delegates to historical constitutional conventions and treaty negotiations, literature reviews from a variety of academic disciplines, summaries of theoretical systems extrapolated in research and speculative fiction, resource guides and org charts displaying the members and progress of internal teams, outlines of dozens of mutually exclusive proposals, and live access to the models Javier and Sofia were building. The breadth and depth of the material could fuel the doctoral theses of a generation of graduate students, and whatever decisions Commonwealth made, whatever experiments they ran, would surely be put under the microscope of history for decades to come. Emily's mind tilted under the weight of the implications.

The feed had remade the world, and now the world would remake the feed.

An incoming call interrupted her contemplation.

"Riz?"

"Mother of God, Pixie, what the living fuck is going on? You know me, I never read the gossip stuff, but then Vasquez comes in here and tells me you're smeared all over the feed and I look it up and holy shit you're right there, you're everywhere, and you're all made up and riding on the back of my new fucking boss and he's got all your glittery shit on him too but you've got a knife to his neck and what happened to staying out of the spotlight and—"

Emily couldn't help it—she laughed. "Riz, Riz, slow down, okay? It's a long story, and I promise I'll tell you the whole thing sometime soon."

"How 'bout now, sunshine?"

"Right now, I have something else for you to think about."

"The fuck is that supposed to mean?"

"There's this exclusive school up in North America that needs an expert martial-arts and self-defense instructor," she said. "It's on an island that's a hell of a lot colder than Camiguin but just as beautiful. The pay's good, they provide housing, and tuition is free for any children of the staff. Do you know anyone who might be interested in a gig like that?"

A long silence.

"Who are you really, Pixie?"

"That's an even longer story, but I promise to tell you that one too."

"Crazy, you're fucking *crazy*," he said, as if to himself.

"That's for sure."

There was a knock on the bedroom door, and Rosa stuck her head in.

"Riz, look, I gotta go," said Emily. "But think about what I said, okay?"

He grunted and she signed off.

"You promised to be careful," said Rosa. "And then you went ahead and started a live broadcast of Armageddon and upended our entire world order." She shook her head. "I mean, I know you can be slow on the uptake sometimes, but that is *not* what *careful* means."

"That's why I need wiser folks than me around to keep me in check," said Emily. "Loose cannon, this one."

"*Loose cannon* doesn't even begin to cover it, you bastard," said Rosa, taking Emily's hands and squeezing them. "Em"—her voice trembled— "I'm so glad you're okay."

Emily squeezed back. "Me too," she said. "I'm glad we're all okay."

Rosa looked around. "So, does this mean you're staying?"

"Actually," said Emily, "I was hoping you'd agree to tour me around the gallery. I want to learn more about your scene, the artists you're bringing up."

"Of course," said Rosa, turning her face away a few degrees. "You're welcome anytime, but I hear from Javi that all of you have way too much to do at the moment, what with the convention and all that. Maybe we can do something once things settle down."

"Nope," said Emily. "I want to go now, or whenever you're able to accommodate me. If history is a guide, things won't ever settle down. So, fuck it, they can wait."

Rosa turned her face back and tilted it to the side and there was an opening there, a glimpse of something amorphous and ineffable that made Emily want to scream and cry and dance.

"All right," said Rosa slowly. "How about we start right now?"

Emily nodded, suddenly tipsy.

"Come on, then," said Rosa. "There's something special I want to show you."

Rosa led her downstairs and into the living room. There was something new built up against the inside wall, a wooden podium displaying a large vase. Its curves were lush, and the dark-green ceramic was lined with golden seams that caught the flickering light from the fireplace.

"It's gorgeous," said Emily, peering this way and that to view it from different angles.

"It's the kintsugi," said Rosa. "The one they delivered to my apartment."

So this was the piece Lowell had convinced Midori to offer Rosa in order to manufacture a plausible excuse for the kidnappers to enter.

Emily remembered taking her own first overwhelming steps into Rosa's apartment, the wonder of seeing her again in the flesh, the terror when the couriers revealed themselves, the crunch of spine under cleaver, and the mad dash to safety.

"In Japanese art, kintsugi refers to the practice of repairing damaged pottery with gold cement," said Rosa. "It dates back to a shogun who sent a tea set to China for repair and was disappointed when the pieces returned with ugly metal staples. Artisans sought to find a more aesthetic approach, and kintsugi was born." Emily could hear the enthusiasm underlying Rosa's words, the echo of years of careful study and appreciation. "I'm not supposed to choose, but it's one of my very favorite forms. It turns an object into a visual history of itself, maintaining its internal narrative fidelity." Emotion swelled in her voice. "Instead of trying to cover up the damage, the repair is illuminated, the imperfections transformed into a source of beauty. I've always seen kintsugi as a physical manifestation of *mono no aware*, the pathos of impermanence, the gentle awareness that everything, all of us, are fragile and transient, that change is the only constant, that we are, at our best, lovingly reconstructed patchworks of our shattered selves."

Reflected in the shimmering lacquer, Emily saw a thousand ghostly faces, the receding silhouettes of dreams realized and squandered, the fatal attraction of hubris, and the poignancy of heartbreak. She heard the roar of fight-club crowds in the throes of bloodlust and the comforting drone of her father's stories. She tasted triumph, betrayal, and teh tarik and felt her mother's calloused hands guiding hers as she reassembled the telescope. Emily wasn't a singular coherent self, she was the many voices competing in her head. She had let one voice dominate, and her identity had calcified. Like Commonwealth itself, her brittle map of the world no longer matched the changing territory, and she had to find new perspectives before life passed her by.

"Can I touch it?" asked Emily in a hushed tone.

"Of course," said Rosa with quiet fervor. "And if you smash it, we'll turn it into something even more breathtaking."

Emily traced a finger along the golden seams. It was possible to be both broken and beautiful at the same time. Restoration was an act of becoming. Every song was a remix. Every tale was a retelling. Creation was reconfiguration. Things that fell apart could be made whole, and even transcend themselves.

AFTERWORD

Although *Breach* is the third Analog Novel, Emily was the first character who revealed herself to me when I began work on the series.

I was hiking through Wildcat Canyon Regional Park with my wife and our conversation teased at the edges of an amorphous story idea. I never know what particular seed will grow into a book, and we talked about the invisible forces shaping world events, odd details we noticed in our lives, and speculative questions about how things might be different. It was from this strange cocktail that Emily emerged.

A teenager forced to fend for herself who develops a keen eye for the hidden rules that influence behavior, subverting them to survive and serve the powerless. A rebel with an anachronistic sense of honor who cannot blind herself to the failures of a broken system. A fighter who loves her friends as fiercely as she hates any sign of weakness in herself, who harbors the vain hope that her ruthless pursuit of perfection might help to balance out the injustice of an imperfect world.

Emily is as hard and brilliant as a polished diamond. I couldn't write her right away. I wasn't ready for her.

And so I did what Emily would do: I looked at the world around me, and squinted a little bit.

Technology is diverting the structure and flow of power. Computers and capital have stitched together a fractured world into a single variegated civilization, even as reactionary forces desperately try to turn back the clock. The companies that built the internet are forging global empires that Alexander the Great would never have been able to imagine. What were once scrappy startups have become geopolitical players on par with nation states.

But with scale comes responsibility, a responsibility that digital luminaries have yet to come to terms with. The miraculous tools they've developed won them the reins of history, but those same reins curse them with exactly what many technologists have spent their lives trying to avoid: politics.

Technology has endowed us with superpowers, but who gets to decide what to do with them? This is the reckoning that *Breach* grapples with. This is the crucible that only someone like Emily could face. Someone as hard and brilliant as a diamond, whose facets transform the harsh light of suffering into coruscating rainbows, who learns that being broken is just the beginning.

If we are to avoid a future of disenfranchisement, we must invent new ways to grant as many people as possible as much agency as possible over their lives. We must take the power we've earned, and share it. In doing so, we might just find that ceding control can be more liberating than seizing it, that perfection is a mirage, that civilization is a work in progress, that the universe demands nothing more than we choose to give.

I chose to give Emily everything I have, and I hope that her journey has given you a small seed to carry with you that might one day grow into a story of its own.

Writers write, but books take flight only when readers tell other readers about them. If *Breach* means something to you, please tell your friends about it. Culture is a strange and beautiful garden nourished by word of mouth.

Onward and upward.

Cheers, Eliot

FURTHER READING

People often ask about the writing process, but I find the reading process much more interesting. Reading is a superpower that we too often take for granted. It is telepathy. It is a time machine. It is a magic door into countless new worlds, hearts, and minds.

I am a reader first and a writer second.

Ever since I can remember, I've loved books. When my parents read me stories as a child, I would stare into the middle distance and lose myself in them indefinitely. Growing up, I would hide among the dusty library stacks until closing time. When high school English teachers passed out assignments, I ignored the curriculum and ventured off on my own. Curiosity is my drug of choice.

Sometimes reading a book stokes my enthusiasm so much that I simply can't wait to dive into a new story. My dearest hope is that *Breach* did that for you. There are so many incredible books out there, fiction and nonfiction, that can entertain, inform, and transform us. Read. Read. Read some more. Oh, and please share your favorites so we can benefit from your discoveries.

After finishing a great book, I often wish I could ask the author what they are reading. What books touch their very core? Where do they find inspiration? Where does their enthusiasm lead them? I've found many of my favorite books thanks to recommendations from my favorite authors.

I'm sure you've realized it by now, but I'm a little crazy. Obsessed, even. But if you just happen to be a little crazy too, then I've got a secret for you.

Every once in a while, I send a simple personal email sharing books that have changed my life. Because reading is such an integral part of my creative process, I often find gems in unlikely places. The goal of the newsletter is to recommend books that crackle and fizz with big ideas, keep us turning pages deep into the night, and help us find meaning in a changing world.

I also share writing updates and respond to every single note from folks on the mailing list, so joining is the best way to get or stay in touch with me. There's nothing I love more than hearing from readers.

Oh, and if you decide to join our little gang, promise me this: when you come across a story that moves you, pay it forward and pass it on.

Sign up here: htttp://www.eliotpeper.com.

ACKNOWLEDGMENTS

I wrote *Breach*, but there is a small army of talent behind every book.

Adrienne Procaccini, Colleen Lindsay, Brittany Russell, Kristin King, and the amazing team at Amazon Publishing shepherded the rough draft into the novel you're holding right now.

DongWon Song, my peerless agent, provided invaluable wisdom at various points along the way.

Tegan Tigani was a keen editor and vastly improved the manuscript. Any surviving errors are mine alone.

Josh Anon, Lucas Carlson, Craig Lauer, and Tim Erickson contributed notes that shaped Emily's journey.

Kevin Barrett Kane and Emma Hall designed the gorgeous cover.

Danny Crichton, Tim Chang, Cyrus Farivar, Josh Elman, Brad Feld, Amy Bachelor, Malka Older, Craig Newmark, Berit Anderson, Nick Farmer, Cory Doctorow, William Gibson, Hugh Howey, Craig Mod, Patrick Tanguay, Ben Casnocha, Jessie Young, Kevin Kelly, Mohsin Hamid, Rick Klau, Robin Sloan, Warren Ellis, Azeem Azhar, Nick Harkaway, Chris Anderson, Becky Thomas, Noah Yuval Harari, George Eiskamp, Mike Masnick, Oliver Morton, Feliz Ventura, Dan Ancona, Shadrach Kabango, Jake Chapman, Om Malik, Jorge Luis Borges, Stewart Brand, Haje Jan Kamps, Peter Nowell, Adam and Jo Gazzaley, Kim Stanley Robinson, Rick Liebling, Tim O'Reilly, Ryan Holiday, Benedict Evans, Neil Gaiman, Kevin Bankston, Noah Smith,

Maria Popova, Nick Greene, Franco Faraudo, Sam Tait, Seth Godin, Andrew Chamberlain, and Ada Palmer provided ideas and inspiration.

Karen and Erik Peper, my parents, encouraged me to fall in love with stories.

Andrea Castillo, my brilliant wife, was my creative partner on every aspect of the book. Our dog, Claire, provided a steady stream of healthy distractions.

Finally, you read *Breach* and brought Emily and her world to life. May she stay with you as you face the next chapter of your own story.

To all, a thousand thanks.

ABOUT THE AUTHOR

Photo © 2014 Russell Edwards

Eliot Peper is the author of *Cumulus, True Blue, Neon Fever Dream,* the Uncommon Series, and the Analog Series. His speculative thrillers have been praised by the *New York Times Book Review, Popular Science, San Francisco Magazine, Businessweek, io9, Boing Boing,* and *Ars Technica.* He has helped build technology businesses, survived dengue fever, translated Virgil's *Aeneid* from the original Latin, worked as an entrepreneur-in-residence at a venture capital firm, and explored the ancient Himalayan kingdom of Mustang. His writing has appeared in *Harvard Business Review,* the *Verge, TechCrunch, VICE,* and the *Chicago Review of Books,* and he has been a speaker at Google, Comic Con, SXSW, Future in Review, and the Conference on World Affairs.

Visit www.eliotpeper.com to learn more—and to sign up for his reading-recommendation newsletter.